left hanging

CINDY DORMINY

Red Adept Publishing
Unlocking New Worlds

Left Hanging
Copyright © 2017 by Cindy Dorminy All rights reserved.
First Print Edition: March 2017

Print ISBN-13: 978-1-940215-93-8
Print ISBN-10: 1-940215-93-5

Red Adept Publishing, LLC
104 Bugenfield Court
Garner, NC 27529
http://RedAdeptPublishing.com/

Cover and Formatting: Streetlight Graphics

To those who never left me hanging

Chapter One
Darla

I T ISN'T UNTIL HE GRINS at me that I realize I'm eyeballing him. That country music star at Bongo Java last month didn't make me gawk this much. This man's green T-shirt matches his smiling eyes, which stand out even from across the room, in contrast to his fair skin. I've never stared at a boy like this before, and getting caught ogling makes my cheeks feel as if they're going to catch fire. Maybe if I hadn't waited until the last week of college to go to a party, I would have a better idea of how to handle frat-boy eye candy.

My stomach is doing this snap, crackle, pop sound that has me second-guessing the chips and salsa I ate earlier. I'm sure everyone at this party hears my heart pounding, even over the "woo-hoos" that erupt when each new guest enters and the wompity-womp music blasting from the speakers.

This must be what it feels like to be in a movie where everything gets fuzzy except for that one thing that stays in focus. That one thing zooms closer… grinning.

He's moving this way, when a dude stops him. He listens to his buddy and nods at appropriate times, but he still holds my gaze. He pats the guy's back then continues in my direction, closing the chasm between us. He runs his hand through his blond hair, messing it up in all the right places, and all I want to do is mess it up more.

"Finally, after all this time, he's going to speak to me," Mallory says.

My roommate's voice startles me back to reality. Oh yeah, she's still here. "What?"

She inches closer to my ear. "That guy coming our way. He's so shy. I've probably hit on him five times this year. I make a point to know when he's at the dining hall. He eats the same food every single blasted day. I mean, what college boy lives on salad and baked chicken? And I say 'hey' to him all the time, but the boy doesn't take a hint."

I lower my eyes to the floor. I thought he was noticing me, when, of course, he was checking her out. If I were a guy, I would be doing the same thing. When I get the nerve to sneak a peek, I lock eyes with him again. *Oh, sh-sugar.* This time, regardless of what Mallory thinks, I'm positive his eyes are really focusing on mine. But that's impossible.

"Darla, don't wait up," she whispers.

I glance over at Mallory before my eyes shift to the dress I'm wearing, the one I borrowed from Mallory. There's no competition when it comes to who would win the getting-the-guy contest. That's why I never play that game. Mallory's legs go on forever, whereas mine barely get started. She loves these social situations so she can flaunt all her perfectness. My appearance isn't shabby, if I do say so myself, but that's because Mallory did my makeup tonight. She also insisted I wear my hair down instead of pulled up into my typical ponytail. *Accentuate the positive* is Mallory's mantra, and she says my positives are dark hair, dark eyes, and dark skin. Flaunt it, don't hide it.

Oh God. I'm at T minus ten seconds before we'll be nose to nose, and he's still smiling at me. Suddenly, the room feels excessively small and cramped, just like all five lobes of my lungs. I've got to get out of this roach motel before he realizes there's something more appealing to stare at. Exhibit A: my roomie. But I can't stop gawking at those gorgeous green eyes. They're like magnets that keep me from focusing on anything else, not that I'm putting up a fight.

When I move to make my exit, my face meets the massive chest of a huge linebacker-type dude carrying about five more drinks than one person should possibly try to hold. The plastic cups slosh beer all over my super cute, borrowed sundress. The cheap brew splashes onto my face and drips down my neck. Sweat and beer make a lovely combination on a humid spring night. My sandal slips in something that might have been food a few months ago. If it is as nasty as it smells, I'll have to burn my sandals after tonight.

Mallory will never let me wear her clothes again. But thankfully, she didn't even notice. She's doing this girlie finger wave in hopes of getting the cute guy's attention. Another guy grabs her around the waist. She squeals, and they rush off toward the kegs. That's typical Mallory. When someone new shows her attention, she forgets her current mission.

"Do you mind?" I yell at linebacker dude, hoping my words rise above the deafening music pouring out of the stereo speakers.

"Not at all, babe. Here, let me help you out."

He reaches toward me to wipe down the front of my dress, causing more beer to pour over the rims of the cups. I smack his hand away. Creepy perv. Not in this universe, bud. I search around and see a room at the top of the stairs that I really hope is a bathroom. God help me if it's someone's bedroom. The way this night's going, it wouldn't surprise me.

Linebacker dude follows right behind me. His beer breath on my neck makes me feel as if somebody is walking over my grave. All eyes watch us climb the stairs. I don't know what I was thinking. I don't belong at a frat party. This place is for happy, outgoing people like Mallory. I need to clean myself up and leave.

Linebacker dude pops my butt, snapping me out of my internal monologue. Oh, he did *not* do that. My nursing professor would call what I'm feeling an irregular heartbeat. If I don't get control of my heart rate soon, someone will have to call 9-1-1. Getting the attention of Cutie Pie followed by getting too much attention from Non-Cutie Pie is more than I can handle in one night.

"Back off, Stevens," someone yells from across the room.

Linebacker dude, a.k.a. Stevens, and I both snap our heads in the direction of the command. *Whoa!* That baritone voice with the southern drawl came from Mr. Smiley Eyes himself. I steal a glance at Mallory, who is busy picking her jaw up off the nasty floor, before I flee into the bathroom upstairs and escape all unwanted advances.

I slam the door shut. Hopefully, Stevens won't follow me in here. He'd better not. Even drunken frat boys have some manners. At least I hope they do. "What am I doing here?" I ask to my reflection in the spittle-covered mirror. Beer drips down Mallory's sundress. The material is now a nice creepy light-amber color over what used to be a really pretty shade of pink. Streaks of mascara trail down my cheek, making me look as though I've been crying. That might happen if I have to face Stevens again on my way out.

I splash cold water onto my face to remove the raccoon eyes my mascara left behind, while doing my best to avoid the collection of hair and unidentifiable objects caught in the drain. I fumble through my purse in search of my hairbrush.

Suddenly, the door swings wide open. I shriek and drop my purse on the nasty, sticky floor. Smiley Eyes rushes in. This night keeps getting crappier. Some one-on-one time with this guy would be awesome in any other setting. But right now, I look more suited for the cover of a Courtney Love CD. Not a great first impression. But at least the guy busting through the door isn't Stevens.

"Shh." He slams the door and locks it.

I back away from him, bumping into the toilet. "What are you doing?"

"Keep your voice down."

"What are you doing?" I ask in a more hushed tone.

"Hiding from that long-legged gal that keeps chasing me." He places his ear to the door.

"Which one?"

"Don't know her name; don't want to know her name." He gawks at me, making my pulse race.

I stare at the mirror, trying to fix my rat's nest of hair. "How did I get talked into coming here?" I ask my reflection.

He leans toward the door and listens for another minute before he deposits himself onto the counter, millimeters away from me. "I was wondering about that. You're kinda like the elephant in the room."

I scrunch my brow.

He stares at the ceiling and groans. "That didn't come out right. It was supposed to be a compliment."

I can't even remember the last time I went on a date, much less had a real boyfriend. School has been my priority, and I really don't need a distraction this close to graduation. But he's so darn cute, and there's something about him that makes my insides tingly when he focuses on me.

I run my brush through my hair once, adding a few new samples to the collection in the sink, while I quickly glance at the cute guy out of the corner of my eye. For some reason, I still hold his attention. My pulse picks up the pace again, and I'm sure it sounds like *The Tell-Tale Heart.* At any minute, my heart is going to explode out of my chest. I'm trying to remember if a beta-blocker or an ACE inhibitor would work better to decrease my heart rate. I don't think either will have a significant effect with this guy so close to me.

"I'll take that compliment."

"Good," he says.

"Good," I reply like a stupid parrot. *Think of something to say, quick.*

He cracks a grin again, and *bam*—a dimple pops out on his right cheek. Have mercy. Now, I know I have pretty good self-control, but a hefty dose of cuteness coupled with that adorable dimple is going to make me drool so fast my head will spin. But that dimple is probably part of his standard operating procedure to make the girls swoon. He has to know how cute he is and what that dimple does to me—I mean, what it does to all girls. I'll bet he gets the once-over all the time and loves it.

He leans down to pick up my purse and hands it to me. When he glides back onto the counter, he dangles his feet like a six-year-old sitting on the side of a swimming pool. So far, he hasn't popped my butt or sloshed beer on me, so he's two points ahead of Stevens in the manners department. At least he has that going for him.

"Thanks."

"Stevens didn't scare you, did he?"

I wave him off. "Nah. You, on the other hand, have me a bit worried."

He laughs. "Hey now. And here I was making sure he didn't follow you in here. I was trying to be a gentleman."

The tingly sensation flutters in my stomach again. I've never had anyone keep a watchful eye out for me, especially a guy that's so kind and easy to talk to. There's definitely more to this person than a pretty face. I can't explain it, but I know I can trust him.

I sit on the counter next to him, but my butt slides into the sink. He catches me, as though it's a natural thing to do, rather than trying to cop a feel. Even through my dress, I can feel the warmth from where his hand touched my waist. Maybe I could fake another sink-slip so he'll grab onto me again. *Darla, get it together and get out of here fast before you let him grab you in other places.*

"Sure you are. Should I take a poll of all the girls downstairs to see how many have been fed that line before?"

He makes this girly "oh my God" face and bats those irresistible eyelashes. "Judge not, lest ye be judged."

I roll my not-so-irresistible eyes. "Quoting scripture doesn't make you a saint."

He stares at me and chuckles.

I switch my focus to the dried beer on my calf. I don't want to stop gaping at the man next to me, but I need to if I want to regain the ability to breathe and speak simultaneously. At least my heartbeat isn't so loud that the people in the next county can hear it anymore.

I take a deep breath and try to sound confident, even though I don't feel it at all. "So, am I going to be trapped in here all night?"

"It appears so."

"Actually, there's nothing to stop me from leaving except you. I think I can take you."

He puffs out his chest and gives me another dimple sighting. "I think you called me small, but I'm going to ignore that comment. Besides, what's the harm in keeping me company? At least until Sally or Tally starts sniffing in another direction."

"Because you were being a gentleman, I'll give you a few more minutes of my time." I sigh and blow a strand of hair out of my eyes. "I smell like beer."

He leans in and sniffs me. How strange and surprisingly... nice.

Goose bumps form on the back of my neck, although his breath isn't creepy like Stevens's ogre breath. It's warm and inviting. And I might let him do that again if he wants to.

"At least it's fresh beer and not recycled."

I crinkle my nose at the thought. "That's... ew."

"What's your name?" he asks.

Oh no. I am not giving him my name. He'll probably spread rumors about me. I know how frat boys work. Nope. Not going to happen. People can say a lot of things about Darla Battle, but one thing's for sure—I am not gullible.

"Juliet," I blurt out. Now he'll think I'm a hopeless romantic.

He snorts. "Really? Juliet?"

I nod and try not to grin, but it's not working, so I cover my mouth with my hand. "So, what's your name?" I cannot believe I asked for his name. I don't want to know his name. Okay, maybe I do.

"Hmm." He stares at the ceiling, and a playful grin slides across his face. "Romeo."

6

I can't help but smile. "Do your parents hate mine?"

He laughs. "I guess so, but I wouldn't let that stop me." He extends a hand that I take without hesitation. "It's nice to meet you, Juliet."

I bite my lip to keep from smiling. He has a nice, warm hand. I hold on to it a bit longer than I should. In fact, I could hold on to his hand for a very long time. I'm drawn to him like a magnet, and I have no plans to resist the feeling.

His gaze wanders down to our hands, which are still wound together. *Oh crap.* I've exceeded the proper allotment of contact time with a complete stranger. I snatch my hand away as if a bolt of lightning suddenly hit me.

"Nice to meet you too, Romeo. But just so you know, I'm not killing myself over you."

His dimple pops out again. "Duly noted."

He stands and stretches as though he's getting ready to run a marathon. Then he claps his hands together as if psyching himself up for a big game.

His actions cause me to snap out of my daze. I blink at him like a fool. A bang on the door startles me, and I jump so high that I almost hit the ceiling.

"You don't wanna come in here," Romeo says. "I need the candle of shame."

"Sorry, man," someone says from the other side of the door.

Romeo glances over his shoulder at me, and his eyes light up. "So, how good are you at Rock-Paper-Scissors?"

He is full of surprises. Instead of plying me full of alcohol and forcing himself on me, he wants to play kid games. He didn't make me feel stupid because I didn't want to give him my real name. Romeo is definitely somebody I think I can trust, somebody I would like to know more about. There's something about him... "I'm a beast."

"Bring it," he says.

I rummage through my purse and find a tube of lipstick. On the mirror, I write *ROMEO* and *JULIET* in block letters. "Let's do this thing."

For the next hour, we play round after round of silly childhood games.

A knock on the door interrupts us.

"Hey, girl, are you in there?"

I mouth to Romeo, "My roommate."

He makes puking noises. "No. Go away."

I cover my mouth with my hand to keep from laughing.

"Okay, but if you see her, tell her I've left with Jason."

"Sure." I can hardly understand his words over his fake retching sounds, and it's all I can do to keep my giggles silent.

I add another notch under the *JULIET* side of the mirror and smirk at him. Watching him is worth the price of admission. I like the way he paces and mumbles under his breath when he loses a game. Each time he sits back down on the counter, he's a wee bit closer to me. His knee taps against mine as we get involved in the next round.

I like it even more that his eyes twinkle when he wins. And he winks at me. *Yikes.* I really like his ritual before each round of thumb wrestling. We start with a handshake. Next, he slowly slides his palm over mine until we lock into position. His soft, strong hand is a stark contrast to the calluses on each of his fingertips.

"Can I go home now? We've worn down two tubes of lipstick already, and unless you carry makeup on you, we're completely out of writing utensils."

He smirks at me.

"Is that a tube of lipstick in your pocket, or are you glad to see me?" I slap a hand over my mouth, trying to force the words back down my throat. I cannot believe I said that. I don't know how to flirt, but with him, it seems natural. I need to take a deep breath and say good-bye before something else crazy spews from my mouth.

"Good one, but no... on the first part." He slides off the counter and places his ear up to the door. "Sounds like a lull in the action. I think we can make a run for it. Let me get you some clean clothes."

Nope. Not a good idea. "That's very nice of you, but—"

He grabs my hand and cracks the door, peeking out before he opens it. Then we dash down the hallway, away from the stairs and toward bedrooms. He scans over his shoulder every few steps with a wide grin spread across his face.

Romeo unlocks a bedroom door, and we slink inside. He kicks off his shoes after he closes the door.

I don't make a habit of being in guys' rooms, but this one is pretty atypical. Aside from the normal socks strewn on the floor, it's kind of orderly. No beer bottles or fast-food containers litter the table. And thank goodness, the standard frat aroma doesn't permeate into his room.

But the oddest thing is the Bible on the nightstand. I certainly don't see *that* every day. He either uses it as a prop to draw in girls, or he's got a spiritual side to him. It wouldn't surprise me if he's the real deal. How nice that would be.

He opens a drawer and removes a T-shirt with "Don't trust atoms. They make up everything." printed on the front. *Oh yay! He's geeky too.*

He tosses the clothing at me. "You can wear that. Oh, and here are some scrubs."

I have to do some serious juggling, but I catch everything without dropping my purse.

"Okay, but I've got my *ion* you," I say, hoping he gets my geeky humor.

His knees buckle. "Ah, talk nerdy to me."

It takes all my willpower not to laugh at his joke. He's funnier than I expected.

"No offense, but how do you live in this frat house? I mean, your room is actually quite clean, but the rest of the place is gross."

"And you saw the clean parts. I kind of wish I'd stayed in the dorm."

"Do you ever leave your room without shoes?"

"Never. Besides, I'm not here much. I'm usually at the library."

I slip off my sandals, and Romeo faces away from me before I even have to ask. He shoves his hands in his pockets and rocks back and forth on his heels. I wriggle out of the sundress and slide on the T-shirt. Then, I take a look-see over my shoulder to make sure he's not looking. He continues to stare at his feet. He's either a perfect gentleman, like he said, or he's not interested in anything more than silly games.

"Sure," I say as I finish changing. "The library."

"I'm serious. If I was smart like my brother, I could party all the time and not worry about my grades. But I got the handsome genes."

I try to stifle a giggle. I don't know why Mallory thinks this guy is shy. He's far from it. He's super easy to talk to. I've only known him an hour, and I feel as though I could tell him anything.

"Actually, he did too, but don't tell him I said that," he adds.

It's getting harder to muffle my laughter.

"And the height. Hell, maybe I should introduce you to him."

The laughter bubbles up in my throat and out my mouth. It feels good to really belt it out. With the stresses of finishing nursing school, I can't even remember the last time I smiled, let alone had a good belly laugh. "I'll pass. You can turn around now."

He grins again, and I melt. "That's better."

I curtsy. Out of the corner of my eye, I notice a dorm refrigerator with a padlock on it next to his bed. "So no one steals your brewskies in the middle of the night?"

He *tsk tsks* at me. "There you go, being judgy again. Am I going to have to whip out my Bible?" He points to the Bible on his nightstand. He either really does know his scripture, or it's a good conversation piece for all the girls he parades through here.

He unlocks the fridge and removes the padlock then opens it to reveal soft drinks, water, orange juice, and vials of some kind of medication. My nursing brain kicks into high gear. A guy his age does not have a refrigerator full of medication unless he is really sick. Glass vials mean he has to inject the drug into his body, and from the amount of medication in the fridge, it seems as though he has to do it often. He retrieves two bottles of water and hands one to me. Before I can even open mine, he has guzzled his down.

"Wow. You were a little thirsty, weren't you? You don't have a stash of beer in here?"

His mouth tilts up on the side in an almost grin. "It's bad for my health." He removes one vial from the refrigerator then grabs a syringe and an Accu-Chek machine from his nightstand. I watch as he wipes an alcohol pad across a finger and pops a lancet over it. He puts a drop of blood on the test strip and slides it into the machine. Now the calluses make sense.

"Type one?" I ask.

"Since I was seven."

"Why don't you have a pump?"

"It's busted." He whips off his shirt.

Oh. My. God. There goes that telltale heart again. I wish he hadn't done that. *Liar.* He's fit and lean, and I'm finding it really hard to focus. I have to blink a few times in order to bring myself back from fantasyland.

He cocks an eyebrow. I've been busted. His whole body tenses when he wipes a spot on his abdomen with an alcohol wipe. "God, that's cold."

After he measures his insulin in a syringe, he hands me the vial to hold.

He flicks the needle into his pinched skin and tosses the used syringe into a Coca-Cola bottle with a handwritten label that reads, "DANGER—DO NOT DRINK."

"You should have been a fly on the wall the last time I told Stella I broke another one. She hit the roof."

"Stella?"

"Stella's my mom."

"You call your mother by her first name?"

"Yeah, she's pretty hip. She'd like you. Anyone who can *almost* whip my butt at one of my own games is golden in her book."

"Shoot, I let you win."

"You did not."

I shrug. He's too adorable. I couldn't bear beating him at his own game.

"You better not hold anything back next time," he says.

Now, it's the telltale heart coupled with a full-blown asthma attack. He said, "next time."

I pick up the insulin vial and roll it between the palms of my hands to keep them from shaking, but mostly I do it to keep from running my hands over his bare chest or through his messy blond hair. I don't think I could be any hotter if the place were burning down around me.

"Here." I hand the vial to him. "You might want to put that back in the fridge."

He takes it and places it on the nightstand. "It can wait."

He leans in and kisses me on the lips. *Oh, sweet Jesus.* His lips are even softer than they appear. He moves away ever so slightly.

I clear my throat. "Do you mind—"

"I'm sorry, I didn't mean—"

I cover his mouth with my hand to shut him up. "Do you mind doing that again?"

I move my hand away from his mouth, revealing an impish grin and that cute dimple. *Not the dimple again. I'm such a goner.*

"I don't mind at all," he whispers. He leans in to kiss me again. He cradles my face in his trembling hands.

I kiss him back. This time, I let my hands slide up his bare chest, causing him to actually purr.

Sigh.

I can count on one finger the number of make-out sessions I've had, and that one was so long ago, I'm sure I wouldn't even recognize the guy without all his pimples. This is not what I expected tonight, but sometimes, a girl deserves to let go and have fun.

In between kisses, he mumbles, "But I might need that OJ in a bit."

I giggle and allow him to lay me down on his bed. I know it's probably a bad idea to be here with him, but I don't want to leave. I don't care what I should or shouldn't be doing. I'm not going anywhere anytime soon.

After all the fun we had playing his silly games, I'm positive we saved the best for last. And because I'm such a good sport about everything, I think I'll let Romeo win the first round of our tongue-wrestling competition. Or maybe it'll be a tie.

Chapter Two
Theo
Seven Years Later

If Mallory lets out one more of her "I'm disgusted with you" sighs, I think I will scream like a nine-year-old girl. My norepinephrine level is probably way out of the normal range by now. When Mallory isn't happy, the whole world knows it.

"I don't understand the attraction of Nashville," she says. "It's so... Nashville. The y'alls, the hats, the music in the grocery store. Anywhere but Nashville."

She shudders and tosses a vase into one of my shipping boxes without even wrapping it. It's not hers, so she doesn't care if it breaks. If I did that, I would get a tongue-lashing to beat all.

"No one is forcing you to move. Besides, I miss my family," I say, hoping I don't come off like the homesick puppy I am. I miss them so much it hurts. The last seven years have been hell with medical school and my residency. I'm worn slap out, and my health has taken a beating. So when a slot opened up at my alma mater, I jumped at the opportunity to return home for my fellowship without even discussing it with Mallory first—an act she hasn't let me forget.

She flips her long blond hair off her shoulder. "Theo, they're all really annoying."

I stop packing and stare at her. She has crossed the line. "Why would you say that?"

She stops stuffing items into her box and places her hands on her slender hips. She sneers at me, indicating she has a list, complete with bullet points, and she is ready to unleash it on me. Knowing Mallory, she has a slide presentation on her cell phone and is ready to beam it onto the wall. I don't even know if that technology exists, but if it does, she would have it and use it on me.

"Well, for starters, your mother—"

"What's wrong with my mother?" How my mom managed to be a mother to us kids and be a preacher's wife is no small undertaking. She's about the coolest person I've ever met. *Almost.*

Mallory stares at me as if I have a wart on the end of my nose. "You must not see her the way I do. She dresses like a bag lady." She wags her head. "How she ever passed the bar is beyond me. And don't get me started about the gaggle of siblings you have, especially that mother-hen big sister of yours."

I grin at her. Peanut butter and mustard go together better than Jennifer and Mallory. They butt heads over everything, even about Jennifer's wedding. Even months later, Mallory was still ranting about how simple their wedding was and that it didn't even make the society pages. She made it clear that when we get married, it's going to be the event of a lifetime. And I made it clear that she's putting the cart before the horse. We are several steps away from taking a walk down the aisle.

"Remember that time she tried to fix your hair?" I ask as I lick my hand and move toward her. "You gotta admit that was funny."

She swats my hand away. "That was *not* funny."

I nod. "Yes, it was."

Mallory bites her upper lip. I think there's a smirk trying to peek out. I can tell it's killing her not to admit how funny that day really was.

"She means well," I say.

Mallory stares at the floor. "I know," she quietly replies.

She removes picture frames from the mantel then rotates one frame around for me to see. It's a photo of the two of us snorkeling at Key Largo.

A moan escapes my throat as I point to it. "If that picture had been taken three hours later, I would have been sporting that massive sunburn."

"It looked painful."

"Says the girl who remembered to wear sunscreen."

"Poor baby," she says with a pouty face. She always points out this picture when she wants to make me feel stupid.

I shudder. "I cried like a baby. It hurt like crap."

She grabs a photo of my family and hands it to me as if it has Ebola covering the frame. I'm not sure why my family is so repulsive to her. They've always been nice to her, but she acts as though their professions are menial. Her attitude toward them is getting really old. Actually, it has been old for quite some time.

"That one's yours," she says. "But it wouldn't matter what box it went in if we were moving to the same apartment, now would it?"

I slump down on the couch, watching her overly dramatic actions as she slings her stuff into boxes. She thinks if she keeps it up, I'll give in and we'll move to Nashville together. It has worked before. After six years of constant whining about wanting to move in with me, she wore me down. Her behavior was starting to affect my ability to concentrate, so I agreed. She knew after an eighteen-hour day at the hospital, I wouldn't have the energy to conjure up a rational excuse.

"If you are hell-bent on moving too, then I think it's best that we have our own apartments," I said for the hundredth time.

She shrugs.

"And I'm gonna be moonlighting in the ER, so I won't be around much at all."

She does her standard-issue Mallory huff.

"It's not important right now. Mallory, neither one of us has been happy for a long time."

I had hoped my love for her would grow stronger with time, but it hasn't. And it's completely obvious that I don't make her happy.

"You'd make me happy if you would try."

I lean back on the couch and stare up at the ceiling. "I haven't tried?"

"If you really loved me, you'd try a little harder."

"Are you kidding me? I spent last Christmas with your family instead of visiting my parents. For my birthday, I stayed out way too late at the concert you wanted to go to and almost fell asleep in clinic. Oh, and don't forget last week, I went to that dinner party with you, and you ignored me the whole time. Don't tell me I don't try to make you happy."

"We could get married."

Here we go again. I pace around the room, stubbing my toe on a box in my way. I mumble a few curse words under my breath. I'm not sure if it's from the pain in my foot or the predicament I'm in. They are equally distressing.

"I can't change the things you don't like about me."

"Like what?" She wraps another picture frame in tissue paper then proceeds to wrap a stack of plates. She grumbles something under her breath as she chucks the plates into a box.

I hold up my index finger. "For starters, my family."

"I like them fine from five hundred miles away. To be fair, the same goes for my family."

I hold up two fingers. "Church, especially Dad's."

She shrugs. "I grew up going to church on holidays. It's not my thing."

I add another finger. "I'm shorter than you as if I did that on purpose."

"Tommy's six feet five. I'm just saying."

Sure, throw my geeky brother into the argument. I'm certain my IQ combined with Mallory's doesn't even come close to his.

I flail my arms in the air in desperation. "I was trying to be funny."

"I wasn't."

I wag my finger in her face. "Blame it on my diabetes, which I'm sure you resent as well."

She swats my hand away.

"And I know that disapproving glower you give me when I take out my Accu-Chek machine."

She sits down in the recliner and crosses her legs and arms. "Now that you mention it, I think you're a bit OCD about it."

I stop in front of her. "OCD? Have you ever been in DKA? It sucks." My pulse is so high right now, I feel as though I'm about to go into V tach.

Mallory waves me off as if she doesn't have a care in the world. "I don't even know what that is."

"Diabetic ketoacidosis. It's very dangerous, Mallory."

My phone rings. The ringtone blares, and an announcer's deep voice says, "Risk, the game of world domination," indicating to me that Tommy is calling. I scrounge around the apartment, searching for my phone. *Thank you, Tommy.* He got my mental SOS in the nick of time. When the ringtone starts again, I find the phone in the couch cushion.

"Don't you answer that," Mallory snaps. "We had a deal—no phone calls until we finish."

"Finish packing or finish breaking up?"

She steels her eyes on me. Before I answer, I peer over at her once more. If I take my brother's call, I won't hear the end of it. If I don't, it will confirm that I am one hundred percent, grade A whipped.

I press the button to send my brother's call straight to voice mail, and Mallory rolls her eyes. I think I'm the one who needs the break, and not only a time-out. I need a complete break, like the humpty-dumpty kind. I sit down and stare at my shoes.

"We need to get this done," she says. "I have a ton of things to do before *my* movers get here."

"It's not working."

"We've already been over this. You don't put in the effort."

I hate it when she starts using that school-teacher tone with me. "You don't love me," I say.

"Don't tell me who I love and don't love."

"What do you love, Mallory? Remember that time I almost quit med school but you talked me into sticking it out?"

She sighs.

"Why? What was your motivation? Did you love me in the beginning, or was it the thought of the MD after my name?"

Bingo. Finally, I've got her attention. Those steel-blue eyes throw daggers at me again. Good thing I wore Mallory Kevlar today, because she and I are in the middle of a massive stare down.

Her lip quivers.

Dammit. I can be such a jerk sometimes. I didn't mean to hurt her feelings, but sometimes, she pushes my buttons.

I run a hand through my crazy hair. "Never mind." I head to the closet. "We're both tired and stressed. I'm sorry I said anything. I didn't mean to be an ass."

I haul all the coats out of the closet and sling them onto the back of the couch. Next, I grab the contents of the top shelf and stare at all my old board games covered in dust. It's like seeing long-lost friends that are crying out how much they've missed me. These games bring back fond memories of Sunday afternoons, growing up. They also make me think of Juliet. *Oh, sweet Juliet.*

I carry the boxes into the living room. "How about we take a break?"

I run my hand over the top of the first box, sending dust particles into the air.

Mallory rubs her nose and lets out a dainty sneeze.

"Bless you. Feel like playing a game?"

Mallory swings around and stares at the stack in my arms. "Seriously?"

"C'mon, it'll be fun."

Mallory lets out another one of her disgusted-with-me sighs. "Theo."

I survey the games, feeling as deflated as a slowly leaking balloon losing its last bit of air. "Never mind."

I put the games in a shipping box. After wrapping up the family photo in a towel, I place it on top of the games. The silence is so loud that it practically ruptures my eardrums. I know what's coming next.

"You're a doctor, remember? It's time you start acting like one." She crosses her arms. "Come on, babe, you're not a kid anymore. Let's get all this stuff packed. I'm exhausted."

"I said never mind." I tape the box shut. "I can't do this anymore."

"Who is she?"

I scrunch my eyebrows together. "Who is who?" I take my frustrations out on the poor tape dispenser. The box only needs one strip of tape, but it gets five. The contents of this box will never fall out.

"Who are you in love with?"

I wish I could answer that question. I knew as soon as I first laid eyes on Juliet that she was the one for me. But I don't know what happened to her. Hell, I don't even know her real name.

"No one, Mallory. There's no one."

She lets out another *exputtered* sigh, as my sister calls it. Jennifer has her own glossary, and sometimes her words describe the situation to a T.

"Oh, all right. I'll play one of your juvenile games."

This is not how I imagined feeling after seven years in a relationship. At first, I was flattered that someone like Mallory would give me the time of day. I mean, she has legs that go on forever, and she's smart as a whip. She put the full-court press on me, and before I knew what had hit me, she had followed me to Johns Hopkins. Lord only knows how she hornswoggled her way into living with me six months ago. It's all a blur to me now.

We did have some fun times. And it was nice to come home to a beautiful girl after a grueling day that sometimes consisted of being on my feet for as much as eighteen hours, nonstop. Even if I was dead tired half the time, I guess the other half was fun for a while. That half isn't enough anymore.

"Okay, I've got a game that won't take long at all." I search around the cluttered apartment until I find a black marker.

"When we get to Nashville, we are going to donate all those board games. I would die of embarrassment if anyone saw those in our apartment."

"We are *not* moving in together. Jesus, Mal, you are so hard-headed."

With no paper in sight, I use the side of a moving box to draw a bunch of blank spaces and a scaffold. I show it to her. It was going to be a cute Hangman game that spelled out "Welcome to Music City," but she has left me no choice but to hammer home the truth. *Here goes nothing.*

_ !

She scrunches up her forehead.

"Pick a letter."

She rolls her eyes but guesses a few letters.

I fill in the letters until we end up with most of the puzzle complete.

We stare at each other.

"R. N. G," she says.

"Hold your horses, Mal."

I A _ B R E A _ I N G U _ _ I _ _ _ O U !

She gasps. "I am breaking up with you."

I kiss her cheek and reply, "Okay." I hate to be such an ass, but she leaves me no choice.

Chapter Three

Darla

"OKAY, STELLA BELLA. TIME FOR beddy-bye." I draw back the covers of my daughter's big-girl bed. It seems like only yesterday she was in a crib with a teddy-bear mobile dangling over her head. Now, she has so many stuffed teddy bears in her bed, there's not much room for her six-year-old body to stretch out.

One thousand one. One thousand two.

"Aw, Mommy, not already."

Two seconds. Wow. I'm impressed. That has to be a world record. But Stella knows if she puts up a fuss, I'll give in and play our little game. I can never resist that cute face and those adorable dimples.

I pat her pillow and point to it. "You don't want to be sleepy for your last day of first grade, do you?"

She climbs into her bed, wearing a pitiful pout on her face. "Please. I promise I'll get up without being a grumpy bear."

I tickle her until she's a big squirmy mess. "Okay, one game."

"Yes," she says, pumping her fist into the air as if she's a teenager. *Oh boy.* That's going to be fun as a single mom.

She talks me into playing every single night. At first, it was a way to teach Stella her letters and how to read. But it has become our little bedtime ritual. It's not as though she has to twist my arm to play, that's for sure. I love playing our game as much as she does. If she only knew how much it means to me, we would be playing it around the clock.

She hands me her dry-erase board that she had hidden under her pillow, waiting for the go-ahead. She can play me like a fiddle, and I love every minute of it.

"You are a rascal. No peeking."

She giggles and covers her eyes while I write out the puzzle. When I'm finished, I snuggle in next to her, tossing a few stuffed animals to the foot of the bed. I show her the puzzle.

– – – – – – – – – – – – – – – – – –

"Choose your first letter, ma'am."

She grins at me. "A."

"I don't know," I say, teasing her before I add the letters.

– – – – – A – – A – – – – – – – – –

She grins at me and picks two more letters.

"You are soooo good at this."

"I know, right?"

"And modest too."

"What's modest?"

"Never mind. Pick a letter."

"T."

S T E _ _ A _ S A S _ E E T _ _ _ _

"Stella is a sweet girl," she says.

"We have a winner," I say, tickling her again. I give her a big kiss and let the board slide to the floor, holding on to her so close that I'm not sure where I end and she begins. My eyes close to drink in her goodness. She has no idea how she saves my life every single day.

"Mommy, why are you always so sad at night?"

I open my eyes. I thought I was better at hiding it. "I'm not sad."

She leans up and puts her sweet little hands on my cheeks. "Your face is sad."

I stare at my precious daughter, who is the spitting image of her father. She even acts like him. He's missing out on so much. I wish I could reach out to him and show him what he's missing. I wish he wanted us.

"How can I be sad when I have you?"

She gives me a suffocating hug that I absorb with all my soul. I cherish every one of these moments because I know that one day, I'm going to blink, and Stella will be all grown up.

"Oh, and guess what?" She releases me so fast, I don't know what hit me. She can change topics faster than the weather changes in Nashville. "Miss Silva said we're going to have a special guest come to our class tomorrow."

"Really?"

She bobs her head up and down, her crazy blond hair going every which way. "Uh-huh. It's her brother, and he's a doctor. He's a ped-a, ped-uh something."

"Pediatrician."

"Yeah, that's it. A kid doctor."

"That's super cool. I wish I could be there, but I gotta work."

She pats my hand. "That's okay. You see doctors all the time, anyway."

"Yep." I kiss her cheek. "Now, bedtime."

"Not before you get the kisses even."

I kiss her left cheek then her right cheek over and over until I get the kisses balanced. On purpose, I keep the kisses unbalanced for a while so I have an excuse to smooch those marshmallow-soft cheeks a few more times. She squeals. I love making her smile. I love anything that has Stella in the subject line. I love that I get to share my life with her.

"I love you," I whisper.

"I love you more," she whispers back.

By the time I leave her room, she's mostly asleep already. I remember when I could sleep that well. I used to sleep through two alarm clocks and my sister's hair dryer. But that was pre-Stella. That was before I had to sleep with one eye open in case the love of my life needed me. I don't care. Sleep is overrated. I would take Stella over a full night's sleep any day, and I have the dark circles under my eyes to prove it.

I meander down the hallway that still has a smidge of crayon drawings on the wall from that one time I wasn't watching her for one minute. Her artwork is too cute to wash off. I may never get my rental deposit back, but it's worth it. The clickity-click of my Chihuahua's toenails on the hardwood floor follow me into the kitchen. Yeti thinks if I'm heading toward the "food" room, it must be treat time. I retrieve a Greenies bone for him, and he takes off with it, clenching it tightly in his mouth in case I have any intentions of stealing it from him. *Yuck.*

I run my hand over the latest addition to my refrigerator art that Stella brought home from school earlier this week. This drawing is of Mickey Mouse. It won't be long until she gets to meet him in person, or in mouse—whatever he is.

There are so many drawings on the refrigerator now, I think I'm going to have to buy a bigger one. I can't seem to part with any of her precious creations. Shelby, my boss, has banned me from posting any of Stella's artwork in my office at the hospital fitness center where I work. She says they're too distracting… for her.

Now that Yeti's late-night munchies have been satisfied, I drag myself into the super quiet living room and collapse onto the second-hand couch. With a deep breath, I stare at the four walls covered with yard-sale "art." Yeti jumps up in my lap and gives me a quick, sloppy kiss on my face. I rub his ears, making him groan. I swear that dog's eyes roll back in his head when I give him ear scratches. I curl up on the couch, and he finds a comfy spot behind my knees. After his typical circling, circling, circling, he settles in and lets out a deep, groaning exhalation.

"I know, buddy."

Stella has no idea how sad I truly am. I try to put on a happy face because she deserves it. I want her to have an uncomplicated life, so if I have to fake my happiness, I'll do it. But I miss her dad so much it hurts. Even though we only had one night together, I thought he loved me.

I wish so many things had worked out differently, but Stella is not one of those things. When I invite myself to one of my pity parties, I have to remember that had it not been for that one and only frat party I went to, she would not even exist. My world would be in perpetual suck mode if it weren't for her.

I only wish he had wanted me, had wanted her.

As sad as it makes me not to have him, I see him every day in her. I see him in her sweet, playful smile. I see him in her messy hair. Her love of playing games she definitely gets from him. Yep, she's definitely the best thing that has ever happened to me.

But it should have been better. It could have been better. Still snuggled in his bed with the party going on below us, I was seconds away from telling him my real name that night, when some jerk caught the place on fire. I should have stuck around outside the house and waited for him. I should have made sure he was safe. But he made me promise to get out of the house and not look back until I got back to my dorm. I was so traumatized, I didn't think straight until everyone had scattered after graduation two days later.

My eyes scanned the droves of people at graduation in hopes that I would miraculously bump into him, but of course, that didn't happen. And by the time I realized I was pregnant, it was too late. He chose Mallory over us. He had already moved on, and it was entirely my fault.

Someday, Stella will hate me for it all. If I do an Internet search on the word "idiot," I will no doubt see my picture staring back at me as the first search result, and I wouldn't even have to click on the "I'm feeling lucky" icon.

On days like today, I really think about him. I thought I saw him today out of the corner of my eye. But when I got a good view of the guy, my hopes faded even though the memories didn't. Right when I think I'm getting my life back together, something will remind me of what Stella and I lost.

A single tear drops out of my eye and slides down my cheek. It's followed by another and yet another. The tears rain down my face faster than I can wipe them away. I don't even try anymore.

Chapter Four

Darla

THE CONSTANT WHIRRING SOUND OF the elliptical machines isn't enough to drown out Shelby's non-stop complaining. I think we all need to take a break and get on the equipment for some stress relief, but Shelby would never go for that. People think since I work in a fitness center, I'm able to exercise any time I want. In actuality, it seems the longer I'm the wellness nurse at the hospital fitness center, the less time I spend actually using the fitness equipment.

I step out of my office and into the main workout area, where Shelby is lining up all our supplies for the screening visit on a table against the wall.

"Isaac Matthew Dupont, the Third, we need more batteries," Shelby says.

Isaac runs from the closet with an armload of supplies. He clutches a box of pens in his mouth as he dodges a guy doing a set of bicep curls. With the ease of the track star he once was, he jumps over a workout bench. He knows if Shelby uses his full name, he'd better snap to it, even if it's the last thing he wants to do. Isaac's real talent is to schmooze with the guests, and it comes naturally for him. With his flawless face and killer grin, he never meets a stranger. Girls are willing to give up practically anything for one date with him, but this dark beauty only has eyes for the guys.

He drops the box of pens out of his mouth. "Hon, I can only be in one place at a time."

Shelby tugs her long blond ponytail tight. "Well, I need you to be in this place right now." If her hair is pulled back, it's best to agree with whatever she says. Men are especially afraid of her when she goes into "take charge" mode. But if guys knew her like I do, they would be falling all over each other to get to her.

Isaac looks at me and wags his head. "Someone didn't get laid last night," he says, avoiding a serious Shelby stare.

I stifle a grin as I throw my supplies down on the table in the corner of the room and go through Shelby's checklist. Isaac should know by now that talking about men, or lack thereof, is off-limits with her.

Nothing is really off-limits with Isaac. He is in constant diarrhea-mouth mode, and I've learned to love it. He has embarrassed the crap out of me more times than I want to remember, but he is a true original, and I'm lucky to call him my best friend. He's the only friend I have left from those awkward middle-school years, and he knows me better than anyone else. But even he doesn't know my darkest secret.

"Someone's going to get castrated if they don't stay out of my love life," Shelby says, making Isaac and I jump. She may be only five foot two, but that doesn't include her attitude. There's not a ruler in the world that can measure that 'tude.

Isaac snarls. "Touchy, touchy, bitchy Barbie."

"Come on, y'all. Focus," Shelby says.

Every year around this time, a fresh crop of doctors converges on the university medical center to complete their training. Before they can get started with their rotations, they have to go through a wellness screening— body composition, cholesterol screen, immunization boosters, whatever they need. Shelby is in charge of this chaos, and the higher her stress level, the twangier her Southern accent gets, if that's even possible. There will be so many "y'alls" and "sugars" today, I know I'm going to want to hurl.

Shelby taps her foot. "Nurse Darla, where's your ID badge?"

Busted. I hate wearing that thing. I shudder thinking about my photo ID. It's five years old and was taken during my short pixie-cut stage. I avoid wearing it as much as I avoid the "who's the father" question.

"Fine. Just a sec." I run back to my office to retrieve my purse. While Shelby continues her toe-tapping, I fish through my purse until I find the ID buried under a crumbled pile of Goldfish crackers, a bubble gum wrapper, and a sticky note reminding me to buy more Goldfish crackers. I peel off a gummy bear that dangles from the clip and eat it. Isaac looks as if he throws up in his mouth. I clip the badge to my blouse, but when Shelby's not looking, I flip it over to hide the hideous picture.

"So, how many young docs have decided to come to Nashville for their residency this year?" I ask Shelby.

"One hundred and ninety-two little pricks."

"Oooh, I love it when she talks dirty," Isaac says as he bags up blood pressure cuffs and stethoscopes.

Shelby cocks an eyebrow. "Please help me get this stuff loaded on the carts, or we'll be late, as usual." She points her finger at him. "And you, mister, are not allowed to make any signs this time."

He feigns shock. "Hurtful."

"Last year, your stupid dyslexic brain had them going to the 'ful' station instead of 'flu' station. Not a good first impression."

"Oopsies."

God love him, but Isaac does tend to get his letters mixed up a lot. Even my first grader notices, so although Stella adores him, she has banished him from helping her with her homework.

We toss the bags onto push carts and head out of the fitness center toward the main hospital building. The best part of days like this is that I get some exercise walking across campus while I'm on the clock. The rest of the day is sure to be exhausting and completely boring.

"Zacc Kendrick," Shelby quietly says, a grin spreading across her face.

"Huh?" I ask.

"The cute one this year is Zacc Kendrick. The name oozes hotness."

"Oooh," Isaac squeals. "I get first dibs."

Nothing he says surprises me anymore. "I wouldn't get in too much of a hurry. You know Shelby's hotness indicator has been broken for quite some time."

"Hey, y'all," she says in protest.

"Yeah, y'all," I reply.

"I know, y'all," Isaac says.

"Come on, y'all," Shelby says.

Oh no. She has said "y'all" three times already, and we haven't even left the fitness center. God help us. Zacc Kendrick had better hide if he knows what's good for him.

Shelby rushes around the room, moving tables and chairs to make stations for all the assessments we will be performing on the doctors. Isaac and I unpack all of our equipment, hoping we didn't forget something. If we did, there will be hell to pay.

Shelby examines our setup, nodding her approval. "Okay, Isaac, you're going to handle the body composition station. Try not to get touchy-feely with the docs. Got it?"

Isaac shows his back to Shelby and rolls his eyes. "Yes, Mother."

I pat his back. I know he has a smart-ass comment waiting to spew, but he's holding it in. Maybe he's learning. I'm so proud of him.

"Darla, you will do the cholesterol screens and the antibody titers."

I square my shoulders, lift my chin, and let out a satisfied sigh. I've been drawing blood for so long, I could do it in my sleep. I almost always hit the vein on the first stick. Even the CEO of the hospital has me draw his blood every year for his routine labs. The first time I drew his blood, I was so afraid I would mess up, I needed a liter of fluids afterward. So I figure if he relies on me, I must be pretty gentle. I take a fleeting glance at Isaac and Shelby and find them staring at me.

"Yeah," Isaac replies. "Every time there's a hunky doc around, you can't stop your hands from shaking. You get so worked up." He fans his face as though he has the vapors.

"I do not."

"Whatever," Shelby replies.

All right, maybe that part is true. I don't make eye contact with good-looking guys for fear they will make me do things I only dream about. Been there, done that, got the baby. Besides, guys have been interested in me so infrequently over the last few years, and the ones that were ran as fast as they could when they realized I had a daughter.

Shelby and Isaac still stare at me.

"Okay, so I'm… shy?"

Isaac wiggles his eyebrows up and down. "Yeah, and I'm a virgin."

Shelby laughs and holds up her hands defensively. "Not going there. You're the wellness center nurse. I need you to do the yucky stuff."

I whine as I take out syringes, alcohol wipes, labels, and my little Sharps container for disposing of used needles. I lay them all out in nice little piles. Tubes? Check. Labels? Check. Needles? Check. Yep, I'm ready to roll.

One by one, I draw two tubes of blood from each physician. I wrap labels around the tubes, and before I know it, I send doc-in-training number one hundred seventy on his way. My back is stiff from leaning over the table, drawing blood for three hours, and my cotton mouth needs a soft drink in the worst way.

"Shelby, I've got to take a break."

She hustles over to me. "Sure thing, sugar, but can you do one more while I call to see where the backups are?"

She takes a quick gander over her shoulder before she leans down and stage-whispers. "I don't know who this hottie is. He wasn't on our list. Trust me, you'll want to hang around for this one. Dr. Stud Muffin is in the house." She waves her arms around in a "whoop whoop" motion as Isaac hands me a soda.

"Thanks." I loosen the cap.

Shelby scampers away, and I reply to her back, "Let Dr. Cutie Patootie draw his own blood." I take a swig from the bottle, and my eyes land on the most beautiful green eyes I have ever seen. I would know those eyes anywhere.

The drink slides down my windpipe instead of my esophagus. I try to stifle a cough, which makes my face feel as if it's on fire. I blow soda out of my nose and all over Isaac. He blinks the drink out of his eyes.

Oh crap. Oh holy crap. No. This. Can. Not. Be. Happening! My heart pounds in my ears. My larynx is so tight, I can only wheeze out a few faint breaths. I'm quickly becoming dehydrated from all the sweat that's pouring off my face and dripping down my neck. I need a liter of anti-anxiety meds, stat.

Romeo cocks his head, and a slight grin tips up one side of his mouth. "Juliet? Is that you?"

Shelby snaps her head toward me. Isaac wipes the soda off his face. My hands tremble like Isaac predicted they would. I fiddle with the tube labels, but my fumbling fingers send them sailing all over Isaac. When I lunge for the labels, my drink springs out of my hand, and a streak of soda flies across Hot Doc's perfectly ironed white business shirt.

"Oh, I'm so sorry." Instead of wiping the soda off his shirt, which is what I really want to do, I lean over to pick up the labels off the floor.

Isaac leans down. "Are you all right?" He helps me up, but I think Dr. Hotness has me by the other arm.

"I'm okay. Only being my usual klutzy self." I have two choices. I can either pretend I don't know him, which is what he deserves, or I can face the fact that my daughter's father is right in front of me after all these years. I think a third option is more appealing—running away.

Shelby rushes over to me. "On second thought, go take your break now." She flashes him a killer grin. "Sugar, can you go to the body comp table and come back to the blood draw station in a few minutes?"

He gives her a thumbs-up and grins at me before he leaves. He inspects his shirt and wags his head. Yep, running away is the best option.

Chapter Five

Theo

A BATHROOM DOOR ISN'T GOING TO stand between me and the one woman I've thought about every day for the past seven years. That deep suntan has made her big brown eyes appear even browner. And she's wearing shorts, so I got a great view of those sexy, curvy legs.

I ease open the door and listen. I don't want to get smacked by a random female trying to do her business. Juliet leans over the sink and splashes water over her face. She mumbles something to herself. I can only make out random words, but most of it could be Pig Latin for all I know. I could stand here and stare at her for hours. I don't know what it is about her, but the sight of her still does it for me. I could have waited until she came out, but I would rather have a few minutes alone with her after all this time, even if it's a risky move.

Through her dark hair, which hides most of her face, she glances my way, not stopping her face washing or babbling. She tries to snatch some paper towels out of the dispenser, and they fly through the air, missing her shaking hands. "Are you lost?" she asks as she kneels down to pick up the mess on the floor.

I take her arm to help her stand.

"This is the women's bathroom, you know," she adds.

Whoa. Not what I expected. Maybe our time together didn't mean very much to her. I thought we had something special. I wanted her real name, a real relationship. But she vanished after the fire, and no one I asked seemed to have a clue who she was. This little reunion is a shock to me too. I would like to know what she's been doing all these years, but I get the feeling she doesn't have the same curiosity.

"Yeah, well, we met in a bathroom, so I thought it was appropriate." I cannot stop the Cheshire Cat grin from spreading across my face.

She stands there, focusing on the hand dryer, the sink, everywhere except my eyes. Cat's got her tongue. I wish this cat did.

"Hello... Romeo." Finally, she speaks.

I throw my head back and chuckle as I lean against the counter, crossing my arms. The edge of my shirt absorbs a puddle of water. "It's you, after all this time."

She throws the paper towels in the trash can, and her eyes flit around the room again. *Sorry, girl. It's only you and me.*

It's as if her hands can't figure out what to do. I can help her with that. Eventually, she's going to have to face me. She crosses her arms and huffs. I enjoy the scenery while she clenches and unclenches her fists. She is as beautiful as I remember. Not model, stop-and-stare beautiful, but purely, completely perfect-for-me beautiful. And she still wears that same uncertain "I'm not good enough" look on her face. But today, it's coupled with a nasty nail-spitting stare. She waxes and wanes from seeming upset to acting as if she's ready to smack me. Maybe I should take a step back in case she wants to make contact, and not the fun kind.

I remember how much her face lit up when she finally realized I really liked her and that I wasn't playing her like some random hookup. We did hook up, but I was already gaga over her by that time. I remember later that night when she woke up in my arms, with one leg slung across mine, dangerously close to the fun zone. It's something I'll never forget. But here we are seven years later, and she seems scared again. Well, let's see what I can do to get rid of that feeling for good.

"So, how long has it been?" She wears a painted-on smile that doesn't reach her eyes.

I'm trying to be nice here, but she's not making it easy. "About seven years, give or take a few months and days." Actually, it's been seven years, one month, and sixteen days, not that I'm counting.

"Nice to see you," she says.

She could have fooled me. I don't have a long history of girlfriends, and I'm certainly not a master of body language, but I'm pretty good at knowing when I'm not wanted.

I take a step toward her anyway, knowing good and well that I might regret it. She steps back, bumping into the paper towel dispenser. I reach out to flip over her ID badge. She has conveniently clipped it on her shirt so her picture and name aren't showing. She swats my hand away.

"Whaaa? I still can't know your real name?"

She crinkles her forehead.

I lean against the counter again, and my entire face lights up. "It's really good to see you." Inside, I'm doing a happy dance and yelling, "Yes." This isn't the happy reunion I imagined we would have one day, but I can work with this.

"Well, I need to get back to work," she whispers. She tries to push past me, but she's not getting away that easily.

I put my hands on her shoulders. "Please."

Her eyes flick to mine for a second before she looks away again. She doesn't need to be afraid of me. It wasn't my fault a fire interrupted the best night of my life.

I run my hands down her arms. "You can't leave before I know your name."

She stretches her lips into a tight line as she averts her eyes from me.

"I thought I'd lost you. You gotta at least give me a name. Preferably, a real name this time."

A tear slides down her cheek. I'm not sure what happened. I hope to God I didn't hurt her.

She shrugs my arms off her and wipes the tear away. "Are you kidding me?"

"Well, crap on a cracker!" a girl says from the bathroom doorway. "Uh, Darla, sorry to interrupt, but we need you out here."

She pushes past me. "I've gotta go."

"Ha!" I pump my fist into the air. "Your name is Darla."

She grins at me. This one lights up her whole face. "Fine. My name is Darla. Are you happy now? Like you didn't know already."

I rub my scruffy bearded chin and saunter toward her until there are only centimeters between us. She sucks in a breath when I lean in to whisper in her ear, "But to make sure we're clear, my name is not Dr. Hotness. Or was it Dr. Cutie Patootie? I can never keep it straight."

Her face loses all expression. "Do you have bionic ears or something?"

And the Cheshire Cat shows itself again.

She race-walks out of the bathroom.

"You want to explain that?" the other girl asks as they scamper away.

"Later."

———◆◇◇◆———

While I pace in the hallway, I roll my shoulders, crack my knuckles, and anything else I can think of to calm my nerves. I can't put it off any longer, so I get in line to have my blood drawn by none other than Juliet a.k.a. Darla. I don't have time for a relationship right now. Hell, I am only weeks out from under Mallory's stranglehold; I don't need to dive into anything else right now. I just need to take a breath and enjoy the view.

But I can't figure out Darla's attitude. *Jeez.* Southern belles sure have changed since I've been gone. In my mind, I keep repeating her words. *"Like you don't know."* Of course, I don't know her name. If I did, our second encounter would have happened a long time ago. Maybe she has some special mind-reading skills from nursing school, something they didn't let us doctors know about, because I'm completely clueless, as usual.

A tall, dark-skinned, perfect specimen of a man helps Darla with the blood samples. The way they chitchat with one another makes it obvious they spend a lot of time together. Okay, so this may be the reason she freaked out. Maybe this guy is her boyfriend, or fiancé, or even worse—husband. *Gah.*

"You want to tell me what happened?" he mumbles through a painted-on smile.

"Not now," she replies in a hushed tone while she jerks her hair into a fast ponytail.

Finally, it's my turn in the barrel to get my blood drawn. In a singsong voice, the dude says, "Dr. Hotness, coming up. I'm getting tingly."

Okay, something tells me I don't have to worry about this dude being her boyfriend or husband. I don't even know him, and he cracks me up. I step up to the table and stare down at her. I hold out my paperwork, which she immediately snatches out of my grip.

She lasers in on the sticker with my name on it. "Well, hello, Romeo… I mean Dr. Theo Edwards. Have a seat." Her tone is all professional as she focuses on her blood-drawing supplies and her neat little stacks of paper.

I sit across from her, trying to hold in how excited I am. "Juliet, a.k.a. Darla, how's it going?"

The dude eyeballs me before making eye contact with Darla. "Am I missing something?" he asks. I can almost see the spinning hamster wheel in his brain.

She shakes her head as she runs her hand down my arm, searching for a good vein. Her touch feels really good. I cannot resist the temptation to curl my fingers so I can brush her arm. A nice tingly feeling circulates through my body. She peeks at me through a strand of hair that has escaped her ponytail. I cock an eyebrow. Perhaps she feels it too, even through her gloves.

When she finally says something, she makes it obvious that she's reading my name off of my newly printed ID badge. "This may hurt a bit, Doctor... Patootie." She adds that last word under her breath.

"I'm a big boy. I've been pricking my finger at least five times a day since I was seven."

The dude giggles at the word "prick."

"Oh yeah, I remember." She fingers my MedicAlert bracelet before she checks out the insulin pump clipped onto my belt. "I see you got a new pump."

"The count is up to five now. I really should buy stock in the company that makes them."

She wipes my arm down with an alcohol pad. The tourniquet she applied makes my bicep muscle flex more than it normally would. I love that she can't seem to tear her eyes away. When she sticks the needle in my arm, I don't even notice because I'm so used to having blood drawn, checking my blood sugar, and giving myself insulin shots. Except now it's Darla sticking me. She's going to make my sugar level spike so much, I'm going to need ten units of Novolog, stat.

She gives the dude a stare down. He has a funny, confused, puppy-dog expression on his face, flip-flopping his attention from me to her, and finally landing on me.

I shrug. "We knew each other in college," I say in the most nonchalant voice I can muster.

"No, we didn't," she replies, her voice ending in a high-pitched squeak. *Denial.* "Did too."

She finishes with the first tube and inserts the second one into the needle. She inverts the first tube before handing it off to the guy. I notice his name tag says Isaac.

"We *met* in college," she clarifies to him. "We did not *know* each other."

"Wow. That's all it was?" *Could have fooled me.*

"Yep."

"I disagree."

She snorts. "We remember things quite differently, don't we?"

Isaac seems as if he's watching a tennis match. He stares at me, waiting for me to reply.

I can't help the impish grin that I am sure is plastered all over my face.

She steels her eyes on me. "Don't go there."

"Go where?" I'm not good at playing dumb. "I was going to say... never mind." My Southern gentleman manners kick in. If she's not comfortable sharing our private time, I'm good with that.

Isaac gasps. "Juliet, have you been holding out on me?"

Her ears transform into a deep sunburn color in two seconds flat. They almost match the color I'm sure is smeared across my face.

"I think we're done here." She hands Isaac the second tube, removes the needle, and slaps a gauze pad on the blood draw site before applying medical tape to my arm. She did it so fast, she really should think about roping calves in a rodeo. The thought of strapping pink Coban tape around a calf's legs makes me chuckle.

"Your results will be ready no later than tomorrow. You can pull them up online."

She removes her gloves and throws them in the waste container. She ducks her head low, hoping her hair covers the grin growing on her face, but she's not successful. When she musters the nerve, her eyes lock on mine. I'm doomed. She nibbles on her bottom lip, and her eyes jet away from my gaze. She may be done with me, but I'm not letting her go that easily, not by a long shot. We'll finish this when there are fewer prying eyes.

She starts packing up her supplies.

The girl who barged in on us in the bathroom stops at the table. "I think we're about finished, thank God. How's it going over here?"

"We're real good," Isaac says. "I've been having the nicest conversation with two star-crossed lovers."

I bust out a loud laugh and fist-bump Isaac as I get up to leave.

Darla groans in frustration.

The girl regards me, glances over at Darla, then looks back at me. "Wait, what?"

Chapter Six

Darla

I CAN TELL ISAAC IS ABOUT to bust a gut, wanting to know all the details. All the way back across the hospital property to the fitness center, he keeps giving me thumbs-up. If he does that one more time, I think I might twist that thumb right off his hand.

Shelby smacks Isaac's hands. "What's that all about? Did *you* find a hot doc today?"

Isaac gives me his toothpaste-commercial smile. "Please, please, please."

"Fine," I say. Sometimes, Isaac makes me feel as if I have another child. Actually, it feels that way all the time.

Isaac bounces up and down. "Darla had sex with Dr. Hotness."

Shelby stops in her tracks. "Today?"

"No! Of course not," I reply, peering around to see if anyone in the parking lot can overhear this humiliating conversation.

Isaac bends over, laughing as he wipes tears from his eyes. I'm glad somebody's getting some enjoyment out of this.

"Apparently, our little darling Darla and Dr. Hot Ass did the nasty when they were in college."

"No way," Shelby yells. "Why didn't you say something?"

Isaac shoots his hand into the air like a second grader. "Oh, please, please, let me tell the story," he begs.

I roll my eyes. "Go ahead. You're enjoying this way more than I am."

Isaac skips over to Shelby in the middle of the parking lot. "Apparently, they didn't exchange names. This is Juliet." He waves his arm toward me as if he's a showcase model on a game show.

Shelby collapses onto the curb, right next to someone's Range Rover. "You have *got* to be kidding me."

"Nope," Isaac says. "Dr. Hot Stuff is Romeo."

Shelby lies flat on the grass. Her whole body quivers with laughter. I let them rollick in their merriment as I stroll toward the building where the fitness center is located. I leave all the equipment for Isaac to haul back to work, and I hope he gets a hernia.

"That was a long time ago. We all have a past, Mr. Popularity."

Shelby holds out a hand for Isaac to help her up off the curb. "At least Darla has good taste. Damn, girl. He's hot in a boy-next-door kind of way. You should have hung on to him."

I tried.

Tears blur my vision, but they aren't from humiliation. I have to admit the PG version of the story sounds funny, but the part they don't know hurts like hell.

Instead of heading back to the fitness center, I make a beeline to my car. I am not in the mood to listen to any more Dr. Hotness stories, and I'm certainly not ready to divulge any more of my past. I text Shelby as soon as I get to my car.

Not feeling well. C U tomorrow.

I lay my head on the steering wheel. The horn blares, making me jump about a foot out of my seat, ramming my head into the car roof. Stella's father is back in Nashville. He's cuter now than he was back in the day, and I made a complete fool of myself. *Ugh.*

And he had the nerve to act as though he didn't know my name. For Pete's sake, I was on the group email Mallory sent out, proclaiming the love of her life to her closest friends. She couldn't wait to introduce everyone to Theo, the medical student.

I should thank Mallory. At least after that, I had a name and an email address. And when I finally got up the nerve, I wrote and told him everything. There's no way I could forget the email I carefully worded as I chewed all ten nails down to their nubs while rubbing my belly that was growing from the "I've gained a few pounds" stage to the "yep, there's no hiding it now, I'm five months pregnant" stage.

I will especially never forget his one and only reply: "Leave me alone."

It broke my heart. Now, I wish I could muster up the courage to scream, but I'm still too freaked out to even cry.

I have rehearsed this moment a thousand times. I had planned to go up to him and tell him he has the most beautiful daughter and he would be a fool not to welcome her into his life. Regardless of him flat-out refusing to have anything to do with us seven years ago, he would be remorseful and beg for forgiveness. Of course, he would scoop us both up, and we would live happily ever after. Either that or he would be a jerk, and I would go about my life as though he was another deadbeat asshole dad. But instead of all that, I got bitchy. It'll be a miracle if he even wants to be associated with me ever again.

I hadn't prepared myself to come face-to-face with the spitting image of my daughter any time soon. And I didn't expect, after all this time, to still go weak in the knees when his face lights up. This is not how I thought my summer would start. But like it or not, he's here, and I'll have to face him at some point. And eventually, he'll have to meet Stella. I have to come up with a plan for them to meet without getting her hopes up. If he breaks her heart like he did mine, I would never forgive myself.

I take out my phone and text Stella's teacher. Jennifer has been such a good friend to me this year, always listening to me go on and on about any topic without issuing judgment. It has been a while since we've had one of our little impromptu parent-teacher conferences, otherwise known as an excuse to commiserate and enjoy ice cream. Boy, I sure could use her company right about now.

R U up for a conference after school?

I lean my head back on the seat, and immediately, my phone chimes.

You know I'd love to. Waiting on my bro to stop by. I'll text back in a snig with est. time.

Love her word choices.

Sounds good. You know where I'll be.

I crank my car and head to the best therapy session in town: Bobbie's Dairy Dip.

Chapter Seven

Theo

BEING INSIDE JENNIFER'S CLASSROOM TAKES me back to when we were little. The eldest kid in our family was born to be a teacher. She used to make us play school all the time when we were little. Tommy liked to trip her up with random facts, and Heather always got called into the principal's office. I was happy hanging out with her, so I did whatever she wanted to do. She and I were two peas in a pod, even though we hardly pass for siblings. The only thing we really share are the God-awful dimples. She and Tommy have long, lanky legs and light-brown hair like our father. Heather and I got the crazy hair and the short genes in the family.

"Class, this is my brother, Dr. Theo." Jennifer's eyes light up when she speaks to her students.

The entire class of miniature humans stares at me, afraid to move. I wave to them, and a few dare to wave back. I'm not going to bite, especially first graders. That would be rude and certainly bad for business.

"He's a pediatrician, and he also has a medical condition that you might find interesting."

A little hand pops up.

"Yes, Kade?" she asks.

Kade pushes his thick glasses up on the bridge of his nose. I can tell he's the kind of kid that loves to ask questions every chance he gets.

"Does he have chronic dry eye?"

I glance at Jennifer. They might give me a run for my money.

"No. No, he does not. At least, not that I know of."

Another hand pops up.

"Molly?" Jennifer asks.

"Does he have a yeast infection?"

"Uh, no," Jennifer replies.

I clench my teeth to keep the chuckle down that's starting to spew through my throat. I stare at my shoes, hoping I can regain my composure. If not, I'm going to need a hefty dose of anti-giggle-biotics.

"What about erectile dysfunction?" another kid asks from the back of the room.

Tell me he didn't ask me that. *Grind, grind, grind.* My molars are going to be little nubs before this is over. *Dear Lord, please help me. Love, Theo.*

"Okay, it's obvious that you kids watch way too much television," Jennifer says.

"Ask your doctor if it's right for you," another one quotes.

"He *is* a doctor," says another kid.

Oh God, here comes the chuckle. Please make these kids stop. I do an about-face and stare at the whiteboard that's covered with math problems. I try to think of something terrible—lost kittens, hunger, war. My body trembles as the laugh escapes.

Jennifer elbows me in the ribs. "Why don't we let Dr. Theo tell us?"

I clear my throat, take a deep breath, and count to three before I have the courage to face the kids again. I silently give her the "you owe me big time" message. She shrugs.

I clap my hands to get myself psyched up for the conversation. "Okay. Would it be all right if we sit on the rug over there?" I point to an old latch rug in the corner of the room.

"Sure," Jennifer says. "Everybody head over to the story-time station."

"Yeah!" they scream as they rush over to find their place on a huge smiley face rug. I'm pretty sure that rug was in Jennifer's bedroom when we were little, because who else would have a grape juice stain in between the eyes of the face?

"You can sit by me," a little boy says.

I kneel down. "Well, thank you."

"Crisscross, apple sauce," a little girl says, smiling.

I nod and try to crisscross my legs under me. I reach into my pocket to retrieve a piece of candy. "Can anyone tell me what this is?"

"Candy!" they all yell.

"And what is candy made of?"

"Sugar!"

"Yep. Did you know that all the food we eat ends up as a type of sugar? But not like the sugar in this candy. It's a sugar called glucose. Can you say glucose?"

"Glucose!" they eagerly reply. I could say Armageddon, and they would gleefully chant it back to me. I should try it.

On second thought, I'd better not.

I take the piece of candy and pretend to eat it. "Now, when I eat it, it goes down my throat into my stomach. What happens next?"

"It makes poop," a red-headed girl says.

Okay, so I set myself up for that one. I should be more specific next time. I sort of remember being six, and I loved to say poop too, so I can't fault them for that.

"Not yet. What's your name?"

"Camille," she replies.

"Well, Camille, it does end up as poop, but there's something before that."

Camille giggles and nudges Kade. "He said poop."

The class sniggers. Using the word "poop" never ceases to be funny. I'm a doctor, and I'm supposed to be all adult-acting, but bathroom humor still brings out a chuckle in me. Jennifer would argue that I have a mental capacity only slightly higher than most of her class, and she's being generous with her assessment.

Jennifer stands. "Guys, this is all fun, but let's calm down, okay?"

"What happens before it becomes poop?" I ask, trying to get them back on target. I am going to write the director of the school system and insist that my sister get a raise. This is one tough job.

"Pee?" a little boy asks.

"Nope, but good guess. What happens between the stomach and making poop?"

There is silence. Jennifer hides her amused expression behind her hand as she sits back to enjoy the show. Finally, after what seems like forever, a little girl with messy light-blond hair raises her hand.

I point to her. "Yes. What's your name?"

"Stella," she replies.

I fix my eyes on Jennifer, and my eyebrows shoot up. The only other person I even know with that name is my mother. I take another gander at the little girl. The name seems to suit her. She is too cute for words.

"Okay, Stella. Do you know?"

She cringes as she says, "Digestion?" Her pretty green eyes beg me to tell her she's right.

"Yes!" I give her a high five. "Digestion is what happens to our food from the time we put it in our mouths until the time we…"

"Poop," the entire class yells.

Facepalm.

"I think we're all clear about that," Jennifer says, interrupting the cheers about poop and pee. "Let Dr. Theo continue. I'm sure he has a point somewhere."

"Yes, I do." I condense my ten-minute adult lecture about what diabetes is and how I have to manage it to a thirty-second, first-grade version. They'll be more interested in the blood-and-guts stuff, anyway.

I wrap up my talk by pointing at my monitor. "And I tell the machine how much insulin I need."

"How do you know how much?" a little girl asks.

"Good question." I take out my Accu-Chek glucose machine from my backpack. "I need a volunteer."

Twenty hands shoot up into the air.

"Um, you. Stella Bella. Come here, and you get to check my blood sugar."

"My mommy calls me that."

"Your mommy has good taste in names."

She giggles as I give her an alcohol wipe packet. "Open that and wipe my finger with the alcohol." I point to my ring finger.

She does exactly as I tell her with the most serious expression.

I put gloves on her that swallow her tiny hands before I give her a safety lancet. "Don't touch that blue button yet." I press the "on" button on my Accu-Chek machine and insert a test strip. "Ready?"

"Yep." Her uncooperative hair falls in her face, causing her to blow the locks out of her eyes.

I hold her hand and push the lancet to my finger, but I let her finger cover the blue button. "Push the blue button." The lancet clicks. "Ow!" I yell and laugh.

The kids scream. Stella grins at me. A cute little dimple appears on her cheek. Together, she and I let a tiny drop of my blood fall onto the test strip.

I point to the "start" button. "Push that button right there."

She does as instructed. I take the safety lancet with the retracted blade and place it in an old soda bottle that is clearly labeled *DANGER*.

I hold a gauze pad on my finger and remove Stella's gloves. "Very good."

She bounces from one foot to the other, enjoying the praise. The other kids crowd around me.

The machine beeps and displays 120. "Not bad, but I need to give myself one unit of the sugar police. Who wants to give me a unit of insulin?"

All hands shoot up again.

I let a kid named Calvin give me insulin through my pump, but I'll bet he's more interested in using it like a video game.

I gasp in mock shock. "You did it."

"Cool," he replies. "What happens if I push the button again?" He reaches for my pump, but I shove my shirt down and stand up from my "crisscross applesauce" position before he can send me into insulin shock.

"Let's don't find out."

Jennifer claps her hands together. "Class, can everyone say thank you to Dr. Theo?"

"Thank you, Dr. Theo!"

"It's time to line up for PE." All the kids jump up and rush toward the door. "John, it's your chance to be the line leader."

John fist-bumps my sister and leads the class into the hallway and out of sight.

I follow Jennifer back to her desk. "They're a funny bunch."

"Oh my God. I thought I would die when they asked you those questions. Do you have chronic dry eye? That was too *spondicious*."

Here she goes again with those made-up words. I sit down on the edge of her desk and wipe my face. "What does that mean?"

She rolls her eyes. "I'm surprised you don't know what it means." She piles her hair on top of her head and runs a clip through it. "It means what you think it means. It's really up to you. That way, I'm relieved of all liability."

I crunch up my brow. "Ooookay."

She pulls out two water bottles from a mini refrigerator under her desk and hands me one.

I take a swig from the bottle.

"Do you think you're going to like being back in Nashville?"

"I think so." *Especially after this morning's turn of events.*

"I know I'm glad you're back. Do you plan on going to Dad's church now that you're back in town?"

I nod. "Absolutely. I've missed his sermons."

His teachings have really saved me from a lot of crap over the years. They didn't keep me out of trouble, but they did help me through it all. And surprisingly, none of us kids ended up like typical PKs, which is short for preacher's kids. I guess the closest any of us came to being a hellion was Tommy, and he's the smartest one of the bunch. Sallister University can't even intimidate the genius of the family. Last, but certainly not the least, is the baby of the family, Heather. So far, she has made it to graduate school without going wild.

Jennifer and I sit in silence. I can tell something is on her mind, and I'm sure she can tell my mind is weighted down also. We've always been good at reading each other.

"How was today?" she asks.

There she goes, trying to read my mind. One time, I scratched the bumper of her car, and before I could even confess, she was asking me what I did. Our connection can be pretty freaky at times. She should moonlight for the psychic network because she could make a killing.

"Good, I guess. I didn't really do anything except get my schedule and go through orientation, get my blood drawn." Thinking about who drew my blood makes my heart skip a beat. *Simmer down. You're not in middle school anymore.* If I tell her about what happened, she'll go all matchmaker on me.

"So the long hours start when?"

"I'm on call next week."

She snarls.

"And... I'm also going to pick up some night shifts in the ER for extra money." I cringe and lean away from her, waiting for the lecture. "But it's for a good cause. You remember. Doctors Without Borders."

"Still, those long hours are not healthy for you. It messes up your sugar levels and gets you all *befizzled*."

I shrug. "I'll try to stay un-*befizzled*. Besides, I knew from the get-go it was going to be rough."

"Yeah, but you're through with your residency. Why didn't you take a job as a pediatrician and be done with it?"

"Because with this fellowship, I can do research and get my specialty in endocrinology. You know, maybe make things better for kids like me in third-world countries."

"My brother is a hero."

I snort. "I'm no hero." I play with the label on the water bottle.

"So, why aren't you happy?" She sits on her knees like a first grader would.

"Oh, I'm happy, I guess. I don't know. Jeez, stop reading my mind." I run my hands through my hair. It's probably standing on end after the day I've had. "You know, Mallory moved here with me, but not really *with* me."

She groans. "Is this the same Mallory that you have nothing in common with? The one that doesn't understand why Mama buys her clothes from the thrift shop or works for the Legal Aid Society?"

I peel the label off my water bottle. "Yep."

"Wait, you told me y'all broke up." She makes a rolling gesture with her hand, signaling for me to explain the nonsense to her.

"We did, but she got a job in town, anyway. She hates this city, but I know what she's up to. This is her way of accidentally-on-purpose bumping into me all the time. I'm glad it's over, but I don't want to be alone the rest of my life." Alone isn't the right word. Being alone at times is therapeutic. Being lonely sucks.

"You don't have to be alone. You're a great person."

"Well, I told her again it was over and if she was hell-bent on moving to Nashville, she needed to get her own apartment." I think back to when I first told Mallory my plans. If I didn't have such quick reflexes, I would still be picking linguini out of my hair. "She was so pissed."

"That's a good first step."

"Yeah. Eventually, it was going to end, anyway. Mallory—most girls, really—always made me feel like I was a stick-in-the-mud for not wanting to party." *Thanks, diabetes.*

"Well, their loss."

I nod. "I know. You're right."

"Now that Mallory's out of the picture, you never know what might happen. You know, when one door closes…"

"Preach on, sister."

She taps my water bottle with hers. "So, what's up?" She nudges me with her shoulder.

Of all the people in this world, Jen is the only one who could help me figure out this crazy situation I'm in. And even though I risk her mothering me to the brink of insanity, I need to talk to her. *Here goes nothing.* "I saw someone I knew in college. I was convinced she was *the one.*"

She leans back to study me and crosses her arms. "How come I didn't know about this girl?"

I grin. "I don't tell you the really good stuff." But my grin fades as I think about Juliet… Darla. I can't get that face, those dark eyes, her silky dark hair, and that gorgeous mouth out of my mind. I finally got one little snicker out of her today, and it almost transformed me into a wet noodle. "It brought back a bunch of memories."

"Good memories?"

I nod. *The best.*

She rubs my arm. "What's wrong with that?"

"I think I really freaked her out. She went from being shocked to angry to sad all in one minute. It was a very strange tilt-a-whirl of emotions. I couldn't keep up. At one point, I thought I was gonna have to call a code on her." Maybe she thought it was a one-night stand, and she was upset because I had the nerve to stir up old thoughts and feelings. Except it wasn't that. *At. All.*

Jennifer stares at me for the longest time before she is able to form words. "Does this have anything to do with the stain on your shirt?"

I chuckle as I remember the earlier incident. "Yeah. It was like she was terrified when she saw me. I could have sworn she felt the same way I did."

"Well, it's been a while since college. Maybe things have changed."

"I hope not." I look up at my sister, but her eyes stay fixed on the floor. "Now, you spill it. What's on your mind?"

She becomes fidgety all of a sudden. "Can we table that for another day?"

"Are you *exputtered?*"

She stands without responding and adjusts a stack of class worksheets.

I love rattling my sister. "Chicken."

She blushes. "Get out of here. I need to go too. Matt and I are leaving for a cruise tomorrow."

"Ah, yes. Is this a 'make a baby' trip?"

She bites her lip. "He wants a baby so badly, but I don't know if I'm ready. I mean, I always thought I was ready, but now that we're seriously talking about it, it makes me nervous."

Whoa. I didn't see that one coming. "What? Sis, you'd make a great mom."

She blinks a tear away. "Thanks. I needed to hear that. It's such a big step. I'm around kids all day long, so you'd think the thought of having one at home would be a no-brainer." She nudges me with her shoulder. "Now, get out of here." After she gives me a hug, she pushes me toward the door.

Seeing her on a regular basis is going to do a world of good for my sanity. I give her a hug before I leave her classroom.

Jen pokes her head out of her room. "Hey, Theo, tell me this girl's name, and I'll pray for the two of you."

I can't keep from smiling. "Her name is Darla."

She gasps and covers her mouth. Before I can ask why she has a deer-in-the-headlights stare, she slams the classroom door. She needs a vacation in the worst way.

I really should ask what that reaction was all about, but if I do, I'll never get any rest before my grueling shifts at the hospital start tomorrow. And I've got a cute wellness nurse I need to get reacquainted with.

Chapter Eight
Darla

I LOVE THIS PLACE. IT MAKES me think of the soda shops in the old fifties movies with its black-and-white square-tile floor, Naugahyde booths, and old jukebox in the back corner that still plays forty-five rpm records. I choose chocolate-mint ice cream in a chocolate-dipped waffle cone, my all-time favorite. *Yum.* It is frozen heaven covered in sinful decadent chocolate. It's Stella's favorite place too. It's a shame she's in after care. I've made the mistake of picking her up before she had adequate playground time, so she'll just have to miss out this time.

I settle into a booth near the back of the store and lean over the Formica table, letting the yummy goodness slide down my throat and hoping it will melt my cares away. *What a day!*

I guess I did not handle Theo's reappearance very well. I think it would have been easier if he had been smug or curt like his email was. But he was as cute and friendly as he was seven years ago. And that has me waxing and waning between wanting to lather his dimples with kisses and wanting to smack that smug smirk off his face.

My phone buzzes, announcing a text message. It's Jennifer.

Sorry. Family stuff came up. Can't make it.

I type a brief response.

No worries.

That's a bummer. She never misses one of our sessions. I start to put my phone back in my purse, when another text comes in from Jennifer.

Give Stella a hug for me.

Aww. Crunching the last bit of my waffle cone, I scoot out of the ice cream parlor to go pick up the coolest kid on the planet. I'm sure I can talk her into an ice cream. My day has definitely been a two-cone kind of day.

———◦◦◦———

By the time I get to the school gymnasium, Stella is deep into a game of foursquare with her after-school buddies. Her hair flies through the air each time she leaps to get the ball before it bounces away from her. When she sees me, she abandons her game and skips to me.

"Mommy, I'm not a first grader anymore."

She wraps her arms around my legs, and my heart swells with joy. Theo should be here. He should want to be here.

Stella tugs on my arm. "I lost my lunchbox again."

This makes the fourth one she's lost this year. "Stella, you're supposed to put it in your backpack after lunch so you won't misplace it."

She runs over to the corner of the gymnasium to retrieve her backpack. Papers and artwork hang out, barely staying in the bag. Any minute, graded homework assignments will be littering the gym floor.

"It's full and..." Her lip quivers. "I'm sorry, Mama. I didn't mean to lose another one."

If losing another lunchbox is the worst thing she ever does, I think I've got it made. I kneel down in front of her and kiss her cheek. "It's okay. It may not be lost. Let's see if the custodian is still here to let us into Mrs. Silva's room."

Her breath hitches. "She's still here."

"No, she's already left."

Stella shakes her head. "She came in here a second ago and gave me a big hug." There goes that lip quiver again. "I made her cry."

Jennifer is still at school, but she told me she had family things to take care of. *Huh.* It's not like her to lie to me. I plaster on my happy mom face. "I'm sure you didn't make her cry."

"Do you think she's upset that I lost my lunchbox?"

I wrap my arms around her little body. I could stay like this all day. "No, baby. I think she's sad because she'll miss you, that's all." *At least I think that's why.* "Come on. Let's find that lunchbox."

Stella races me down the hallway, and when we get to her classroom, she bolts through the door. Jennifer jumps. She wipes her eyes and turns away from us, erasing the whiteboard that has nothing written on it.

She clears her throat. "Hey."

Stella skips over to her desk and peeks inside. "Mommy, I found it!" Beaming with pride, she holds out her *Finding Nemo* lunchbox.

"Yay. That deserves ice cream."

Jennifer bites her lip while diverting her gaze into a box of books. "Sorry about bailing. I had…" She's a terrible liar.

"Family stuff. I understand." I'll give her the benefit of the doubt because she seems very upset about something. Maybe she did have family stuff, and it didn't go well. "You okay?"

She stares at the box. "I'm not sure. How are you?"

Stella tugs on my shirttail. "Mommy, ice cream?"

"Why don't you finish your foursquare game, and afterward, we'll get that ice cream."

"Okay. Bye, Mrs. Silva." She hugs Jennifer's waist.

More tears fall from Jennifer's eyes. She crouches down and envelops Stella in a whole-body hug. "I…"

Stella pries herself away from the hug and runs out of the classroom.

Jennifer faces away from me and wipes her face.

"Do you get this emotional at the end of every school year?"

She sniffles. "Yes, that's all it is. I'll miss them so much."

Jennifer is usually perky and fun. I've never seen her this emotional, but I'm sure saying good-bye to twenty people in one day would take a toll on me too.

She readjusts the books in the box for the third time. "You? Anything new?" She nibbles on a fingernail, never making eye contact.

I laugh as I pace the room, checking the hallway to make sure Stella isn't anywhere nearby. "You could say that." I know Jennifer bailed on me earlier, but I need to get an unbiased opinion on today's events, and it looks as though she might need a good distraction. "Did I ever tell you about Stella's father?"

She drops the book in her hand. "Uh, you never said anything, and I didn't want to pry."

I pick up the book and hand it to Jennifer. "We met in college, and I knew right away he was the one for me."

She looks like a fish on dry land, trying to suck in a mouthful of water. "Oh. What happened?"

I sit in Stella's little chair and think back to my night with Theo. "It's complicated."

She picks up some artwork that a child left behind. "Is he involved in Stella's life?"

"Nope. He didn't want anything to do with her."

Her back stiffens. "Why?"

"He had a girlfriend, and he told me to leave him alone."

She stuffs the artwork in the trash can. "That's awful. Are you sure?"

"Yeah. But now, he's back in town, and I don't know what to do."

She picks up her purse and glances at her watch.

I guess this conversation is over. "Sorry. I shouldn't have thrown all that on you. You're clearly stressed about something. This is very insensitive of me."

"Oh, Darla. I'm sure it will be okay." She hugs me and mumbles something I cannot make out. "I need to go, but… I need to go."

I nod. "Thank you so much for this year. I'll make sure Stella visits you from time to time."

She swipes more tears away. "Please do. She's so special."

Yes, she is. And one day, when I work up the nerve to tell him, Theo's going to think so too. There's no way he'll be able to look at Stella's sweet face and not fall madly in love with her.

I don't know how to fix this. All I know is I have to try.

Chapter Nine

Theo

I'T'S GOING TO TAKE MORE than a fresh pair of hospital-issue scrubs to get me ready for my first all-night shift in the ER. I have to keep my eye on the prize. Each shift gets me a few dollars closer to my goal. Maybe when my three-year fellowship is up, I'll have enough cash saved to take that Doctors Without Borders trip. I hope I can survive that long.

I'm going to need as much caffeine as possible in my bloodstream to make it through the night. That and a Foley catheter because I'll have to pee every thirty minutes. I fumble my way to the cafeteria and grab the largest cup I can find. If they had one of those sixty-four-ounce bladder-buster cups, I would get it. Clutching my diabetic kit under my arm, I fill the cup to the brim and survey the room to see if anyone's watching before I try to slurp down the coffee without scalding my tongue.

Gag. It tastes like coffee I would find in a truck stop. It's awful, but it does the trick even before I douse it with all kinds of unhealthy additives. I refill my cup before I schlep to the cashier. *Wow.* I'm such a rebel, living on the edge. I'm so tired, I don't really care if I get arrested for topping off my coffee.

As I slip the lid on my cup, Isaac from the fitness center appears. He looks at me and clucks his tongue as he cocks his head to the side. I've been busted by the health police. But I could get him in just as much trouble with that bear claw pastry *and* large coffee he's carrying. So my only offense is that I plan to pay for a large coffee when I should be paying for an IV bolus supply.

Isaac gets in line to pay, and I stand right behind him. He turns and wiggles his eyebrows at me. "Interesting couple of days, huh?"

"You could say that. You're here late."

"Yeah, had a lot of paperwork to do from the orientation session yesterday, especially since Darla hightailed it out of there after y'all's meet and greet."

I must have really made her mad, but I don't know why.

"Hey, Janie," Isaac says to the cashier.

She holds her hands out. "Now, Isaac, I know I've said it before, but I'm going to get to the fitness center. I promise."

He smiles at her. "Sure you will."

"You know everyone, don't you?" I ask him.

"Pretty much. It's part of my job. Hey, Janie, I've got his too." He pays for our coffees.

"Thanks. So... you know Darla very well?" It spills out before I know what I'm saying, but maybe he'll know what I did wrong. Beating around the bush has never gotten me anywhere. Hence the reason Mallory still thinks we're going to get back together.

Isaac motions for me to follow him to a table in the far corner of the cafeteria. I sit across from him and sprinkle sugar substitute into my coffee.

"I've known Darla since we were kids, but not like *you* know her, if that's what you're thinking."

I crack a grin.

He cackles with laughter. "What do you want to know?"

I glance around the cafeteria before blowing on my coffee. "She didn't seem too happy to see me. That's for sure."

Isaac shrugs. He waves at the man cleaning a nearby table. "She doesn't tell me everything. Some things are locked up tight in that pretty head of hers. Darla and her older sister, Diane, were my neighbors growing up. I even dated Diane briefly, but obviously that was a disaster," he singsongs.

I can't help but like this guy. He's so friendly and genuine. I'm glad Darla has a friend like him in her life. If I didn't have my brother and sisters, I don't know what I would do.

Isaac's happy expression fades. "I don't know anything, but I have never seen her get this messed up over anyone before. I sense there was something special there. Maybe still is."

I knew it. She feels it too. *Sweet.*

He leans in and whispers, "Don't say I said this, but I think she really likes you. She might be afraid."

"Of what? Have you looked at me? I'm not very scary. She could probably take me in a fight. What could she possibly be afraid of?"

"I don't know. Maybe it's you popping back into her life, or maybe it's something buried deep that no one knows." He rakes his teeth over his bottom lip. "Heck if I know. Damn, she's goofy as hell, but she's golden and about the finest person I know."

I lean back and close my eyes. If I sit here too long, I'll fall asleep. "I recently got out of a toxic long-term relationship, one that would have never happened in the first place if I'd had only a few more minutes with Darla. You have no idea how much I've thought about her over the years."

He chomps down on his bear claw and gulps down a swallow of coffee. "Be honest with me. Do you want to pick up where you left off?"

"Yes!" I guess I said that with a little bit too much enthusiasm. Several families at nearby tables swivel their heads in our direction. "But she does seem fragile... not to mention mad at me for something. I don't want to scare her off. Yep. I should approach this really slowly."

"But not too slowly." He snaps his fingers. "Her office is in the fitness center. Stop by and let her get used to you. You can find time to work out, can't you?"

"Are you a walking advertisement?"

He shrugs. "And if you need Uncle Isaac or the Fairy Godmother to knock some sense into her, we can do that."

A warm feeling runs through my veins, and it's not the caffeine. I think back to the one night Darla and I had together. I was ready to have her meet my family; I was certain that she was the one for me. "No, I think I can handle this one on my own."

We fist-bump.

"I'm sure you can."

Not that I needed one more item on my schedule, but working out is for a good cause. I have to get another dose of the Darla drug soon, or I'll go through withdrawals again.

Chapter Ten
Darla

I RAMBLE AROUND MY GALLEY KITCHEN in my favorite comfy clothes—a pair of ratty surgical scrubs, my old gray university sweatshirt, and my favorite flip-flops. To celebrate the last day of school, I am making Mexican food. Stella loves to make tacos. If I didn't know better, I would think she was descended from the Aztecs. She eats chips like other kids eat french fries.

"You better hold off on those jalapeños. They're killers," I say to her as she pops another salsa-laden chip in her mouth. She seems completely unfazed by the heat, even though beads of sweat are already forming on her forehead.

"I know what else will kill you," she says.

I take out the ingredients for our meal. "Yeah? What's that?"

"A spinning wheel."

I stare at her.

"It's true. That's what happened to Sleeping Beauty."

"Ahh. It's a good thing we don't have a spinning wheel."

"I know." She bounces on one foot then the other. "Can I shred the cheese?" She blows a strand of hair out of her face.

I have absolutely no self-control around her. It has been the two of us for so long that it would be really weird to have a traditional household—a mom, a dad, two point five kids, and a dog. I'm so used to doing everything myself that I'm not sure if I could hand over some of that control.

At first, it was overwhelming because I had to take all the day and night feedings. I was the one who had to make a mad dash to the store during a tornado warning with a three-month-old in tow because I ran out of diapers. And I paced the floor alone, praying that God would let her fever break.

But we survived, and every day got better and better. Eventually, I found my groove, and with help from friends like Isaac, we've done pretty well on our own. He really stepped up to the plate since my father didn't want anything to do with me and my illegitimate child, and my crazy sister had already moved to Los Angeles.

Isaac was there through it all—the pregnancy, the delivery, the post-partum anxiety, and all those times I needed someone to fall back on. He even helped out by watching Stella when I had to work the night shifts as a staff nurse. But the missing piece of the puzzle has always been the daddy-sized elephant in the room.

I tried to date, but that faded over time. It wasn't worth the effort. The bar had been set so high that even an astronaut would have had trouble reaching it. The only person that would fit all my criteria was tucked neatly away in medical school, living the life he wanted.

He has some nerve, waltzing back in and acting as if life is peachy, as if he doesn't even remember that one night. It's as though he doesn't even remember he has a daughter. Medical school must have zapped all his memory cells for him to forget something like that. The party, the baby, the emails, the rejection. It breaks my heart to think he has so little respect for the life he created when she is absolutely wonderful.

I hand Stella the shredder. "Here, make sure you don't shred your knuckles this time."

"Oh, Mommy, I only did that once."

She takes the chunk of cheddar in her tiny hand and slowly starts making little bits of crumbled cheese. I don't care if the shreds are imperfect. Cheese is cheese. Most of it lands on the floor, which Yeti willingly cleans up. I brown the ground beef on the stove, keeping one eye peeled over my shoulder to make sure she doesn't get her little hands too close to the shredder's sharp edges.

"I like lots of cheese. Daddy does too." She must have been a fly on the wall, watching the recent turn of events.

"What makes you think that?"

She shrugs. "Don't all daddies? Can we watch a movie tonight?"

I grin at my daughter. Sometimes I can't keep up with her rapid shifts in conversations. She can go from what happened at school to some current event to that pretty butterfly outside the window in less than thirty seconds. All the while, I'm still trying to work my way through what happened at school. She sure does keep me on my toes.

"Sure."

"Kade has a great daddy."

And we're back to daddy talk. This is starting to get freaky. If she has the ability to read my mind, we are going to be in a world of trouble when she's sixteen.

"When do you think Daddy will be finished with that special, secret job he has?"

Not soon enough. "Soon, or at least I hope so."

Every time she mentions my little white lie, my blood pressure rises ten points. I wish I could blame this on someone else, but it falls one hundred percent on my shoulders. A few years ago, she started asking about her daddy, and I couldn't look at that precious face and tell her he didn't want her. To protect her until she was old enough to understand the situation better, I went with the fib about him being away working, which wasn't entirely a lie.

"But hey, we're doing good, you and me, right?"

She shrugs. "You won't get me a pony."

I can hardly afford to feed the two of us, let alone a huge beast. And Stella has it in her mind that a pony can live in our postage-stamp-sized backyard. The neighbors would love that.

It's time for me to change the subject. "Hey, Aunt Diane will be here in a few days. Remember, you're going to spend a few weeks with her."

Stella's eyes get as big as saucers. "Oh yeah! She promised me she'd take me to Disneyland." All her worries about spinning wheels and finding her daddy are forgotten like a dandelion after the seeds have been blown into the breeze.

I wish I could be more like a six-year-old. I'm still kicking myself for agreeing to this little adventure with my sister. When Stella found out she could meet princesses and Mickey Mouse, the battle was more than I could handle. I mean, Stella's puppy-dog eyes *and* Mickey Mouse? My sister knew I wasn't going to win this time. I like being in control, and I lost control to Mickey Mouse of all people. Darn that rodent and his high-pitched voice.

"I know. It's the original park. The one in California near where Aunt Diane lives. You're going to have so much fun." My sister fell in love with a movie producer eight years ago when he was in town filming an episode of *Nashville*. Within three months, they were married and living happily ever after in Los Angeles. I do my best, but sometimes, my fifty shades of green peek through. But Stella's time away might give me time to formulate a "meet your daughter" event.

"What did you do today at work?" she asks.

She always wants to know all about work—every detail of everything. She can finish the game of Twenty Questions before breakfast every morning. Mrs. Silva says needing to know every single detail of everything is a sign of intelligence. Stella must have inherited that curiosity from her father, because she sure didn't get it from me.

"Well, I took the day off because... I wasn't feeling well, but yesterday was very busy. You know I work at a teaching hospital, so every year about this time, new doctors come to work at the hospital to finish their training. They've finished school but need to learn all the skills that go with it. Miss Shelby, Uncle Isaac, and I help to make sure they've had all their shots, check their cholesterol, blood pressure, stuff like that."

She giggles as she grabs two paper plates and places taco shells on them. "Uncle Isaac's funny."

He hasn't been recently.

"Do you like him?" she asks.

I stop chopping vegetables. "Of course I do. We've been buddies for as long as I can remember."

"Do you want to marry him?"

"I love working with him, but he's more like a brother to me. And he's been a bad boy."

"Did he spit food on somebody?"

I laugh out loud. "No, but I'm sure he's done that at some point."

"Kade does that sometimes in the cafeteria. It's gross. And you can't marry Uncle Isaac. When Daddy comes home, you'll want to marry him."

God love her. "We'll see."

We inhale the tacos and lounge on the couch, downing chips as we watch a movie. Yeti sits at our feet, expecting every third chip to be tossed his way.

The doorbell rings, causing Yeti to go ballistic. Good thing his bark is louder than his bite. He may only be a ten-pound Chihuahua, but if anyone tries to take his treat away from him, he transforms into a Doberman. He runs to the door, doing circles as if he's rallying the troops for battle.

Stella sprints to the door. "I'll get it."

"No, I'll get it. You can't even see out of the peephole." I scoot her out of the way and peek through to see Isaac's eye. It's creepy. God, I hate when he does that. At least it wasn't his tongue this time.

As soon as I open the door, Isaac says, "Romeo, oh, Romeo. Wherefore art thou, Romeo?" He's still dressed in his khakis and polo shirt, looking as though he came straight from work. *Oops.* I guess my faux illness caused him to work overtime in order to get all the data from the physician screening entered into the database. I should apologize, but he's in the doghouse, so I don't feel too bad. Yeti barks at Isaac as if to say he's glad some other old dog has entered his home.

"Down, Bigfoot," Isaac says, petting the top of Yeti's head.

Stella bounces up and down. "Uncle Isaac. Uncle Isaac."

He plops his messenger bag by the door and scoops her up to run through the living room with her on his back, sliding on the fake Oriental rug in front of the fireplace. Both of them scream, "Whee!"

When Isaac visits, it's like having two children in the house. He and Stella play so well together that it's sometimes hard to remember he's not her age. At least Stella can hit the toilet when she goes to the bathroom, which is more than I can say for Isaac.

"What did you bring me?" Stella asks.

"Stella," I scold. "Manners."

"Oh, it's okay. I would never drop by without something." And when Isaac wants the scoop, the "something" he brings is usually really good. He backs up toward the front door and points to his messenger bag.

Stella bounces again from one foot to the other.

"I've got… cookies from Becca's Bakery." He takes out a big paper sack from his messenger bag. At least it's not a pony.

Stella squeals again. Oh, he has brought out the big guns. If he splurged for Becca's Bakery, I know he's serious. He holds the bag a bit higher than Stella can reach. She jumps for it over and over but never quite gets it.

No matter how mad he made me earlier, I know he would never do anything to hurt me, not on purpose, anyway. It's time to get him up to speed on some details I've kept from everyone, even my best friend.

Stella reaches for the bag. "Mommy said you spit food on somebody today."

He cocks his head to the side. "What?"

While Isaac is distracted, I snatch the bag from him and run into the kitchen. They both chase after me and tackle me to the ground. Yeti jumps in on the action.

———————◦✕◦———————

The three of us settle in on the couch to watch Stella's favorite movie, *Finding Nemo*, and munch on cookies dunked in milk. This is my slice of heaven. I can forget all my troubles because all I ever need is right beside me on this couch.

"I love this movie," Isaac says.

"Are you going to cry?" Stella asks.

He dabs his eyes. "Maybe."

"Stella, he cries at movies... a lot. I thought he was going to make a scene during that romantic comedy we saw once."

"Hey," Isaac says. "Jonah's mom dies, and he wants a new wife for his dad. It's so sweet." He snatches another tissue and dabs the tears from the corners of his eyes.

"Hey, Isaac," Stella says. "Maybe we can go find my daddy."

Isaac's eyes widen.

"Okay, sweetie, time for bed."

"Aww," Isaac and Stella moan.

"Bed," I say. They both head to her bedroom, heads hanging low.

"I meant Stella."

Isaac gives her a smooch and runs back to the couch to fumble through the bag of cookies.

After I have Stella neatly tucked into her bed, I stand over Isaac, tapping my toe. "Checking up on me?"

"Well, after the whole *Romeo and Juliet* scene, I needed to make sure you were okay... and to apologize for laughing at you. That was evil." He leans back on the couch, looking as if he has confessed to a triple homicide. Boy, that whole apology thing wasn't easy for him to spit out.

I focus on anything but his face. "Apology accepted."

"What is it with this guy?"

I groan. Isaac pats the seat cushion next to him, and in a split second, my anger toward him is gone. I need to tell him everything.

I take one more peek down the hallway toward Stella's room. "Okay. I'll tell you."

He flings his shoes off and folds his legs under him. If I didn't know any better, I would think we were having a sleepover like we did back in the day. The only things missing are pillow fights and prank calls to old boyfriends. But the night is still young.

———— ◦◦◦ ————

Isaac bats the tears from his eyes. I roll mine. He's the most emotional person I've ever known, and I love him for it.

He fans his face. "That's the most romantic thing ever."

"Oh, please. It's cute, but romantic?"

"Why haven't you ever told me that story before?"

I shrug. "I guess I didn't want to relive it. It's embarrassing."

All of a sudden, he gasps so loudly, it sounds as if he is sucking in all the air in the room. I sneak a peek over my shoulder to make sure he hasn't woken up Stella.

"Oh! My! God! That's why you named her Stella."

I nod. "It was all I had of him. I wanted her to have some connection to him, regardless of whether he wanted us or not."

He wraps his arms around me. "That is so sweet. I remember trying to convince you to name her a dozen different names, but you were hell-bent on naming her Stella. Makes sense now. You know, I spent so much time scratching my head, trying to figure things out. You weren't the type to sleep around. None of it made sense to me. But who am I to judge? I kept my opinions to myself and helped any way I could."

After what feels like an eternity, I finally continue. "I know it all sounds crazy, but I really liked him. I had only known him a few hours, but I felt like I had known him my whole life. He was different. He made me feel something I had never felt before."

"That's not crazy. That's love."

I snort. "I have no idea what love feels like. All I know is that seeing him again after all this time sent a shockwave of emotions back into my soul."

"That's good, right?"

I sigh. "I don't know."

Isaac puts on his shoes and takes out his keys. "But you have one thing wrong in your story. You said you really liked him."

"I did like him."

He wags his index finger in front of my nose. "Your eyes dance when you talk about him. You *like* him. Present tense."

I rub my face with my hands. I know it's true, but Theo chose medical school and Mallory. He flat-out didn't want us, even after I sent him a picture of the sonogram. I thought that even if he didn't care about me anymore, he would at least want to be in his daughter's life. I've kept a copy of the "leave me alone" email all these years. It's dog-eared and tear-stained, but I can't throw it away. I wasn't enough for him seven years ago, and I'm still not enough for him today, not even with a precious child as a bonus prize.

"Maybe. But it doesn't matter how I feel."

Isaac gives me a hug. "Would it make a difference if I told you I talked to him in the cafeteria a little while ago?"

I push him away and swat at his arm. "You didn't."

"Ow. It wasn't planned, but I can tell you this—he's really glad he found you. And… he's not in a relationship anymore."

Heat rushes up my neck. I need some Propranolol, stat. "Really?"

He rubs his arm where I hit him. "I know what you should do." His eyebrows dance up and down, and he makes kissie faces at me.

I push him out the door. "Go home."

He giggles all the way to his car. "Don't be afraid of being happy," he calls back at me. "You deserve it."

Aww. I love my buddy.

"Bye, Juliet."

I put my finger to my lips to remind him not to tell anyone. He does the same. Even though he sometimes has loose lips, I know he would never hurt me by telling something as sensitive as what I've confessed to him.

As he drives away, I think about the story I told him. Remembering was fun. But of course, I left out some parts—like the way Theo kept eye contact with me and kissed me as if he really loved me. He was either good at pretending, or he really felt something between us too. I remember that he wasn't in any hurry for me to leave. He was perfectly content to sleep curled up with me. And it was the best sleep I have ever had in my life. I just wish our beginning wasn't also our ending. I wish I had been good enough for him.

All those questions Stella was asking tonight confirm to me that she needs to know her father. Even if he didn't think he wanted her before she was born, he won't be able to resist her now. I deserve answers, and he deserves a second chance to know his daughter. How I'm going to do this... I have no idea. Perhaps with a friendly conversation over a hot cup of coffee and maybe a game of Truth or Dare sprinkled in.

Chapter Eleven

Theo

"MAKE SURE YOU PICK UP the mail every day," Jennifer says.

"Okay," I reply as I drag her luggage to the check-in counter at the airport. Matt follows behind us, lugging more bags.

"Oh, and Wednesdays are trash days."

"Got it."

We've gone over this a dozen times, she's left me a detailed list on her refrigerator, *and* she's sent it to me by email... twice. We've moved up in line a mere inch. This is going to take a while. I could find a cure for some rare diseases faster than this.

I eyeball Matt, Jennifer's husband. Even ten years out of college, he still maintains his quarterback physique. I'll never forget the way he couldn't get enough of my sister at their wedding. He looked at her as though she were the only person in the church, his beginning and end.

Jennifer says it wasn't his handsome face she was attracted to, even though he is a damn fine-looking dude if I say so myself. She said it was his eyes that got her. His pale-blue eyes would sparkle and make her feel as though she were the most important person in the world, no matter what she did or said. And she likes his hands. I don't even know what that means. Maybe I don't want to know. All I do know is that he adores my sister even when she mother-hens us, like she's doing right now. Matt grins at me. He knows as well as I do that I know all these details already, but I let her ramble. She's my big sister, and neither of us would trade her thoroughness for all the tea in China.

"Darlin', everything will be fine," Matt says.

She takes a deep breath. His warm Southern drawl is the only thing that can calm her down.

I scan the airport to distance myself from Jen's chatter. One of the kids from her class is in another line, holding an ice cream cone. If I point her out to Jen, my sister will get out of line, and we'll have to start this process all over again, so I keep it to myself. It's the little girl that helped me check my blood sugar. She's with a tall female that could be a dark-haired version of Mallory from what I can see. The fancy purse and watch the woman wears are probably worth enough to pay off my student loans. The lady flips her hair around as she chats on her phone.

The little girl sits on her Dora the Explorer suitcase and takes a long lick of her ice cream cone. She catches my eye and grins. I wave to her, and she gives me the cutest little finger wave back.

Matt bumps me to move forward. *Yes! Progress.* Finally, Jen and Matt are at the counter. My services of taxi and valet are complete. Matt and I knuckle-bump.

"Let me know if you need me to call in a prescription for promethazine. Nausea can be bad with those big waves."

He chuckles. "I'm hoping we'll be making our own waves."

Jen pops him on the arm. "Matt. I can't believe you said that."

I give her a hug, enjoying the pink flush across her neck. "You got all weird on me the other day at your school, and you've ignored my texts every time I've brought it up. What's up?" I wish she was going to be around this summer. I would love for it to be like it used to be before I went off to med school.

She searches her purse and her pockets and withdraws her plane ticket. She stares at her feet and crumples her ticket in her tightly fisted hand.

"They may need that in one piece."

She flattens it out.

While Matt is checking his bags, I put my hands on her shoulders. "Talk to me."

Her eyes are trained on the floor. "Did you ever wish you could unsee or unhear something?"

"Like the time I walked in on you and..."

She pushes me away. "Don't go there."

"Honey, they need your boarding pass and ID," Matt says.

Jennifer's gaze moves from me to Matt then back to me. She wraps me in a big hug. "I have to go. I love you so much."

Matt shrugs.

"I know." I pry myself away from her. "The freak-out happened right after I mentioned Darla."

As soon as I utter Darla's name, Jennifer gets that deer-in-the-headlights gaze again.

A few gears click into place, but my brain cells run dry. "You don't... nah. Impossible."

Matt places his hands on her shoulders and rotates Jennifer to face the check-in counter. "What's possible is you're going to make all those passengers behind us miss their planes."

"Have a great trip," I say to them.

She stares at me and opens her mouth to say something. Then she closes it and takes a deep breath. "We do need to talk, but I guess it will have to wait until I get back."

She stares at me as if she wants me to read her mind. Usually, I can read her like yesterday's news, but this expression is new. I wish I could steal her away for five minutes to download her thoughts, but if I do, I will impede the progress of getting them through security. So I smile and act as though I'm oblivious, which isn't hard for me.

She sighs. "I'll try to call or text you if I get cell service."

"Have fun," I say as I make my way toward the security gates.

My phone buzzes, and I unclip it from my waistband to read the text. I glance around to see if I'm being pranked before I read it again.

> *It's no longer Juliet. The name is now known.*
> *Wouldn't you like to make her your own?*
> *She has a big secret, not sure how to spill.*
> *She doesn't know how you'll really feel.*
> *Go back to the beginning is how this quest starts.*
> *Head straight to the ruins where it all fell apart.*
> *Shhhh.*

"What the heck?" I check the phone number. It's not one I recognize. I dial the number, and it goes straight to an anonymous voice mail.

I replace the phone on my waistband clip, when someone yells, "Watch it!"

My attention is so fixed on my phone that I'm not paying attention to my surroundings. Before I know it, I plow right over the little girl from Jennifer's class, knocking her onto her bottom. She still holds her cone, but the ice cream lies in a blob next to her suitcase. The little girl's bottom lip quivers.

"Ugh," the lady says, rolling her eyes.

Yep, she's a Mallory clone. I offer my hand to help the little girl to her feet, but her mother swats my hand away.

"Why don't you watch where you're going? You almost ran over her."

The little girl wipes some ice cream off her dress.

"I'm so sorry I messed up your ice cream." Man, I would rather get my foot run over by a car than make this cute thing sad.

She holds out her empty cone to me. "That's okay, Dr. Theo."

She remembered my name? *Aw. Adorable.*

"You know him?" the lady asks her.

"Uh-huh," the little girl replies.

She rolls her eyes. "It figures in this town. I hate Nashville."

"He has diabetes."

"Very good," I reply. "You're... Stella, right?"

Her eyes light up when she realizes I remember her, and she bounces. Yes, I remember the eyes and the bounce.

I open my wallet and hand her a ten-dollar bill. "How about as soon as you get through security, you buy yourself another ice cream? Eat one for me too."

She takes the money, and her eyes flick up to her mother.

The woman snatches it out of Stella's hand and shoves it back into mine. "Nope. Please get out of the way. I'll buy her one later."

"I'll be sure to check my sugar before I eat it," Stella says.

I whistle in frustration at the little girl's mom. "You do that."

Her mother gives her watch a once-over before her attention lands back on Stella.

"Sorry, ma'am, for any inconvenience," I say.

She takes Stella by the hand and scampers down the concourse. Before they're out of sight, Stella takes one more look at me over her shoulder. We exchange waves before the Mallory clone whisks her away.

I clear my throat and sneak away, hoping I don't get chewed out by anyone else today.

———— ◦✕◦ ————

All afternoon, I stay busy seeing patients in the clinic, but every thirty minutes, I get a reminder text to go back to the beginning, the frat house where Darla and I met. I'm not going to fall for a prank. I will *not* fall for a prank. Nope, I'm not going to where the frat house used to be. Not going to do it.

Okay, maybe a peek. Whoever sent this to me knows I can't resist a game. I don't care if Mallory thought they were childish. They're fun, and I love the challenge. Besides, this game has to do with Darla, my favorite game partner.

When I'm done in the clinic, I saunter through the university campus, which is right next to the medical center. I head toward fraternity row, my old stomping ground. I mean, it is on the way to the parking lot... sort of. I walk down the street and see the empty lot where my fraternity house used to stand. Nothing has been built there since the fire. I saunter across the street, surveying the neighborhood behind me, in front of me, to my left, and to my right. I will not be pranked. I swear, if someone is playing a joke on me, I'm going to be pissed. The texts have to be from Darla. I can't think of anyone else who knows where we met and how I can't resist a game. She doesn't have to go to all this trouble to tell me a secret, but I do love a good puzzle.

I stop in my tracks when I notice an envelope nailed to a tree in the middle of the yard. Checking out the surroundings, I creep over to the tree and see the name Romeo typed on the envelope. I snatch up the envelope, open it, and peer over my shoulder one more time before reading the contents.

I knew you couldn't sit this one out.
Your interest is piqued, there's no doubt.
You'll get a text in an hour or so.
With details on how this fun game will go.

I chuckle as I stash the note in my pocket and walk to my car, where I should have gone in the first place. "That's real cute, Darla."

The pitiful rhyme sticks in my brain the entire drive home, and as soon as I enter my apartment complex, my phone buzzes. I retrieve it from my pocket and read the text.

> *Rumor has it, you like to play games.*
> *Especially when it's one special dame.*
> *So brush off your skills, if you think you can.*
> *Let's play a fun game of Hangman.*
> *_ _ _ _ _ _ _ _ _ _ _ _ _ _ _*
> *Choose your first letter.*

The message is signed, *I'm not a stalker.* I switch off the car and focus on the sentence. I'm good at this. I crack my knuckles and tap my fingers on the steering wheel.

"Hmm." I type the letter A and hit send. Before I take two steps away from my car, I receive another message.

> *Good first choice. More chances to play coming*
> *soon after this message from our sponsor.*
> *_ _ _ _ A _ _ A _ _ _ _ _ _ _*

"Oh, I'm good. Bahaha!"

> *No cheating. If you tell anyone about this*
> *game, you'll lose the grand prize.*

Damn, she's serious.

Chapter Twelve
Darla

SHELBY CLUTCHES HER CHEST AND collapses into the chair next to my desk. "Dr. Hotness is her father?" Her voice ends in a high-pitched shrill.

"Yep."

She scans the wellness center from my office doorway. Barely above a whisper, she asks, "Does Stella know?"

"It all happened so fast. She was leaving with Diane, so I couldn't simply spring something like this on her and then say, 'See ya in a few weeks.' Besides, I need to talk to him first."

"Does he know?"

I throw my hands up in frustration. "I thought he did, but he acts completely clueless."

"Oh. My. God."

"It's a lot to process."

Shelby has a refreshed appearance after finishing her morning run on the treadmill. "Ya think?"

Isaac leans against the doorframe. "I take it you told her." He gives me a thumbs-up.

Shelby swats at him, but he jumps out of hitting range. "If you knew, why didn't you tell me?"

"Hey now. A promise is a promise. Sorry, Boss."

She closes her eyes and exhales. "Okay, I can't take all this in right now. We've got to get ready for new staff orientation."

Isaac groans.

I stand and stretch my arms over my head. "Think of it this way. This week can't get any worse, right?"

They both stare at me as if I've jinxed all of us.

We trek across campus with our oversized storage-bags-on-wheels stuffed with all our equipment.

As we enter the hospital lobby, Isaac whispers, "Dr. Stud Muffin, dead ahead."

Before I even realize I'm looking, my eyes find him coming my way. His cheerful expression makes it hard not to watch. As he passes without seeing me, I continue to follow him with my eyes, not watching where I'm going. Someone rushes past me and whacks me with a very large purse, sending me to the floor.

Isaac helps me up. "You okay?"

"Rude," I say to the blur that keeps going.

I watch the blur for a moment. *No! Unbelievable.*

My mouth drops, and I am frozen in place. I need a sinkhole to open up and swallow me whole. It's the best thing that can happen at this point. I thought he wasn't with her anymore.

Mallory runs up to Theo and links her arm through his. He rotates his head and jerks his arm away. At that very moment, he catches my eye. I can't stop gaping. He grins at me. She keeps chatting into his ear, but he continues to hold my gaze.

"Help me," he mouths.

Holy cow.

We settle in to our little section of the orientation room. Isaac slides two tables together and arranges chairs for us to sit in one long line on one side of the tables. In front of the tables, he arranges another set of chairs for the new employees to sit in while we do their wellness assessments. I'm always at the end so I can draw blood and be near the Sharps disposal containers. Like three little robots, we organize our supplies and set up for the day. I think all of us could do this in our sleep, except today it's a nightmare. Thank goodness I hid behind Isaac so Mallory didn't see me. With any luck, she's long gone by now.

"Whoever schedules all these orientations back-to-back should be shot," Shelby snaps as she throws brochures and forms on the table.

I nibble on my fingernail as I pace back and forth across the room. I cannot believe Mallory is here and with him. This is not good. This is nothing near good. I think I'm going to hurl. Maybe I thought the gods of mercy would cut me some slack, but it seems as if they're taking a smoke break.

"Amen, sister," Isaac replies.

"I'm serious. It's too much for one week. I mean, hello? We have other things to do. And we have a nighttime screening session coming up for the evening staff."

"I say let the newbies figure it out for themselves," Isaac says.

I nod, not really following the conversation. I keep replaying the hallway scene over and over in my head. He's here. She's here. They're still together. The idea makes the bile bubble up from my stomach. The last time I saw Mallory, we did the obligatory graduation photo together and made "let's stay in touch" promises, which we did for a while. But when I realized she and Theo were a couple, I couldn't keep up the pleasantries. So I replied less and less to her emails, and she eventually stopped writing.

"Couldn't have said it better myself. Drinks are on me tonight." Shelby holds up a stack of brochures as if it's a shot glass. A shot would be helpful right now.

"Yes!" Isaac cheers.

"Darla," Shelby says. "You're awfully quiet."

Mallory is here. She still has those legs that go on for days and that perfect shade of blond hair. And she's... well, she's still... perfect in every possible way. And she is still with him. Of course she is. Mallory always gets what she wants. She stalks her prey and pounces. When that happens, it's best to either surrender or play dead.

"Maybe she's worried another lover from her past will show up," Isaac says.

"No chance of that," I reply, plastering on a fake smirk.

I stack up the tubes near the Sharps container and get set for a long morning. I'm hoping that by keeping my hands busy, my mind won't stay stuck on the perpetual Theo-Mallory wheel.

I pull Isaac aside and lower my voice to a whisper. "You said he wasn't in a relationship anymore. Does your dyslexia get facts backwards too?"

He chuckles. "No. That's what he said."

I inspect my supplies to make sure everything is in place. I can whip right through two hundred new employees in three hours if I'm all organized. That's what I need to stay focused on—work. If I don't think of something else soon, I'm going to need a paper bag to breathe into. *Please tell me she didn't get a job here too.*

Isaac stands in front of us and starts his traditional deep-breathing exercises. This is his way of getting psyched up to be nice to everyone that stops by. Shelby and I follow suit. It actually does help. Isaac says if he doesn't do this, he cannot stand answering the same questions two hundred times.

The crowd filters into the room and quiets down as the orientation film plays on the screen. A new wave of nausea threatens to take control. Mallory sits on the back row, phone in hand, fingers flying across the keyboard. *Shit.* She *is* a new employee. *Ugh.*

I could fake a stomach virus. Or maybe I can lie and say I left my favorite stethoscope in the office. That should take at least two hours to fetch.

Suddenly, I don't think I'm going to have to fake that stomach virus. I am going to need a gallon of Maalox to get through this morning. Maalox combined with Xanax and a shot of whiskey might do the trick.

When the crowd breaks up into small groups, Mallory heads directly to our station, of course. *Open wound. Pour salt. Kill me now.* At least I'll get this face-to-face over with, and I can check it off my "people I want to see the least" list.

Mallory sees me and freezes. She grins and cocks her head to one side. "Darla?" she asks with a syrupy sweetness to her voice.

I paint on the fakest, prettiest smile I can manage. "Hi, Mallory."

She runs around the table. With her long legs and four-inch heels, she towers over me. She grabs my shoulders and does a bouncy happy dance. "Oh my God! Oh my God! I cannot believe it's *you!*"

"It's me."

"It's her," Isaac and Shelby say with as little enthusiasm as I did.

She takes in my appearance. "You look fantastic. Absolutely adorbs."

She starts with my hair, which hasn't been trimmed in months, and scans all the way to my sneakers, which have seen better days. Yep. That's Mallory. She always analyzed my choice of clothing. I look as though I'm ready to take a yoga class, and she's dressed as if she owns a yoga studio. It's easy to feel inferior in her presence without her even trying. It's not that she purposefully tries to make people feel a few levels lower on the food chain. She just has this way about her. She can criticize me while she has a beauty-queen smile plastered on her face. And I don't even realize the jab until ten minutes later after she has moved on to someone else.

Had it not been a random roommate pairing freshman year, we probably would have never even known each other's names. We had zero friends in common. But I did enjoy her perpetual perkiness. Otherwise, I would have requested a new roommate the first chance I got. Besides, she was gone partying so much, it felt as though I had the dorm room to myself most of the time. Mallory was always, and I'm sure still is, the life of the party. There's never a dull moment when she's around. Except sometimes, dull is good. I'm really good at being dull.

I've often wondered over the years if she really did try to help me find my Romeo before we graduated. Now that I have had time to think about it, I realize it's possible that she intentionally kept information from me so she could snatch him for herself. She seemed sincere at the time, but only a few months after graduation, she had him, and all I had were memories of what I could only assume he thought was a one-night stand.

But the only thing I can think of right now is the last communication from her. It was that email Christmas card showing off the love of her life. I was still pregnant, and my hormones were off the charts, so I didn't take it well, to say the least. I guess I should thank her for sending that email to everyone, including Theo. It gave me the opportunity to reach out to him, even if he flat-out refused to accept responsibility. I didn't copy Mallory on the email because I never was good at standing up for myself when it came to her. My plan was to tell Theo, and together, we could talk to Mallory. But my plan took a nosedive when he rejected me and his baby.

"You haven't changed," I said, trying to keep my smile in place. "What are you doing here?" *Oh God.* I can't believe I asked her that. *Just get this little meet and greet over with. Don't make eye contact. Don't ask. Don't tell. Don't pursue.*

"Well, my fiancé is doing a fellowship here, and…"

And that's all I remember from the conversation. She said fiancé. She didn't say boyfriend or friend or roommate or even cousin. I think I could handle any—well, most—of those words. But she said fiancé.

Shelby assesses the situation with a thin-lipped grin. "You two know each other, I assume."

Behind Mallory's back, Shelby mimics gagging herself with her finger. I stifle a grin. *Thanks, Shelby. I owe you one.*

"Yes, of course," Mallory replies. "We were roommates all through college."

She gives me another squeeze around the neck, and I fake a grin. It's such a good grin that I could get an award, although I think I will have to massage my cheeks to release the cramps I'm getting.

"Yeah, we kind of lost contact somewhere along the way," I say.

"I know, and I don't think you ever got to meet the love of my life."

I bite my lip. She has a lot of nerve. "Guess not." Boy, talk about an Oscar-worthy performance. Of course, I've met him. She must have seen Theo staring at me the night of the party, and we did some incredible things that I'm glad she didn't see. He's the only man I've ever wanted, and somehow, she managed to squirm her way into his life. On top of that, it appears as though she has a strong choke hold on him now. She knew who he was and kept it from me on purpose. I'm certain of it now.

She hugs me again. "Now that we're back in town, the three of us have to get together, unless you have someone special too."

I glance at Isaac and Shelby, who aren't missing any part of this conversation. "Actually, I do, but she's out of town right now."

Mallory's face goes blank. "Oh, that's okay. I've got lots of gay friends. Well, not lots, but you know what I mean."

She tugs on one of the three necklaces she has around her neck. I think she's going to choke herself. *By all means, please continue.*

I glance over at Isaac. "She's my daughter."

"Oh, thank God." She lets out a huge breath. "You have a daughter? I cannot wait to meet her."

Yeah, that will go over nicely. Showing her a child with the same eyes and dimples as her fiancé is *not* on my bucket list. *Uh, nope. Not gonna happen.*

"Are congratulations in order?" Isaac takes her left hand and flips it over to examine her finger. He makes a "tsk tsk" sound. "Where's the ring?" he asks with a scolding tone.

Ha! She got busted by the prince of observation. The Mallorys of the world would have a massive rock to show off to the world if they were engaged, and she doesn't have one.

She snatches her hand back. "It's not official. He's going to work additional shifts in the ER to make some extra money. So it won't be long." She claps her hands like a cheerleader and cocks her head to the side—a tick of hers I learned a long time ago that signals when she's bullshitting her way through a conversation.

"Well, it's really... good to see you again." I try hard not to throw up on her blouse.

Mallory continues to bounce. How in the world can she do that while wearing four-inch heels? And those fake boobs are going to put somebody's eye out.

"We have got to do lunch." Her phone rings. "I've got to take this. Toodles."

"Toodles," Isaac and Shelby say together.

Isaac watches Mallory until she is out of the room then turns to me. "Girl, you should have gone to college with me. I would have made a much better roomie."

Shelby points to Isaac. "What he said."

I'm more confused than ever. Theo told Isaac he wasn't in a relationship anymore, and the lack of an engagement ring corroborates his story. But I don't think Mallory got the memo.

There's only one way to find out—put Theo in the hot seat.

Chapter Thirteen

Darla

Isaac and Shelby don't know it yet, but they are about to enter a brainstorming session to help me figure out how to deal with my Theo problem. But first, I need some face time with my baby girl.

When her sweet face fills my screen, I can barely keep the tears away. It has only been a few days, but I already miss her. I can't breathe without this kid in my life. She's having the time of her life with my sister, but that doesn't mean I have to like it.

"Hey, Mommy."

That voice. It can melt the hardest of hearts and make me forget all my troubles.

"Hey, sweet girl. Are you having fun?"

"Yep. We went to the pool today."

Shocker. "That sounds like fun. The sun is a lot stronger in LA, so please make sure Aunt Diane puts a ton of sunscreen on you."

"I will," my sister says offscreen. "You are such a worrywart."

She would understand if she had a child of her own.

"I miss you." On purpose, I move my phone so she doesn't see me wipe tears off my face.

"Miss you too." Her lip quivers. "I did something really bad."

"It can't be that bad, honey. What is it?"

Stella's gaze roams around the room. "I was listening when you and Uncle Isaac were talking the other night."

Shit. No air can get into my lungs. I have to think of something fast. "We weren't talking about anything." *Liar.*

She wipes a tear away. "Yes, you were. You told him you found my daddy, but I think I found him too."

My phone drops to the floor.

"Mommy?"

"Yeah, sorry." I scramble to pick up my phone. "What did you say?"

Her face leaves the screen, and Diane's appears. "Yeah, she's been saying this all day long. It's nothing. Don't worry about it."

Oh yeah, I'm not going to worry about it, not at all. "Why does she think that?"

Diane shrugs. "Something to do with this jerk that plowed her over in the airport. She thinks her daddy's special secret job is in the airport."

"It is," Stella says, grabbing for Diane's phone again. "That's where he's been all this time. Go find him, Mommy."

"Why in the world would you think you found your daddy at the airport?"

"'Cause... well, we both like ice cream." *That eliminates about zero potential fathers.* "Oh, and he called me Stella Bella, just like you."

"You also thought the UPS driver was your father because he delivered a package for you on your birthday."

"Mommy, it's him."

"Okay, baby. That's real sweet, but it's not likely. I'll look into it."

Thank God Theo doesn't work at the airport.

⸺⊷⊶⊷⸺

Since it's a pretty day with surprisingly low humidity, Shelby, Isaac, and I sit outside on the fitness center's patio for lunch. Butterflies surround the Buddleia bush and will be drunk on its nectar before the day is over. I bet if Stella were here, all she would have to do is hold out her finger close to the bush, and one of those beautiful Monarchs would gladly rest on it. God, I miss that sweet girl. Only two weeks, and I'll have her back. That is two weeks too long.

Shelby picks through her salad, and Isaac inhales a pizza... as usual. I sit cross-legged on a yoga mat and munch on a turkey club sandwich and some pretzels.

"We are so boring," Isaac says. "We have the same lunch at the same time at the same place every day. Can't we ever do anything different?"

"Here's something different. I need some ideas on how to deal with this"—I lower my voice—"baby-daddy problem."

Isaac lifts his hands in praise. "You have come to the right place. But first, let me make sure I have all the facts straight. Theo's the cute baby daddy."

"Super cute," Shelby adds, smiling at me.

Isaac gives Shelby the stare down. "Don't interrupt unless you have something important to add."

She giggles. "That was important."

Isaac stares at her.

She lowers her eyes. "Sorry. Please continue."

"Back to my rundown. He's the father. He was with Mallory. He's not anymore, but she seems to live in an alternate reality."

"Don't remind me."

Isaac walks to the glass door that leads from the sundeck to the fitness center and leans against it. "She's a piece of work. You need to figure something out before she sinks those acrylic nails into him again."

Isaac peers into the fitness center. When he catches me staring at him, he raises his eyebrows, giving me a "what did I do" look, and stuffs his pizza into his mouth. He'd better not be up to anything.

I take a gulp from my water bottle. "I thought about maybe asking him to meet for coffee one day, but that seems too casual for this kind of conversation. The setting needs to be private in case he decides to be an asshole."

Isaac tiptoes into the fitness center, peers around, and comes back out to the deck. "How are you going to spill the beans?"

I ignore his question and narrow my eyes. "What are you up to?"

He shrugs. "Looking for someone."

"What did you do?"

He scratches behind his ear. "Greased the wheels."

Shelby crosses her arms. "Details."

He cringes. "I might have mentioned that Theo should stop by and—"

"Isaac, I can handle this," I say through gritted teeth.

"I was doing my job… as a fitness consultant."

Sure, he was.

Oh crap. Theo might stop by here. I have to get myself together.

"You need to tell him, and the sooner, the better." Shelby points her finger at me, which tells me her advice is more than a suggestion.

I let out a sigh. "He knows, remember? Do you think he forgot?"

"That's not something you easily forget," Isaac says.

Shelby sighs and rolls her eyes. "Let's take this one step at a time. You did tell him, face-to-face, right?"

"I emailed him… multiple times."

She lets out an exasperated sigh. "And you're sure he got the email? I know I rarely check my spam folder. Maybe it went there." Shelby slides on her sunglasses and lounges back in her lawn chair for a lunchtime vitamin D session.

"I know he read them. I had the 'delivered' and 'read' notifications enabled. Long story short. Mallory sent an email and a picture right before Christmas. She had her arms wrapped around him like a python. He was copied on the email, so I had a name and an addy. I worked up the nerve to write him."

I take another bite of my sandwich, trying to calm my nerves. I'm surprised I haven't thrown up all over myself.

Shelby's mouth slips downward. "I take it that didn't go over well."

"Not well at all." This conversation has made me lose my appetite. Maybe some deep breaths will center me. "The first few emails were ignored. It wasn't until I sent him a picture of the sonogram that I actually got a reply. He told me to leave him alone. I never wrote him again."

Isaac cocks his head to the side like a puppy.

"Hmm," Shelby says. "Do you think it was because of her?"

"I suppose."

Isaac pinches the bridge of his nose. "Something's not jiving. He doesn't have the deadbeat vibe to him."

"He chose her over you and his baby?" Shelby asks.

"Yep." I sit back down on the mat as I think about the lowest point of my life. Never in a million years did I think he would do that to us.

Shelby is slack-jawed. "I'm so sorry."

Isaac stomps his foot on the ground. "I'm telling you, they aren't a couple anymore. And you always said you didn't know the father."

"If anyone asked, I pretended I didn't know who the father was. It was less humiliating than being rejected. But I cyberstalked him in case Stella ever wanted to know about him. I knew when he graduated, where he went for his residency. I did *not* know he was coming back to Vanderbilt, though. Last I heard, he was staying at Johns Hopkins." I promised myself I wouldn't make contact with him until Stella was old enough to understand what she wanted.

I wipe a tear from my face. Isaac squeezes my shoulder. I've kept all of it locked away so deep for so many years, it hardly even sounds real now. But it is, and it sounds even more depressing when I say it out loud.

"And this week, he didn't ask about our child. He didn't act awkward. He acted…" My lip quivers. It hurts so much to admit that he doesn't care. Another tear slides down my face.

Shelby leans down and hugs me. "He acted like it never happened."

"Maybe his brain is so full with medical facts that something had to slip out," Isaac says.

We both stare at him.

"Hey, I saw on TV where that's a real medical condition. Some people can only hold so many facts. When they learn a new one, one leaves them."

"Would you shut up?" Shelby yells at him before I have a chance to do the same thing. She focuses her attention back on me. "But if he wants to pick up where you two left off, you can't let him pretend she doesn't exist."

"I've decided I'm going to use the time Stella's in California to let him get used to the idea of being a dad again. If he's remorseful, he can see her when she gets back. And I deserve an apology. He needs to explain to me what he was thinking."

My path gets clearer in my mind. "I know what I want. Shelby, you're the planner. What should I say to him?"

She stands and stretches her arms over her head. "Step one—you march up to Dr. Hotness."

"He's got a name. It's Theo."

"I like Dr. Hotness better," Isaac says.

"Not helping," I reply.

"Step two," Shelby continues. "Give Dr. Hotness a huge smack on the lips. Use lots of tongue. The more tongue, the better."

His tongue was *pretty talented.*

"I agree," Isaac says.

"Step three—say, 'You have a daughter. Deal with it.' Bam! You're done."

She takes a bow. Isaac claps.

I can't help but crack a smile. "That's a little in-your-face. I'll figure something out."

"If I see him again, I might smack that dimple off *his* face," Shelby says.

I try not to react. That dimple is irresistible. As much as I would like to agree with Shelby, I do like the dimple. That dimple draws me in and makes me forget his shortcomings. And Stella has his dimple, among other things. All he has to do is answer two not-so-simple questions: Why did he reject us, and is Mallory still in the picture? Now, all I have to figure out is when this conversation is going to take place. I could wait around like a middle-school kid to see if he makes the first move, or I could coax him to the fitness center so we could talk on my turf.

Yes. Asking him to meet me here for a fitness assessment might be just the ticket.

Chapter Fourteen

Theo

M Y NURSE CAUGHT ME SNORING twice today. I think it's Tuesday, but I'm not quite sure because I pulled another overnight ER shift. I can hardly keep my eyes open. To everyone else, it's time to clock in and start the day. For me, it's the end of eighteen straight hours of nonstop work. This killer schedule is going to be the death of me. I grab my diabetic kit and keys, ready to leave the ER. Hello, snoozy time.

My buzzing phone makes me whine. I love my job, but please, not another emergency today. I examine the display and see that it's another message from *I'm not a stalker*.

"Not now."

On my way to the door, I decide I can't let it go. I have to read the text. It's like a hangnail waiting to be ripped off.

> *Stop by the gym as soon as you're fit.*
> *And accidentally leave your diabetic kit.*
> *One letter you'll gain if it's left in her room.*
> *A second one's yours if she returns it by noon.*

I whimper. I want sleep. Darla, you had better be glad you're cute. As if I'm on autopilot, I drag myself across campus to the fitness center. I swipe in and shuffle inside like a zombie. I have no business being here, and I certainly don't need to leave my kit lying around. If I weren't leaving it in the hands of a licensed medical professional, I would never even consider it.

I peek inside an office and see Darla pecking away on her computer, humming to the tune coming out of her stereo. I can't make my feet move, so I lean against the doorframe. Her office is rather bland, no personal items at all except for one small picture of a toddler perched on the edge of her desk. She's a mom. That must mean she's married. *Crapity crap crap crap.*

I clear my throat, finally catching her attention.

Her posture stiffens. "Oh."

"So, is this where you hide out during the day?"

She waves her hand through the air. "Yeah. My home away from home—when I'm not playing vampire, that is." She bites her lip, making me salivate.

"Can I come in?"

"Uh, sure. Have a seat," she says, nibbling on a fingernail.

I slide into the chair next to her desk. I'm not sure what to do or say now that I'm here. She may be the one behind these messages and getting a thrill out of making me do these things. But on the other hand, she may be totally clueless, no pun intended.

"To be completely clear, I'm not stalking you." *Hint, hint. Come on, Darla. Give me a sign that you're my anonymous messenger.*

She grins. "Never crossed my mind."

Bummer. She didn't give me one twitchy, nervous reaction.

"So…" She tries repeatedly to tuck a strand of hair behind her ear. She gives up and blows the hair out of her eyes. "Are you getting settled in?"

I cannot get near this girl without her reacting nervously. *Calm down, Juliet. I won't bite.* I mean, I might bite, but it would definitely be consensual. "Yeah. Everyone's been very helpful. Already working my ass off."

"Anything unexpected?" she asks.

Yeah. You could say that. It's a Hangman puzzle you sent me. "Uh, no."

Her lips are stretched into a tight straight line. "That's good. Great. Good." She drums her fingers on her desk.

We stare at each other. I need to find a way to break the ice. I point at my diabetes bag. "Do you mind if I check my sugar before I work out?"

She blinks. "Of course not. Do you need an Accu-Chek?" She starts to get up.

I wink at her while I fish through my pack. "I come prepared." *And I'm leaving it in your office like your message instructed me to.* I take out the glucose-testing machine and place a test strip in the slot. "This is my lifeline. Never go anywhere without it, but I do need a pen. Can I borrow one?"

She stares at me while she rummages around in her desk drawer. "Here." She holds out a tampon for me to write with.

"Uh, I don't think I'll need one of those anytime soon."

She crinkles up her brow and takes a quick peek down. A horrified expression crosses her face.

"Oh shit," she screeches and slams the tampon back into the drawer. She throws a pen at me then slaps her hands over her face, peeking at me between her fingers. She's so cute trying to hide her beet-red face.

A chuckle escapes my lips as my eyes roam the small office. I wipe my finger with an alcohol pad and prick it with a lancet. I nod toward the frame on her desk. "Nice picture."

She lowers her hands. "Huh?"

I motion with my head toward the picture of the toddler dressed in a Princess Leia outfit and holding a trick-or-treat bucket.

Then I focus back on my finger and force the drop of blood onto the test strip.

"Oh," she says and slides the picture into her desk drawer.

That's odd. "Yours?" *Please say "no." Please say it's a niece.*

She growls at me. "Yes. I have a daughter." She stares a hole through me. She pastes on a cavity-producing sugary smile, while I try not to show how defeated I feel.

"Congratulations." *Gah.* I can't stop my runaway mouth. This has to be her secret. *Dang.* Game over before it ever got started. "She's beautiful."

"Thanks."

"She doesn't look anything like you." *Way to go, Casanova.* That didn't come out right.

She blinks and nibbles on her fingernail again.

I squeeze my eyes closed for a second and take a calming breath. "That's not what I meant. I meant that she doesn't favor you. Maybe your husband?"

If she says "yes," I might throw up all over her desk and shoot the messenger. The entire premise of the game makes no sense if she's married.

"Nope."

Hallelujah! And I'm back in the game.

"Divorced?" Boy, I sure am nosy. The Accu-Chek beeps, making me jump.

"No, never been married, okay?"

"Oh. Good, I guess." That was stupid. Way to go, Mr. Diarrhea Mouth. Now she has *my* nerves all whacked.

She cocks an eyebrow. "Don't you think you should go work out?"

"Yeah, guess so. Do you mind if I leave my kit here?"

"Why?"

Like you don't know. "It has my emergency glucagon in it. I need it close by in case my sugar drops too low."

"Oh, sure. No problem. But I'm heading to a meeting soon. I'll leave the door unlocked so you can get it before you leave. Get your kit after you get fit." She laughs at her own joke. "It rhymes. Kit and fit... never mind."

I quirk an eyebrow.

"Seriously, it will be safe in my office, but I wouldn't want you to be without it if you need it."

Maybe she isn't the one sending me the game. Before this conversation, I was sure it was her. But now, I don't know.

I write down my glucose value on my log sheet. "Good. Thanks."

I don't want to move, but I force my legs to leave her office. "Good to see you again, Juliet. Thanks for the... pen."

She lets out a relieved laugh, as if she was holding her breath during the entire conversation. I start to leave when she says, "Have a good workout, Romeo."

I chuckle as I wave good-bye. I sneak a peek back toward her office and find her beating her head against her desk. God, she is absolutely adorable, and I am absolutely doomed. I situate myself on a bench and start pumping out a set of bicep curls. Isaac wanders around the workout area. When he sees me, he waves.

It's him. Isaac has to be the culprit. During our coffee time, he mentioned that coming to the gym could be a way to ease back into Darla's life. It's him. It has to be.

"How's it going? Theo? Or is it Romeo?"

I laugh and nearly drop the dumbbells. In my state of exhaustion, I really shouldn't be using anything heavier than two-pounders. Even those might feel heavy. I'm such a wimp.

"You're not stalking me, are you?"

Isaac scrunches up his brow. "Come again?"

I wave him off. "Never mind zombie boy over here."

"So," he whispers. "You here to work out or for the scenery?" He nods his head toward Darla's office.

I put the dumbbells back on the rack. "Considering I can hardly keep my eyes open, I'm going with door number two and say the scenery."

Isaac laughs. "Maybe you'll win the grand prize." He waves to another fitness member. "Take it easy. See you soon." He strolls away.

My two prime suspects act clueless in regards to the Hangman puzzle. I'll find out who's sending them to me eventually. But most importantly, I'm going to get some more letters to that puzzle.

I manage to push my body through thirty minutes of a half-assed workout before I can't take it anymore. I peek inside Darla's vacant office. My bag sits right where I left it. I snicker to myself as I tiptoe out of the fitness center and head home. Let's see if she takes the bait. Whatever happens, I have a pillow calling my name.

Chapter Fifteen
Theo

*T*AP, TAP, TAP. MY HEAD barely hit the pillow; it can't be time to wake up already. *Tap, tap, tap.* There it is again. *Crap.* I untangle myself from the sheet and stumble to the door. This had better be good. A few good hours of sleep isn't too much to ask for.

"Coming." If it's Mallory, I'm going to be pissed. She knows it's over. She has shown up twice this week, and it's getting annoying.

I swing open the door. Suddenly, I'm not pissed anymore. Darla is standing on the other side. I try to show how happy I am, but I'm butt-ugly tired. "Hey." It's all I can manage.

"I, uh…" she stutters and holds out my diabetic kit.

I glance down at my watch. It's 11:45. *Ka-ching!* I scored two letters. I take it from her.

"Did I wake you?" she asks.

"It's okay. Want to come in? Sorry about the mess," I say, pointing to the stack of moving boxes in the living room as I retreat back inside.

I turn around to see her staring at my chest. *Oops.* I forgot to put on a shirt. I take a gander at my body to make sure I'm wearing pants. One never knows. Scanning the room, I spot a T-shirt on the floor. I grab it and sniff it to see how many days it has been lying there before I fling it over my head.

Darla's lips slide downward a tad. Her disappointment over my covered body pleases the hell out of me. I would grin, but it's almost impossible to smile and yawn at the same time.

"Thanks for my bag. I forgot I left it there. Have a seat. Want something to drink?"

She perches on the edge of the couch, and her knee bobs up and down. "No, thanks. A shot of whiskey might be nice."

I rotate toward her, and my eyebrows shoot up.

"Kidding. I really should go."

I collapse on the couch beside her and rub the sleep out of my eyes. Another yawn slips out. "Come on. You ruined a perfectly good snooze, and you're going to leave?"

She scans my messy apartment. Maybe she's trying to find all of her possible exit routes in case she needs to scram. "I'm sorry. I was trying to do the right thing, and I stopped by your clinic, and you were gone. They told me where you lived. I didn't want you to be without your—"

"Calm down. I'm kidding."

She blows a lock of hair out of her eyes.

"Why do I make you so nervous?"

She slouches and covers her face with her hands. "I don't know, but you make my heart race every time I see you."

This could be fun. I wiggle my eyebrows, and she rewards me with a whack on the shoulder. I act as if it hurts.

"I didn't mean it like that."

Bummer. She pinches my bicep.

"Ow! What was that for?"

"That was for telling Isaac that we had sex in college."

"Oh. Actually, I didn't say that. He read between the lines."

She goes in for round two, but I block her.

She peers over my shoulder. "Where's your girlfriend?"

"What makes you think I have a girlfriend?"

"Mallory? I saw her on her first day of work."

I shake my head. "First, she moves here. Then, she has to get a job at the same hospital as me." *Mallory is going to be the death of me.*

"She's quite delightful. She couldn't wait to tell me about her boyfriend." She holds up a finger. "No, wait. She said fiancé. So, when's the wedding?"

"We. Are. *Not.* Engaged!"

She stares at the ceiling. "Will I be invited?"

Now, she's making *my* heart race. "Again, we are not engaged. I don't know why she told you that." *Dammit.* This has to stop. Mallory thinks if she keeps pushing the issue, it will be fact, but that is not happening.

"Kind of touchy, aren't you?"

I rub a hand through my hair. "No. Yes. Maybe. Jeez. Of all people, how did you run into her?"

Darla's eyes dance. She's enjoying this way too much. But it's got her talking to me, so I'll go along with the conversation.

"She says you're working extra hours in the ER to buy her a ring."

I chuckle. "I'm not surprised. It's not even close to why I need the money."

"Drugs?"

"Yeah, that's my style." I close my eyes, but not for long, fearing I might fall asleep. "Mallory was not a good match for me. We aren't together anymore."

"Well, she wasn't a good match for a college roommate either, but I survived."

I almost break my neck, yanking it around to gape at her. "You've got to be kidding me."

"Nope."

I sit up, bury my head in my hands, and moan. "You were at the party together, weren't you?"

"Yep."

Suddenly, I remember something. I point my finger at her. She swats it away.

"You know, she talked about you a few times. She wanted to fix you up with some ugly-ass guy at her work."

Mallory doesn't have many female friends; she doesn't like the competition. I could never figure out why she wanted to fix this particular friend up all of a sudden. If Mallory knew I had been with Darla at the party, she must have been attempting to mark her territory by trying to fix Darla up with some other dude. To think, I could have been with Darla this whole time. The thought of all those wasted years makes my stomach churn. Bile creeps up my esophagus.

She shudders. "That would have been awkward, huh?"

"No shit. But I wish she had."

"Thanks a lot."

"Hey, at least it would have been a chance to get together again."

She narrows her eyes.

Uh-oh. I've pushed the wrong button. "Not to do *that*, but hey, you talked me into it once before, or was it twice, so…"

Her eyes get big. "You're awful." Her ears are a nice shade of pink.

Talking about that night has me wide-awake now. I cover her hand with mine. Hers is so tiny and soft, I could hold on to it forever. Like a good boy, I let go. Her gaze floats from my hand to my eyes.

"I'm joking, but I wish things had been different. I really do."

After the fire, I spent the next few days in the hospital for smoke inhalation and burns to my feet. My diabetes didn't like that and was uncontrollable. By the time I got out of the hospital, everyone had left for the summer. All I had left was the memory of my Juliet and oozing blisters on the soles of my feet.

"And by the way, she doesn't live here," I say, pointing to my apartment. "Besides"—I lean in close to her ear—"she's taller than me. I can't have that now, can I?"

I swear she sniffed me. *Sweet.*

"That wouldn't do." She sighs deeply. "Actually, I know why you make me nervous. But I won't say."

"Why not?"

She focuses on her feet. "You really don't know, do you?"

"Know what?" If Mallory told her another lie, I might come unhinged.

She stares at me, and her jaw drops. She glances down at her tremulous hands. "I guess I have a secret. A really big one. I don't know how to tell you."

I nudge her shoulder. "I already know about your daughter, remember?"

She gasps. "You do?"

"Yeah, the picture on your desk."

Her shoulders slump, and she lets out a groan. "This is so weird. Are you one hundred percent positive you do not know anything else?"

Women are so confusing sometimes. "I have no idea what you could be talking about. Let it spew. I can take it."

"I can't. I'm sorry. I thought this would be easy, but it's not."

This has to tie into the Hangman game. It has to. "How about you tell me in a Hangman game?" *Not very subtle.*

Her mouth drops. "Are you kidding me? No. Absolutely not. This isn't a game to me. It's so big, I'm afraid it will make you run away."

"So, you don't want me to run away?"

She shrugs and fidgets with her name tag.

Okay, this conversation is getting too serious. "You rob banks."

She furrows her brow. "What?"

"That's your secret. You rob banks."

She giggles. "Uh, no."

"Steal diamonds?"

"Nope."

"You're a chicken hawk."

She bursts out laughing then stares at me, her face all perplexed. "I don't even know what that is. I could be one and not even know it."

I stand and strut around the coffee table. I am the dorkiest chicken impersonator ever, but if it makes her laugh, I'll do it. I'll dress up like a chicken if it keeps that expression on her face. "You know, from *Looney Tunes*. Foghorn Leghorn. 'Ah say, boy, ah say.'"

She giggles and tugs on the hem of my T-shirt, pulling me down and giving me a chance to get a little closer to her. My leg brushes against hers. This time, she doesn't bristle at my touch. She doesn't jump away. I think I'm getting the hang of this.

"I am not a chicken hawk, and I can promise you that I have never done anything illegal."

I lean in to her, and we make eye contact. "Well, how bad could it be?"

"Bad. I'm confused right now. I thought you knew. But when I get the courage to tell you after all this time, you'll probably make a beeline outta here."

"Nonsense. I live here. I'm not going anywhere."

Her jovial expression fades. "Are you sure there's no conversation, perhaps by email, that we need to finish having?"

I throw my hands in the air. "I have no idea what you're talking about."

That stupid fire messed everything up. After that, it all kind of fell apart. I never saw her again. I wished every day that I had told her to wait outside on the sidewalk instead of telling her to go back to her dorm. That way, I would have spent the last seven years with the woman I am madly in love with instead of with a person that filled a gap.

I'm positive I saw her leave the burning building unharmed, so she couldn't have been injured unless she came back in looking for me. If she did that, if she was in a hospital bed right down the hall from me, I think I'll throw up.

"Ah." I snap my fingers. "I get it."

Those big, brown eyes make me weak in the knees. In my best French accent, I say, "You're reeling me in with your seductive ways, and when I fall for you, you'll snap the trap." I snap my hands together in front of her face, making her jump. I snap them over and over.

She can't contain her laughter. It's great, infectious. She should do it more often. I want to make her laugh more often.

"That's my MO, all right."

"Trap snapper," I say again, snapping my hands in front of her face.

She pushes them away, still laughing. "It shows how little you know about me. I'm about the least seductive person there is."

All I want to do is take her to my bedroom and be with her. Screw sleeping. Sleeping is overrated. I swipe a strand of hair away from her eyes and tuck it behind her ear. She swallows hard.

"Don't sell yourself short."

She focuses on her trembling hands.

God. There I go again, getting too serious-sounding.

"But seriously, you tell me whenever you feel like it, or never. It doesn't matter."

"But it does matter," she whispers. "Theo? The night at the party... any regrets?"

Hell no. No regrets. Is she kidding me? "Hmm." I try to sound calm, cool, and collected. "I have regrets."

She reaches for her purse and starts to stand.

Crap. That didn't come out right. I grab her arm. "Let me finish." I run a hand through my bedhead, making it even more of a mess. "Do you believe in love at first sight?" The words spew from my mouth like verbal vomit.

"That's a girly thing to ask."

I chuckle. "I guess, but I believe in it. My dad's a minister, and he always tells me I will know when God puts the right one in front of me."

Her mouth drops. "So, at the party—"

"I'm not talking about the party. I'm talking about microbiology our junior year."

She leans back. "We had micro together?"

I nod. "I used to watch you play with your hair. You'd bring it over your head and twirl it around, like you're doing right now."

She stops and grins. "Sorry. Habit."

"I had to meet you, but there had to be over one hundred people in that class."

"Yep. It was in one of those big auditoriums."

"You made me get a C in that class. I had to retake it in the summer, thank you very much."

"Me? What did I do?" She leans in closer to me.

I blink to regain my thought processes. She smells like fresh laundry and baby lotion. I want to breathe her in deeper, experience more of her.

"I couldn't concentrate, but I didn't care. Do you know I asked to switch my lab time twice so I could be with you? But I never got in your lab."

She snickers. "That's because I took the lab a different semester."

I lean back and groan. As red as her face is, she must be about to burst out laughing again.

"Go ahead. Laugh away."

She leans over and puts her head on my shoulder then laughs until a tear trickles down her cheek.

I think I'm going to die, but I'll die a happy man. I could get used to her resting her head on my shoulder. "You blew my theory about love at first sight. I couldn't find you. It's a big campus, so I sort of gave up. But when you waltzed into that party a year later, all those feelings came back."

She moves away from me. Her cheeks are pink. She wipes her face and sneaks a peek at me between her fingers. "I think it was the beer-soaked dress. It was the latest from Calvin Klein."

"Ah, that's it. But I saw Stevens heading your way, and I was like, 'No way, man.'"

"So why didn't you ask me for my name?"

"Ma'am, your memory must be slipping. I did, but you wouldn't tell me, so that's when you became Juliet. But if I thought for a second it would be seven years before I saw you again, I would have pressed the issue a bit more."

"So you mean it wasn't another hookup?"

My mouth drops, and she gingerly pops my jaw shut.

"That's what you thought?"

"Why else would someone like you"—she points to me—"be interested in someone like me?" She points to herself.

I sigh and close my eyes. "I saw you head to the bathroom. I made up that story about hiding from you-know-who. I needed something that would keep you hostage for a few hours."

That didn't come out right. I cringe, waiting for her response, which could be anything from a punch to a hug.

She puts her hands on her hips. *Oh crap, here it comes.*

"Okay, I didn't plan on *that* happening." Heat rises up my neck. "But to answer your original question, I don't regret it. Not one single thing."

She doesn't say anything.

"I know our first... whatever you want to call it... was a bit rushed before it came to a screeching halt, but that wasn't anyone's fault, was it?"

She shakes her head. When she peers up at me again, her eyes sparkle.

My heart pounds through my chest, but I need her to know our night together was special to me, not a random hookup. "And in case you were wondering... you were my first."

A beautiful pink blush spreads across her cheeks. She covers her face with her hands. "You were mine too." She peeks at me through her fingers. "You were very talented." She closes her fingers. "God, I cannot believe I said that."

I peel one hand away from her face and hold it. On instinct, I rub the back of her knuckles with my thumb. "I could say the same thing about you. To tell you the truth, I didn't know what the heck I was doing. I knew what felt right at the time."

She leans back on the couch and focuses on the ceiling. A slow, deep chuckle comes out of her mouth. My shoulder touches hers when I lean back. Her hand rests on my thigh. A warm feeling that I thought I would never feel again rushes through my veins.

She leans her head on my shoulder. "Nothing like your first, huh?"

You got that right.

"So, why don't we start over? I know you're a single parent and that's priority one for you. I get it. I respect that. But... I want to try."

There. I've said it. It's out there. Even though I have zero hours for a relationship and I'm in debt up to my eyeballs, I've put myself out there. No take-backs now.

It seems as though she's holding her breath. She exhales slowly. "What about this secret of mine?"

"Tell me when you think the time is right."

"Even if it's a really, really big secret?"

I nod. Nothing she could tell me would change the way I feel about her.

"Okay, but what about Mallory?"

Whoa. She agreed with me. I thought I would get the runaround. Forget about sleep. Suddenly, I'm not sleepy anymore. But I can't rush things again. This time, it needs to be right—slow, sweet, perfect. "I told you, we're not a couple anymore. You see that box over there?"

I point to the large pile of moving boxes I haven't unpacked.

Darla tilts her head.

"What does the writing on that one say?" I ask.

She squints to read my scribbling, then a very boisterous laugh bursts out. "You broke up with her by playing Hangman?"

"Yeah. I should at least get bonus points for originality."

She rolls her eyes, but her smile doesn't fade. "Only you would do that."

"We've been growing apart for some time. I'll be fine. She'll be fine. You, on the other hand, might face the wrath of Mallory's temper."

She rolls her eyes. "Nice words of encouragement."

I take her hand and help her stand then start down the hallway.

"Uh, where are we going?" Her voice trembles.

I try not to grin, but it's hard to hide my smile. "The bathroom. Isn't that where it all started?"

Stopping, she puts her hands on her hips and bites her lip. She's trying not to smile, but she is failing miserably. I love that I'm able to put the smile back on her face. I get the impression she doesn't do that very often. That's a shame, because when she's happy, her entire face lights up.

"I better let you get some rest," she says.

I shrug. "If you must."

I move toward her. She backs up against the wall. I take another step closer. We are only inches apart. All it would take is a slight tilt of the Earth's axis, and I would be up against her. It's taking all my willpower not to reach out and touch her face.

"See you tomorrow?" I ask. *Please say yes.*

She nods. I take both of her wrists in my hands and slide my fingers around until I find her radial pulse. She's right. I do make her heart race. I lean down and kiss her on the cheek, and the years we've spent apart vanish. Her breath hitches. I want to make her do that and more all day long, but not so soon...

In her ear, I whisper, "I have a secret too."

She blinks. "Huh?"

This is going better than I expected. She slides her hands up my chest. Now, *I'm* having trouble focusing, and my heart rate is way beyond my maximum target range.

I smirk. "I kind of left my diabetes bag on purpose."

She snarls at me. "You are evil."

"It worked, didn't it?"

She throws her head back and cracks up. She pats my chest and wipes her face with her hands. "I've got to get back to work. See you soon." She moves to leave and runs smack-dab into the wall. "Ouch."

"I've been meaning to get that wall removed."

Her face is suffused with a pretty shade of pink, and she mumbles something under her breath.

"See ya."

She picks up her purse and leaves. I watch her from the front door as she gets into her old Ford Escape. She waves as she backs out into the parking lot. I wave back.

After she drives away, I take out the Hangman puzzle I printed out from my front pocket. It's like a drug calling my name. There's no harm in finishing the puzzle. If she's the one sending me the messages, we'll get a big kick out of it.

However, if she's not the one and someone else is trying to facilitate me in figuring out her secret before she's ready to tell me, I risk hurting her. I should throw the puzzle away and enjoy the grand prize. I fold the paper and stuff it back in my pocket. I can't let a game go unfinished.

Chapter Sixteen
Theo

"SETH, YOUR HEMOGLOBIN A1C LEVEL is great. Your glucose control is so good for a teenager."

I glance up from his chart to see him strutting around the exam room. If I didn't know better, I would think I was seeing a younger version of myself. Seeing how proud he is makes me happy. I know it's not easy to keep diabetes in such a tight check at that age. As long as I had a normal routine, I was good. But nothing is normal about those teen years.

"Now if I could only get a girl to check me out, my life would be perfect."

"Seriously? You don't have the girls fighting over you?"

Seth slides back onto the exam table and stares at his swinging legs. "Nope. They all think I'm dying."

I sigh and run my hand through my hair. Boy, do I know what that feels like. I roll my stool over to him. "Seth, if there's anyone that knows what you're going through, it's me."

He raises his head. I can see the sadness in his big eyes. He's sixteen. All the other guys his age have girlfriends and are out partying. Seth feels as though he's missing out.

"They can make you feel like damaged goods."

He bobs his head. "Exactly. Pisses me off. Sorry, I shouldn't have said that."

I grin at him. "No, it pisses you off, and it pisses me off too. I had a girlfriend who wanted me to wear my shirt untucked all the time to hide my pump."

"Dude, that's so wrong."

Mallory made me promise not to mention my disease the first time I met her parents. They didn't want her to date a guy who was sick, and she didn't want to upset dear ole dad. "But trust me, you'll find someone that sees you for who you are and not just one part of you."

"Hope so. I guess you don't have that problem anymore, do you?"

I wish I could lie to him. It would be easier. But I would hate myself if I did. "It's complicated."

He lies back on the exam table, making the paper barrier crinkle. He covers his eyes with his arm. "Why do adults always say 'it's complicated' when they don't want to tell the truth?"

I groan. "Truth is, I recently got out of a relationship because she's not the right one for me. The one I want is terrified of me. Not my diabetes, but me. She's my complication."

Seth chuckles. "You seem pretty harmless to me."

"I know, right?"

My cell phone buzzes with a message.

Good job. You get two letters.

Maybe it's Shelby. She seems like the pushy "go get it" type. I need to interrogate her next time I see her.

"Hey, Seth, you want to help me out with something?"

He sits up. "Huh?"

"The complication has a secret, and someone—not sure who yet—is sending me clues to help me figure out what it is. You want to help me select some letters to the puzzle?"

Seth grins. "Dude, this is so cool." He peers over my shoulder at the puzzle. "Hmm, how about O and E?"

I rub my hands together before I type O and E and hit send. "Thanks, man. You have a good summer. See you in six months."

Seth leaves the exam room, and my phone buzzes again. I really should ignore it, but I love a puzzle. I check my phone, and the text message has the Hangman puzzle with some pieces filled in.

– O – – A – E A – O – – – – E –
Good job!
I knew you would think this is fun.

But wouldn't you like your lunch in the sun?
I know what would put you in a good mood.
A noontime visit with you, Darla, and food.

Okay… whoever is doing this sucks at rhyming. But it is a nice day for a picnic, and I'm free until my afternoon clinic. I have to eat anyway, and I could certainly use some pretty company to go along with it. I click open my email and send her an instant message.

Hey, Juliet, did you bring your lunch today?

I finish Seth's history and physical report. When my computer beeps that I have a new message, I grin.

> **Darla:** *Yep*
> **Me:** *Me too. How about I meet you somewhere?*
> **Darla:** *Maybe another day.*
> **Me:** *Chicken*
> **Darla:** *Ha! I thought I was a chicken hawk.*
> **Me:** *Oh yeah. My bad. I have some free time around 11:30. See you at the big magnolia by the library.*
> **Darla:** *I didn't say I was coming.*
> **Me:** *I know. See you there.*
> **Darla:** *You are exhausting.*
> **Me:** *;)*

When I head toward the magnolia tree, Darla is already there. She's doing some kind of yoga stretch. They are all the same to me. Her shoes are off, and her feet grip her yoga mat, showing off her pink toenails. My mouth goes dry as I watch her. She catches me gawking and grins. The summer heat couldn't melt me more than that face.

"You're late."

I cock my head. "I figured you'd chicken out."

"Me, chicken? Nope. I'm hungry."

I chuckle and sit next to her on her mat. I drop my diabetes kit and lunch next to me on the grass. I slip off my shoes and peel out of my socks. My toes enjoy the freedom even though they aren't anywhere near as cute as Darla's.

Her eyes dance. "Did you clear this lunch date with your betrothed?"

"She's not my betrothed. So, this is a date?"

She growls at me. "That's not what I meant."

"It's what you said." I retrieve my sandwich and take a bite out of it.

She rolls her eyes. "It's lunch. Where's Mallory?"

Ah, the green-eyed monster makes an appearance. I wipe her cheek with my napkin. "Something's on your face. It's green... oh, could it be... jealousy?"

She smacks my hand away. "Answer the question, Romeo."

I groan. "How many times do I have to tell you? It's over between us."

She focuses on her yoga mat.

"I don't want to be with her, but I also don't want to hurt her."

"You're a good guy. It's your kryptonite."

"She's been fun... a lot of fun, but—"

Darla covers her ears. "Too much information. Sorry I brought it up."

I sneak a peek at her. "I just realized I know nothing about you."

She stretches her feet out in front of her, and I admire those cute pink toenails again. She bends down until her chest rests completely on the front of her thighs. If I did that, I would never be able to stand up again.

"There's not much to tell."

"Parents?"

Her shoulders slump. "Mom died when I was little. Dad never got over losing her. He passed away a few years ago."

"I'm sorry," I say.

She opens a yogurt cup and fishes out a spoon. "Not your fault. He was not the nicest of fathers."

From my lunch bag, I remove a container of baby carrots.

"Did you check your sugar?"

"Yes, Mother."

"Sorry. I guess moms are never off the clock."

I stretch out on my back, staring up at her. It feels so good to relax and feel the warm breeze blowing across my face. Only peace and quiet and... Darla. "So, tell me about your daughter."

She snatches a few blades of grass out of the ground and twirls them around between her fingers. "Well, she's uh—"

My phone buzzes, and I hold up a finger. "Wait a sec." I fire off a text message to the clinic nurse. "Sorry. Where were we?"

"I was about to ask you about your family."

Now, that's a topic I never get tired of talking about. "Let's see. My mom is the coolest person on the planet. You'd like her. She's a hippy-chick, lawyer hybrid."

Darla snickers. "That's going from one extreme to the other."

I nod. "I know, and she's everything in between too. My dad is a minister. I think I already mentioned that."

Scraping the last bit of yogurt out of the cup, she nods. She takes out a bag of grapes and pops one into her mouth before offering me some. I take one and chomp on it.

"And there's us kids. I have one older sister, one younger brother, and a baby sister."

"That's a houseful. I bet your parents did a lot of praying."

"Whenever we had a fight, my dad would make us stand hand in hand and pray for each other out loud."

She laughs.

I shudder at the memory. "It was worse than any beating we could ever get." Heather's prayers were always the most creative. *Oh, Lord, please give Theo the wisdom to understand that he can never outdo me in an argument.* Tommy always tried his best to crunch my fingers together. I don't remember ever having a fight with Jennifer.

"Do you get to see them much?"

"Some. Tommy is at Sallister University in Boston, and Heather's at the University of Tennessee. They're both in graduate school. But my big sister lives here, and Mom and Dad still live here too."

She stops mid-bite on a grape. "Here?" She spits out the grape and wipes her mouth.

"Yeah. Dad's church is down the road. I guess I figured you knew that already."

"I cannot believe you grew up here!" she squeals, punctuating each syllable by bombing me with grapes.

I catch a few, which makes her even more annoyed. "What's the problem with that?"

"Ugh. So did I!" she replies.

"No way," I say, using my best girly voice.

I throw grapes back at her, and she giggles as she tries to dodge them.

"What high school? Please don't say Hillsboro. If you say Hillsboro, I will scream."

I shake my head. "Montgomery Bell Academy."

"Oh. You went to a private all boys' school. It suits you."

I wear my snootiest smirk and scrunch up my nose. "I see you are a commoner and went to public schools. I must not associate with such low class."

"Shut up." She pushes me over and pummels me with sissy punches.

I roll over on my back, laughing like a hyena. "Okay, if you stop, I'll let you wipe the mud from my shoes."

She climbs on top of me and finds my tickle spot. She remembers that sensitive area under my floating rib. This is going better than I imagined.

"Stop. Oh. Not there. Stop," I beg through my laughter. But inside, I'm thinking, "Don't stop. Oh, there. Yeah, do it again."

Suddenly, she stops. I think she finally registers the position she's in. She's been in this position before, and it was fantastic. I slide my hands to her waist. When I try to bring her down for a kiss, her phone rings. She snaps out of her daze and drags herself off me.

"Saved by the cell," she says.

She crawls over to her purse and finds her phone. I grab her foot to snatch her back. She tries to wrestle free, but I grab the other foot and tickle it. She giggles as she answers the phone, and I lose my grip on her foot.

I sit up on an elbow to watch her.

"Hey, baby. Are you having fun?" The smile on her face reaches her eyes, and she radiates. "That sounds like fun. You did? Will you get Aunt Diane to send me a picture? I miss you so much. Okay. Can I talk to Aunt Di? I love you. Call me tonight."

She holds up a finger to indicate it will be a minute. I try to grab her foot again, but she tucks both of them under her body. She wags her index finger at me while she talks on the phone. I love how her voice became all singsongy when she talked to her daughter. *Cute.*

She hangs up the phone. "She's spending part of the summer with my sister in California. They're at Disneyland. Di loves her, but when she gets home, I'll have to deprogram the little critter." She puts her phone away and sits back down.

I cock my head to the side. "Would a child that young enjoy a theme park?"

Darla laughs. "You're never too young for Mickey."

I look at Darla and can't stop staring at her.

"What?" she asks. "Do I have something on my face?" She wipes her mouth with the back of her hand.

"You're a good mom."

She shrugs. "I don't know about that. I do know that it's the only thing that makes me happy."

Her face lights up when she talks about her baby. Boy, do I wish I were in her shoes. It would make me as happy as she seems to have a mini-me to love and dote on. I want that so badly. I think I would be a good dad. At least I would love the opportunity, but it's not in the cards for me. "You're blessed."

"I know I am. I didn't do the 'marry first, have a baby second,' but it worked out all right."

"Enjoy her."

"I do."

"Lots of people can't have kids."

"I know."

"People like me."

Her eyes get misty. I'm not sure she gets it. I'm saying that it's a good time for her to cut and run before she gets involved with me. It's better for her to know early on so no one gets hurt. I would never want to lead her on, so it's best she knows these things before she invests too much time and effort in me. If she wants more kids, it's not going to happen with me.

"Why?"

"Diabetes. It makes it really hard for dudes to father children."

Her hands tremble. *Shit.* I've scared her. She would like more kids, and she knows it's out of the question with me. I knew she was too good to be true.

"Damn. I shouldn't have said that. Few women want to be with someone when they know the chance of kids is extremely rare."

"You don't know that for sure." Her voice is hardly above a whisper.

I slide on my socks and shoes. She does the same. We were having fun. She was letting go of her reservations, and I messed it up. *Stupid. Stupid. Stupid.*

"It's enough to scare people away," I say.

She hugs her knees to her chest. "It didn't scare off Mallory."

I soak in the warm summer sun while I scan her profile. "It's because she didn't really want children." I focus on the grass. "But I do."

She buries her face in her hands and groans. She mumbles something, but all I can make out is "do it" and "idiot." I pick up my lunch bag and my diabetes kit and stand. The deafening sound of a robin singing comes from the magnolia tree. Darla looks away, and I wave my hand in front of her face. She rolls up her mat and tries to take my hand, but I keep moving it to mess with her. She finally grabs on to it, allowing me to hoist her to her feet.

"Are you scared?" I ask.

She takes a deep breath. "I'm not scared."

"By the way, you never told me what your daughter's name is."

"It's uh…" She looks down at her watch. "I have to get back to work." She points in the direction of the fitness center building.

First, she doesn't tell me her name for seven years. Now, she's going to withhold her daughter's name. She is one strange but wonderful person. I kiss her hand. She leans down and picks up some grapes on the ground.

"See you soon?" I ask, hoping for the truth.

"Sure," she says casually before strolling away.

As I turn to leave, I feel something hit my back. A grape rolls by on the path.

"No fair," I yell at her.

"Oh, like you always play by the rules. I seem to remember that you like to make them up as you go, Romeo." She waves and rushes off.

I can't tell if I scared her. Her reaction was certainly not typical. She was surprised but not turned off. She didn't give me a "poor dear" look or a "get the hell away from me" look. It was more as if she didn't believe me, which is even weirder. She has me so messed up, I don't know if I'm coming or going.

For a first date with a girl I've already had sex with, I think it went pretty darn well. If we keep this up, who knows where we'll be in a few weeks. She might even tell me her secret. She acted only slightly weird about the fact that I can't have kids. And I'm certainly not backing off because she has a toddler. Maybe, just maybe, this will go somewhere. I would love to have Darla and a baby. Talk about winning the grand prize.

Chapter Seventeen
Darla

HERE WE GO AGAIN, LUGGING the equipment across campus for a screening. But this time, Shelby scheduled the screening in the evening. So no matter how long we've been at work already, we still have to work into the wee hours of the night to do screenings on the nursing staff that work the night shift. I'm not a night owl, so this is torture.

Since Mallory has an administrative job, the chances of her being at the hospital at this hour are slim to none. Theo is a different story, and with my luck, anything is possible. I want to see him again and again, but I get so tongue-tied around him. At this pace, I'll never work up the courage to tell him about Stella.

I still cannot get the last conversation I had with Theo out of my mind. He really doesn't know about Stella. He's totally clueless. He would certainly remember something this important, especially since he wants kids so much. And the fact that he thinks he can't have kids when he actually has one is more than I can process right now. We were having so much fun on our picnic that it would have been the perfect opportunity to tell him. But I could not make my mouth say the words. The longer I wait, the harder it is going to be. I'm so afraid he'll freak, and I don't know if I can handle rejection again.

I know he got my emails, though. I know he replied to me. He didn't want anything to do with us. But something does not add up. I mean, come on. He remembered everything about our one night together, even the fact that we had sex twice. Maybe he had someone else checking his email for him. It is possible Mallory deleted them before he had a chance to read them, but when I ran into her, she didn't act as though she was trying to hide anything. And I know Mallory—she's not a good actress. She would have given me a clue that she saw something. So if he didn't tell me to bugger off, I can't imagine who it could have been.

I've lived in a pit of sorrow for seven years because I thought he didn't want us. Somehow, I knew he couldn't be that callous. I knew he wouldn't ignore us. Even so, he's here now, and I have the chance to make it all right. If it wasn't Mallory, it had to be someone in his family. Maybe it was his preacher father. The man could have been trying to protect his image. Or it could have been his mother. She may have thought I would try to get child support from him.

"You're lucky Stella's out of town, or I wouldn't be able to do this," I say to Shelby as we lug our equipment up the sidewalk.

"Why do you think I scheduled it this week?" Shelby asks. "I've got to squeeze every ounce of opportunity I can. Keeps you from missing her."

"How about a movie next time?" Isaac suggests.

I agree. "Yeah, a movie sounds really good right now. Or face time with my sweet girl."

"Let's just get this behind us," Shelby says.

※

We push our carts through the hospital and onto the elevators up to the ninth floor. Another boring session of tuberculosis skin tests, immunizations, and whatever else the nurses need to be compliant with hospital regulations. Next, we move down to the eighth floor. At least the tests go quickly and smoothly. By midnight, we are finally done. Fluffy pillows call my name. And I didn't run into Mallory or Theo, so it wasn't completely awful. After a midnight shift, I look and smell like death warmed over. The only thing making me cringe is Isaac's latest earworm. If I never hear Vanilla Ice again, it will be too soon.

Shelby collapses onto a couch in the nurses' lounge. "Thank God that's over."

Isaac yawns so big, I can see past his molars. Even yawning, he still bobs his head to the tune of "Ice Ice Baby." He takes in the break room, scrunching his nose. "No offense to you, Juliet, but nurses are messy as hell."

He doesn't deserve an eye roll. Talking trash about my profession and calling me *that*? I'll have to give him a nasty pinch when I'm fully conscious.

He grimaces and points to a slice of pizza sitting on the table.

I shrug. "Nurses rarely get to finish a meal, so they eat what they can when they can."

"Let's hope they wash their hands before entering patients' rooms, because they don't practice good hygiene in here."

Shelby gasps. "Unprofessional."

"The least they could do is clean up after themselves. That slice of pizza needs a shave. No telling how long it's been sitting there. I bet you could manufacture enough penicillin from that single slice to treat this whole hospital unit."

I laugh. That's gross but funny at the same time. "Throw it away if it bothers you so much." I finish packing my supplies into the cart and stretch out my back. My sore muscles sure could use a massage right about now. And I know the perfect hands for the job. *Stop it.*

"Nu-uh. I might get hepatitis or encephalitis or some other form of itis."

Shelby giggles. "I think you already have."

He sticks his tongue out at her. "Juliet, you're a nurse. You throw it away."

Groaning, I massage my temples. "I will if you'll stop calling me that."

He claps, knowing he has won this battle.

"Oh, for crying out loud." I toss it into the trash.

"I can still see it."

"Ugh. You could never be a nurse or a mother." I snatch some paper towels off the counter to cover my hand and shove the pizza down farther into the trash. A sharp pain shoots through my hand, and I jerk it back. My hand is covered in red, and it's not pizza sauce.

"Oh no." I hold up my left hand, displaying a deep, jagged cut on my palm. Blood is seeping out of it. On a scale of one to ten, this is an eleven.

Shelby rushes to me. "Jesus Christ. What happened?"

I grab more paper towels and cover my hand with them. Blood soaks through them within seconds and trickles down my arm.

Isaac backs away from me. "I think I'm going to be sick."

Shelby pushes me into a chair and rips more paper towels out of the dispenser. She covers my hand with them and holds my arm in the air. "Isaac, go get Bonnie, the charge nurse, now."

He rushes out of the room. I think he's relieved he got to leave.

"I'm okay," I say to Shelby. "No big deal." The throbbing pain takes my breath away.

Shelby cringes. "I don't know. It seems pretty bad." She inspects the contents of the trash can. "A tuna can got you."

"I'm an idiot."

"No, Isaac's the idiot."

"Am not," he says, returning to the lounge with Bonnie.

She plants a wheelchair next to the door. I don't need that.

Bonnie leans down in front of me. "Let's take a peek." She peels off the paper towels, and more blood gushes out.

I suck in a breath. *Shit, that hurts.*

"Okay, that wasn't a good idea," she says.

"I think a butterfly bandage should do the trick," I say to her.

She presses a gauze bandage to my hand and goes into full nurse mode. "You need stitches."

"I'm fine." I stand up, and the room spins.

Shelby catches me. The charge nurse plants my butt in the wheelchair and pushes me out of the lounge, into the elevator, and down to the emergency room.

Chapter Eighteen
Theo

M Y PHONE RINGS... AGAIN. *So much for a nap.* It's the ER letting me know another patient has shown up in the waiting room: a laceration with profuse bleeding. As I round the corner, I screech on the brakes when I see Isaac and Shelby in the waiting room. Isaac locks eyes with me.

I rush up to him. "Where is she?"

Isaac can't stop pacing. "Oh God. This is all my fault."

"Where is she?"

He points to the bay the staff took her to. I pat his arm and push through the curtain. I let out a sigh of relief when I see Darla sitting on a gurney, swinging her feet like a little girl. She holds her bloody hand in the air. I cock my head to the side as I take her in.

Her eyes get big when she sees me. "Of course, *you* would be working tonight."

"It must be your lucky day."

She waves her wounded hand toward me and cringes. "Don't think so."

I wash my hands and don gloves. "Maybe it's *my* lucky day."

Monica, the ER nurse, enters the bay and hands me a package of gauze and a kit of sterile instruments.

"You know, if you wanted to see me, all you had to do is call."

Monica laughs. Darla's mouth tips upward a tad on one side.

I roll over to her on my wheeled stool. "Let's see what you did."

She holds her hand out. "I think the culprit was the lid off a tuna can."

I grimace, knowing that had to hurt, but I've seen worse. She's lucky it didn't hit an artery. She would be pulsating blood all over the place if that were the case.

"Monica, could you get me some sterile water, one cc of lidocaine, five hundred units of Bacitracin, and the superglue?"

"Sure thing."

"Superglue?" Darla asks.

"It's not really superglue, but it's pretty much the same thing. Better than stitches. Comes in real *handy*. Get it?"

"Don't make me laugh." She sucks in a breath, and a tear trickles down her cheek. She wipes it away with her good hand.

"Are you allergic to penicillin?"

"N-n-no."

I gaze into her eyes. "By the stink Isaac was causing out there, I thought you'd been hit by a car."

She rolls her eyes. "Tell me about it. I told them I didn't need to be here. Ouch."

"Sorry, but I have to get this clean. You need to be here. I'm glad you're here."

"Me too," she says, barely above a whisper.

I move to sit on the side of the gurney. Our knees touch, reminding me of when we sat on the edge of the bathroom sink at that college party. "I've got you, sweetie."

She leans over and rests her forehead on mine while I hold her wound closed, waiting on Monica to return with the meds. I'll hold it all night long if I need to, but I have to assess the damage.

"Can you move your fingers?"

She grits her teeth but is able to move all the fingers on her left hand.

"Good. I don't think you hit a tendon or a nerve."

Her hand trembles, or it might be mine. I hold hers tight again.

"You should be more careful where you put your hand."

"Got any suggestions?" Her eyes get big as she realizes how I will take that. "I cannot believe I said that."

I chuckle and clear my throat. "Nurse Battle, you have a dirty mind. I'm shocked."

Monica enters the room, giggling. "I'm going to pretend I didn't hear any of that."

"That's why you're my favorite work nurse." I wink at Darla, my favorite wellness nurse. "I'm going to write you a prescription for antibiotics and pain meds. And to be sure it's healing properly, I think I should hold your hand for the next few days. You know… physical therapy."

Her eyes snap to mine, and she swallows deeply. "Doctor's orders… I guess."

My eyes get big. That was easy.

Darla moans through clenched teeth as I clean out her wound and close it up. I let Monica bandage her hand; she's way better at it than I am. She says I use five times the amount of bandage needed and that even a cut on the pinky finger ends up looking like a mummy.

"Why don't you lie back while I get your prescriptions filled?"

"Thanks, Doc."

I reward her with a wink.

"When can I go home?"

"You can't drive on pain meds. I guess you'll have to wait until I'm off-duty." I wiggle my eyebrows.

"Where's Shelby?"

Wow. She shot me down. Hurtful. "She took the supplies to the office, but she said she'd be back soon. And I shooed Isaac away. He was making a scene."

Darla's eyes are glassy. The pain meds have definitely kicked in.

"Lie back and get some rest. I'll let you know when she's here."

She curls up, propping her bandaged hand on the pillow. Her eyelids are heavy. "Oh, Romeo, Romeo…"

My cheeks hurt from the big smile on my face.

"I need to talk to Stella. She'll be…"

"You want to talk to my mother?"

She mumbles something through a very large yawn. "'Ice Ice Baby.'"

I never took her for a Vanilla Ice fan. It would be unprofessional to laugh at my patient, but she's so damn funny on drugs.

She drifts off to sleep before I can tease her about her ramblings. I raise the bed rail and move the call button closer to her good hand. I kiss her cheek before I make myself comfortable in a chair beside her bed.

For an hour, Darla sleeps. Her chest rises and falls in a slow rhythm as she rests. It's a nice excuse to stare at her without her knowing. I can take in all her features without seeming like a stalker. Her mouth is a bit open, and it makes me want to kiss those pillowy soft cheeks so badly. It's really hard to keep my distance. I can't thank Monica enough for taking me off-duty until Darla goes home.

She stirs. *Dang it.*

I sit down on her bed, soaking in every detail of her face—her full lips and those dark lashes that do a terrible job at hiding her emotions. Her hair is splayed across the pillow, tempting my itchy fingers to run through those strands. When I'm around her, I feel warm and fuzzy. I can't quite find the right words to express my feelings, so I do what I do best. I stare at her.

"What?"

"Nothing. I'm... glad you're okay."

She exhales. "That makes two of us. But I was in good hands. Get it? Hands?" She waves her bandaged hand in my face. She closes her eyes and yawns.

"That was really... bad." I reach out to touch her right hand and bring it to my lips.

She places her bandaged hand on my cheek. Then she blinks and snatches her hands away as if my skin burned her.

"Did I say anything? I have a tendency to ramble when I'm doped up."

"You wanted to talk to Stella."

She gulps, and her normal dark complexion fades to pale. "What did I say?"

"You wanted to talk to her."

She stares at the wall, and I sure do wish I could download that monologue she's having in her head right now.

"This is good. I need to get this off my chest." She attempts to sit up and tilts to the side. Her face goes from pale to an eerie-green tint. "Oh no."

I have a nanosecond to reach for the emesis basin before she tosses her cookies all over the place. The only thing I can do is hold her hair back and order Zofran.

Monica zips in seconds after I hit the call button and takes over puke duty.

My phone rings, interrupting me from staring at Darla. She waves her injured hand as she and Shelby proceed out of the emergency room and down the long hallway that leads to the elevators. By the sound of the ringtone, I already know it's Jennifer. She would only call me this time of morning if it was urgent or if she has her time zones mixed up.

"You know it's four a.m. here."

"I figured you'd be working, and I finally got cell service."

I scoot out into the hallway so as not to disturb anyone. "Are you pregnant yet?"

She sighs. "And to think I was missing you. But now that you've mentioned it, how would that make you feel?"

"Huh?" My sister is insane. Only she would be asking me this, and in the middle of the night, no less.

"How would you feel if you suddenly found out you were going to be an uncle?"

"I'd be thrilled, of course. Why?"

She giggles. "I'm working on it."

"What are you saying?"

"I'm saying I'm not afraid anymore."

"Does this mean…"

"Yep. This time next year, maybe you'll be an uncle."

"That's fantastic, Jen."

She gets all giggly again. "Matt, stop it."

I grin. It sounds as though they're having fun. Maybe someday I'll have time to have fun with someone I care about.

"I know I would be glad if I found out I was going to be an aunt," she says.

I lean up against the wall and cross one leg over the other.

"Theo, I'm sorry. That was insensitive."

"It's all right. The day you find out you're going to be an aunt will be the day you have to pick me up off the floor."

"From shock or fear?" she asks.

I shrug even though I know she can't see me. "Both, I guess."

"Aw, come on. You'd be excited, wouldn't you?"

I scratch the back of my neck. It's been a long night, and I don't need any crazy talk from my sister. "Did you call for a specific reason?"

"Uh, any progress with that girl you ran into?"

I glance down the hallway and see Darla and Shelby waiting for the elevator. "A little. At least she's not afraid of me anymore."

"That's good," she says. "Anything I need to know about?"

I roll my eyes. "No, Nosy Nelly. Jeez, you can be so—"

"Never mind. We'll talk about it later."

I close my eyes. When she goes all mother hen on me, it's hard to get her to stop. "Why don't you go get naked in a hot tub? Get to working on that baby-making."

She giggles. "You are awful."

She tells Matt what I said, and his voice is loud and clear in the background. "Yeah! That's what I'm talkin' about."

The phone call ends. My family is so strange. Before I put my phone in my pocket, I send a quick text to Darla.

"Hey, Doc," Monica says from the emergency room triage station.

I nod at her as I finish my text.

> *Take it easy the next few days.*
> *No Tylenol while on the meds I prescribed.*
> *Be safe and later gator.*
> *P.S. I don't mind house calls :)*

"You two make a cute couple," Monica says. "I can tell she likes you."

My grin overtakes my face. "Well, can you blame her?"

Monica rolls her eyes. "Seriously, why do I even bother?"

"Because if it weren't for me, you'd be working with Dr. Fredrickson and his chronic halitosis." I shiver.

"Good point."

Right before I slide my phone into my pocket, it buzzes to notify me of an incoming text... from Darla.

> *I nevr gt 2 tale u.*

Darla Battle on pain meds—adorable.

Chapter Nineteen

Darla

I STARE AT THE CEILING, TRYING to catch my breath. This week alone, I've had that dream three times. I can still smell the smoke. The screams rattle through my ears. And Theo's last kiss before pushing me out of the house still lingers on my lips. He wasn't going to leave until he made sure everyone was out of the house. If he hadn't been so selfless, we would have escaped together, and everything might have worked out fine. It makes me play the "what if" game over and over in my mind. If there hadn't been a fire, if I had given him my real name, things might have been different.

I untangle myself from the sheet and head to the bathroom. Splashing cold water on my face with my uninjured hand jolts me back to reality. Yeti spins in circles at my feet.

"All right, all right, I see you. Let's go outside."

When I open the door to let him out so he can take care of business, he slides right between two human legs. Yeti unceremoniously hikes a leg and pisses all over Theo's foot and leg.

"Shit, what are you doing here?" I ask him.

He stands there, peering down at the wet spot on the frayed hem of his jeans. Then he looks back up at me and holds out a bouquet of flowers.

"Uh, Yeti, stop it."

"Your dog's name is Yeti? Like Bigfoot?"

I motion for him to come inside. He follows me in and stares at me. *Crap.* I forgot I had on a short nightgown and no robe. I instinctively cross my arms. His eyebrow shoots up into his hairline. *Not so fast, buster.*

"Yeah. Isaac named him."

"Shocker."

"Have a seat," I say, keeping an eye out for Yeti. "I'm so sorry about your jeans. I can wash them if you want."

"Nah, don't worry about it. Besides, what would I wear while they were in the washer?"

"Uh, I didn't think that far ahead. I wouldn't want you to be standing around in your panties." I would bet he looks every bit as yummy as he used to... or even better.

"I don't wear panties. I wear... uh, well... you know what I wear."

"Okay, that's enough." He sure knows how to make me squirm. Finally, Yeti prisses back into the house.

"Yeti, this is Theo. He is not your personal fire hydrant. Be nice."

Yeti growls and heads for the bedroom.

"Stay put while I go get dressed."

"I could help."

"Would you stop it?" I scamper down the hallway, and when I get to my bedroom, I peer over my shoulder. He is standing at Stella's bedroom door.

"What are you doing?"

He shrugs. "Killing time."

Losing my nerve to let him know about her, I push him away from her room, and pain slices through my hurt hand.

"Darla, I know you have a baby. It's all right."

"No, it's not all right. Don't nose around in my personal life."

He backs up against the wall, slack-jawed. Flower petals fall to the floor. "Whoa. Not my intention at all."

He chews on the inside of his jaw, and I can only imagine that Mallory has treated him like this a time or two. If I want him to want us, I'm sucking at it.

"Sorry. It's uh... very messy." *Gah. Tell him.*

He holds out the flowers to me again.

Now I feel like a big jerk for overreacting. "These are so pretty. What's the occasion?"

"Seriously?"

"Yeah," I say before it hits me. It's my birthday. Jeez, I totally forgot. "Theo, how did you know?"

"I have my ways. You don't celebrate your birthday?"

I shrug. It's another day on the calendar. My life started the day Stella was born, so that's more worthy of celebrating.

"Do you want to do something this year? It'll be fun."

"What are we going to do?"

"It's a surprise."

I bite my lip. "I don't like surprises."

He nudges me toward my bedroom. "Go get dressed. You might want to wear those sexy yoga pants." He wiggles his eyebrows.

I move to leave. "Let me take a shower."

He grabs my arm. "No time. You don't smell too bad." He sniffs my armpit. I cannot believe he did that, and I can't believe I let him. Something is seriously wrong with me.

"Manners." Jeez, it's like I'm talking to Stella.

"Go. We're burning daylight."

"All right, all right, Mr. Bossy. Stay put. I'm a little slow getting dressed with my gimpy hand, so be patient."

"I promise to only snoop through your purse." He winks at me, and I might need help moving down the hallway.

I rush back into my bedroom and try to think of something to wear. *It's not a date. It's not a date.* It's a friendly day with a gorgeous guy, who happens to be Stella's father. That's all. Yoga pants implies something casual, thank goodness. I toss on a T-shirt that has "Do you want to talk to the doctor in charge or the nurse who knows what's going on?" printed on the front.

I hop on one leg down the hallway back to the living room and slide the other shoe on my foot. Theo stares at my chest. I snap my fingers, and his gaze takes its time getting back to my face.

"Your shirt… not funny."

I grin. "But it's true."

He rolls his eyes and takes me by the hand to escort me out of the house and toward his car.

"Not on call today?" I ask.

"Nope. Shocker. I'm totally free. I threatened the call center that they dare not ring me unless it's a five-car pileup."

He leads me to his car, which is nothing like I expected. It's an old Subaru Outback with a dent in the fender and some rust around the edge of the hood. A plethora of bumper stickers covers his back window—everything from "Shit Happens" to a 26.2 sticker.

He opens the passenger door. Everything imaginable falls out onto my driveway and litters the seat and floorboard. "Oh, let me move some things. I'm not used to anyone sitting there."

I pick up an empty water bottle about to roll under his car. "This could take some time. Perhaps I could go take a shower while you tidy up."

"I got it." He tosses used paper coffee cups, journal articles, an open bag of peppermints, and an old, worn Bible into the back. He wipes crumbs off the seat and scratches his head. "And you were afraid your house was messy. As you can tell, I practically live in my car."

He motions for me to get in. I sit and take in all the stuff he threw in the backseat as he slides into the driver's seat and buckles in.

"You have journal articles and a Bible in your car. Quite a range of genres you got going there." I might need that Bible to help me confess my sins.

He laughs. "No romance novels or nudie magazines, I promise. You ready?"

I put my hand on his. "I didn't mean to snap at you. I don't let many people into my life." I lean over and kiss him on the cheek.

A cute shade of pink creeps up his neck to his right ear.

"I am sorry."

That mischievous grin that I love so much takes over his face. "I think one more kiss would help me forgive you."

I lean over the gearshift, but my hurt hand slips and jams into the emergency break. I suck in a breath through my teeth. He takes my hand and peppers it with kisses. "To be continued."

Absolutely. "Where are we going?"

"A place you probably haven't been to in a long time."

"By the looks of my chariot, I'm hoping it's a car wash."

"Ha. No. I'll give you a hint. It has something to do with what you said when you were on pain meds."

Shit. No telling what all I blabbered on about. It could be anything. If I messed this up for Stella, I'll never forgive myself.

Chapter Twenty

Darla

WHEN WE DRIVE UP TO the ice-skating rink, I almost bounce out of my seat. "I love ice-skating."

Before he can answer, I'm out of the car and doing a jig on the pavement. If I wasn't afraid of reinjuring my hand, I would do a cartwheel.

Theo's body quakes with laughter. "I guess this means you approve? I didn't think about your hand. Will you be all right to do this?"

I jump into his arms. "Yes. I haven't skated in years. Did I ever tell you I used to take lessons?"

"Really?"

I nod. "Uh-huh. I took lessons for five years."

He pouts like a kid that got his football taken away from him.

"What's wrong?"

"I was hoping you'd have to hold on to me to keep from falling."

"Poor baby." I pat his cheeks. "I'll let you catch me when I attempt a double."

His jaw drops. "You're *that* good?"

"*Was* that good. It's been a long time. Come on." I drag him into the rink.

After he tightens my laces, he wobbles to the rink.

I point to his blades. "You know, those are hockey skates."

"I know."

He gets on the ice, while I stand at the doorway watching. In a flash, he races around the rink. When he gets back to where I'm standing, he ices me with a hockey stop. I put my hands on my hips.

He has a twinkle in his eyes. "Did I mention that I used to play hockey?"

"I think you skipped that part."

He grabs my good hand, and we go buzzing around the rink. He's too fast for me, so I decide to cut through the middle to catch up.

"Cheater," he yells, switching directions. I try to keep up, but his longer legs have much more speed than mine do. I stand in the middle of the rink, watching him buzz by.

It's been a while since I've been on skates, and I wonder what I can still do. First, I try back crossovers. *Not bad.* Next, I try a spiral and a shoot-the-duck. I slide to the ice on that one, as usual. It was always hard for me to balance on one bent leg with the other straight out in front of me.

Theo skates up to me and helps me stand. "Let's see what you got."

I skate around him and set up for a toe loop. It's only a single, but I land it. I'll blame the wobbly landing on the rental skates.

He claps and skates toward me. "Nice job, Tara Lipinski."

I bow. He holds my hand, and we skate together. After a few laps, I skate in front of him and switch to skating in reverse so we are facing each other. It's as though we are dancing on ice. We skate in sync until a group of kids invade the ice and mess up our rhythm.

"Why didn't my mom insist on me skating like this?" he asks. "Way more fun than playing hockey."

"And we don't smell as bad."

He grins. "Well, the figure skaters that actually decide to take showers, that is."

I shove him, and he almost falls. I pivot and grab him by the arm before he splats on the ice, which causes him to slam up against me. I like the way he feels up against me. He nudges my chin up with his nose and kisses my cheek.

"Ewwww, PDA," a kid says as he skates past us, making me giggle. Theo seems completely unfazed.

"You're really good," I tell him.

"Thanks, but my ankles are killing me."

"I'm so glad you said that. Mine are too." We slide toward the edge of the rink, when I skid to a halt. "Let's take a selfie." I take out my phone, and we head to the middle of the rink. Theo pulls me down onto the ice. We scrunch close, and he wraps his arms around me so my head isn't directly on the cold surface.

"Say 'Ice Ice Baby,'" he says.

I gasp. "That's what I said when I was on pain meds, wasn't it?" The next time I see Isaac, I'm going to force him to listen to some Adele so I can get a new earworm.

"Yep. Smile."

We examine the photo, neither one of us in any hurry to get off the cold rink. Breaking the trance we're in, Theo hobbles to his feet and helps me up.

I look at him as we head off the rink. "This was awesome. Thank you so much."

"You're welcome." He winks at me, and that cute dimple pops out. He unlaces my skates and gives both of my feet a nice massage before heading to the skate rental counter to retrieve our shoes. I'm left watching his tight ass stride away from me.

He totally rocks surgical scrubs. He can definitely fill out dress slacks like no other. His butt looks mighty fine in a pair of jeans. And I don't need to get started on how nice the scenery is *without* jeans, because it's a sight to behold. I'm glad he has to stand in line at the skate return, because it gives me time to wipe the drool from my face and cool the hot flash rising up my neck. I love re-falling in love with this man.

<hr />

Afterward, he says he needs to make a quick stop, then we can get ice cream if I want. *Heck yeah.*

"You'll have to give me plenty of advance notice when your birthday rolls around."

He doesn't say anything. He keeps his eyes straight ahead, both hands on the wheel.

"Don't tell me you recently had your birthday."

He cringes.

"Why didn't you say anything?"

He shrugs. "No big deal." He takes a gulp of his iced tea. "Besides, where I'm going is my birthday tradition."

"Oh. What is it?"

"Not telling."

"Skydiving?" I ask.

Please say anything but skydiving. I would even be okay with seeing whatever action-packed, bloody, senseless, and violent movie happens to be in the theatres. Theo is so unpredictable; it's probably something like scrapbooking.

"Nope."

"Stealing diamonds?"

He laughs. "Good one, but no. You'll see."

We drive downtown into a run-down neighborhood. The tiny shotgun houses have shingles missing from the roofs, and the wood siding doesn't look as though it has been painted in decades. He drives up to a faded-green house with a rickety fence around the yard. The car in the driveway is on concrete blocks.

Theo and I get out of the car, and he pops the trunk. He hands me a bag containing canned goods, a loaf of bread, and a bag of cookies that don't look store-bought. I stand there eyeing the cookies, while he retrieves a large cooler, leaving a small bag behind. We ramble up what used to be a sidewalk. If he's bringing me home to meet his parents, the least he could have done was let me brush my hair first.

An elderly Hispanic woman waddles out onto the front porch and clutches her chest. "Chico. Mi Chico."

"Buenos dias, Señora."

"Your mom said you were home." She grabs Theo into a big hug and kisses him on the cheek.

He motions for me to stand nearer to them. "Mrs. Lopez, I'd like you to meet Darla." His eyes twinkle. "Darla, this is Mrs. Lopez, an old family friend."

She swats at his arms. "Chico, I'm old, but not that old." The corners of her eyes crinkle up with her big grin.

Theo takes the bag from me and places it next to her.

Tears stream down her face. "Miss Stella and The Reverend raised some good children."

He hands her an envelope, and she sobs into her hands. "It's not much, but maybe it will help until Mr. Lopez is out of the hospital."

She falls into him and weeps. "Te amo. Te amo."

Theo's eyes brim with tears. So do mine. He kisses her cheek. "We have to go, but I'll be back tomorrow to give you a checkup and bring your medicines. Okay?"

She nods and covers his face with kisses. She embraces me, even though I haven't done anything to deserve it. My heart grows bigger for this man that is the father of my child.

It's settled. As soon as Stella comes home, she's going to meet her daddy.

Chapter Twenty-One
Darla

WE JUMP OUT OF THE car and race each other to the counter like a couple of ten-year-olds. After we get our cones, we sit outside on one of the picnic tables. I am so tired, but I'm wired all the same. I try to keep ahead of my ever-melting ice cream, but I'm not very successful in this summer heat. Stella would love an ice cream on a day like this.

While we lick our ice cream, Theo grabs my unbandaged hand and presses my thumb down to start a game of thumb wrestling. I'm distracted by ice cream and eye candy. He beats me at another thumb war, but I don't care who wins. I like holding his hand. I think that's why he likes the game too.

When he writes out a Hangman puzzle on a napkin, I roll my eyes. "You're getting soft on me. 'Ice Ice Baby.'"

He shrugs. "You caught me on a bad day."

"Slacker."

"This is exactly what I needed," he mumbles with a mouth full of ice cream.

"The ice cream?"

He winks at me. "That and other things." *Eep.*

"So tell me, who is Mrs. Lopez?"

He takes a long lick of his mint double fudge ice cream cone and closes his eyes tight.

"Brain freeze? Stick your thumb to the roof of your mouth."

He slides back into the booth, still squinting. "You want me to look like I'm sucking my thumb?"

I chuckle. "Try it. I promise it works."

He shrugs and sticks his thumb in his mouth right as I click a photo of him with my phone.

"Oh, you are dead."

"What?" I bat my eyes. "Are you going to get all macho on me?" I wink at him. It could be fun if he did.

He holds his hand out for my phone. "You wish."

"Oh, all right." I relinquish it. "Party pooper."

He deletes the photo. "Let's do another selfie." He leans over the table, and we butt heads. "Ow," he says with a laugh. "Say 'ice cream.'"

"Ice cream," I say. But before he takes the photo, he rubs his cone on my nose. I squeal. I cannot believe I fell for that. It's something an eighth grader would do. I grab for my phone, but he leans back in the booth so I can't reach him.

"Done. I sent it to myself."

I wipe my face with a napkin. Oh, I know how to get him back, and it doesn't involve ice cream. It doesn't involve photos or even a cell phone. "That's too bad. And I was about to ask you if you wanted to stay the night." After seeing this side of him, I want him to stay a whole bunch of nights.

And boom! The grin, the laughter, and the joke are over as his hands scramble around with my phone. "Oh crap. How do you unsend, delete. Come on, there has to be an undo button on this stupid thing." His fingers fly across my phone screen as he begs me with his eyes. "Uh, you were kidding, right?"

I shrug. "You'll never know now, will you?"

He scrunches his eyebrows together. "You don't play fair."

"Aw, poor baby has met his match," I say while I pinch his cheek.

He swats my hand away. "Back to your question about Mrs. Lopez, you evil beast. When I was in middle school, my mother met her at Goodwill. And when you meet my mother, you'll find out she never meets a stranger. It wasn't long before she and Mrs. Lopez became half-price thrift-store buddies every Wednesday. She's been in our lives ever since."

He gets this faraway look in his eyes. "My parents knew her family didn't have much, but they were very proud, so we adopted her. You know, we would have the standard birthday parties but did something for her on our birthdays also. Sometimes, they would come to our house for the holidays, and other times, we'd surprise them with food. We would bake dinner—well, Tommy would do most of the baking—and we'd buy gifts for her kids, rake her leaves, stuff like that." He shrugs as though it's no big deal.

I can't keep my eyes off him. If God ever created a perfect human being, Theo is it. He has such deep compassion.

"We still do what we can for her, especially on our birthdays."

"That's why you work the extra shifts in the ER."

"Among other things, but not for an engagement ring for you-know-who." He winks. He finishes his ice cream and stares at me. "Do you know why I went to medical school?"

"I'm guessing you want to help people."

"Sure. This country's flooded with doctors, but in Africa and other parts of the world, it's not that way." He's staring at my eyes, but he's peering much deeper, way deeper, right into my soul. He's trying to tell me something.

"I'm not sure what you mean."

"I want to be a part of Doctors Without Borders."

I sit back. "That's wonderful," I say when I can find my voice again. I'm not sure I mean it. "I toyed with the idea of doing something like that, but it's not possible being a single parent. Speaking of being a parent..." I wipe my mouth with my napkin in case there's a trail of melted ice cream anywhere.

"You see, that's the beauty of not having to answer to anyone."

The nerve of him. Right when I'm on the verge of telling him about Stella, he goes and says something so insensitive. Maybe I was wrong about how he would take the news.

"Excuse me? I find that having to consider another human in my choices to be... beautiful and very worthwhile."

He sits back in his chair. "I didn't mean it like that."

I hold my hand out to stop him from speaking. "What you mean is you enjoy doing whatever you want at the drop of a hat. Right?"

His mouth opens, but no words come out.

"You can fly off to Haiti or the Ivory Coast or Guatemala on a moment's notice."

"Well—"

"And people like me, a single parent, can't make choices like that. Our decisions are made for us." My face is on fire. I don't know how many times I've had to defend myself because what I wanted to do conflicted with what I needed to do. And until Theo has run a mile in my size-six Nikes, he'll never get it. While he was off doing who knows what with Mallory, I was changing dirty diapers, kissing boo-boos, and having to justify my single-mommy status every step of the way.

He swallows. "I, uh, no matter what I say, it isn't going to take back the fact that I was being kind of high-and-mighty. All I can say is I'm sorry. I didn't mean it that way."

I fold and unfold my napkin, managing a slight nod.

He clears his throat. "Not to change the subject, but the whole family will be in town this weekend, so Mom wants to have a cookout. Want to come?"

"Uh, sure." I'm completely shocked that he wants to be in the same county as me after the two scoldings I have given him today.

"Great. I'll let you know. But just so you know, it's not a birthday party." He takes my hand and kisses each knuckle. I guess it's a nonverbal "I'm sorry" gesture.

I don't know what I'm going to do. A few hours earlier, I was ready to tell him everything. But now that I know he plans to head off for months at a time, I'm not sure that would be fair to Stella. Meeting him when he plans on leaving might break her heart. And I don't know if he can handle being in our lives full time. Stella deserves no less than everything, and if he can't give her that, I don't know if he deserves any of it.

Chapter Twenty-Two
Theo

SILENCE LOOMS OVER US ON the drive back to her house. Darla stares out the passenger window. She doesn't even crack up when I purposely sing off-key to every tune on the radio. I thought we were having fun, but things went south fast, and I don't know how to fix it. I don't like to apologize for wanting to volunteer, but it's obvious I struck a nerve with her.

When I stop the car in her driveway, I get out, but I'm not ready to say good-bye. I don't want the day to end this way. She slides out of the car and starts up the driveway.

Oh crap. The gift. "I almost forgot."

She turns back toward me.

I retrieve a gift bag and hand it to her. "Happy birthday."

"You didn't have to do this," she says, not making eye contact. She flings tissue paper all over the driveway and takes out a DVD of *Romeo and Juliet*. She squeals with laughter. Maybe I haven't ruined everything after all.

"This is perfect. But I didn't get you anything for your birthday."

I scrunch my forehead. "Sure, you did. Spending time with you is all I could ever ask for. It's something I should have done a long time ago." I wink at her. "Did you enjoy your birthday?"

She wraps her arms around my neck and whispers, "Yes, thank you."

I slide my arms around her waist and tug her closer. "You're welcome. I'm so sorry about what I said earlier."

She bows her head. "I have no idea how hard it's been for you, the sacrifices you make every day. Please forgive me." She wipes a tear away and leans back, but I don't let go. "I'm sorry for being so touchy."

"I've already forgotten it."

She swallows hard. "Why did you do all this?"

I stare at her. "You don't know?" I lean in to kiss her, but she pivots her head.

"Please don't," she says softly.

"Not even a little peck? Aw, come on. Why not?"

"Because I don't want you to fall in love with me."

A warm sensation fills my entire body. I rub her shoulders. "Uh, too late."

She sucks in a breath. Again, I go in for a kiss, but she covers my mouth with her hand.

"If you kiss me, I know I'll fall in love with you all over again, and I don't want this to end."

"Why would it end? Because I want to..." I knew it. I knew it was too good to be true. That's why she got so quiet in the car. Africa is a total buzzkill, and she didn't know how to tell me. I let her go and lean up against my car. I took a chance telling her about my desire to be part of Doctors Without Borders, and it backfired on me. It's fricking volunteer work; it's in my DNA.

"Because of what I need to tell you. It might influence your plans, and I can't make you feel guilty over your choices."

"Tell me."

"Trust me. You'll hate me. I... God, why can't I spit it out?" She rests her head on my chest.

I tilt her head up and press her forehead to mine. I stare into her eyes. They are filled with such sadness. I wish I knew how to fix what was wrong so she would be happy.

"You said again."

She closes her eyes. "Huh?"

"You said you would fall in love with me... again. Again implies there was a before, so I'm guessing..." She was in love with me. I knew it. It wasn't one-sided.

She buries her face in my shirt. "You know what I mean."

"I know exactly what you mean." I hold on to her for a moment longer, breathing her breaths, smelling her baby-lotion scent, and soaking it all in. When I come up for air again, I abruptly let go. I rumble around in the backseat to fish out my Bible. It's my source of comfort, my source of inspiration, and it's the only place I can turn that will give me the words I know I have to say. I pace in front of my car, flipping through the pages until I find the scripture passage I'm searching for.

I lean back against the hood of my car. "I want to read something to you. First Corinthians, chapter thirteen, verses four through eight."

I stop to clear the crud that has built up in my throat and blink my vision clear. I can't believe I'm going to say this, but it's exactly how I feel. She needs to know how much she means to me.

"Love is patient. Love is kind. It does not envy. It does not boast. It is not proud. It does not dishonor others. It is not self-seeking. It is not easily angered. It keeps no record of wrongs. Love does not delight in evil but rejoices with the truth. It always protects, always trusts, always hopes, always perseveres. Love never fails."

I close my Bible and toss it through the open car window. Tears streak down her cheeks. I take her face in my hands and wipe away the teardrops I've caused.

"I love you, Darla. Whatever you have to tell me and whenever you tell me, I promise I will not be easily angered, and I won't keep record of wrongdoings, and I won't delight in evil. I will rejoice in the truth. I will always protect you. And you, my sweet love, can always trust me. I won't fail you."

She stands there with her mouth open. I softly close it with my finger and cup her face with my hands.

Her lip quivers. "That was the most beautiful…" Her body trembles, so I hold her close.

I kiss her so softly at first. This is really finally happening. I wrap my arms around her. I kiss her over and over again, my tongue exploring that familiar mouth of hers that I have missed so much. My hands run under her shirt, touching her warm, soft back. She lets out a slight moan, and her hands grip my shoulders. I don't care what happens next. Right now, I love her, and I know she has never stopped loving me.

It's quite obvious where this is heading, and I certainly have no plans to stop it. Suddenly, a lion roars, and I realize my phone is ringing.

"Shit, shit, shit," I shout. I lean back against my car, coming up for air. I think my lips are bruised from the passion of our kisses. I snatch my phone from my pocket.

Darla stumbles backward, out of breath. Her poor cheek is raw from my sandpaper-rough near-beard. She leans over my car's hood and sucks in air.

"Sorry, it's work. I have to take this." I swipe my hand over the phone and snap at the innocent person on the other end of the call. "What?"

"Hi, Dr. Edwards, this is Carmen from the ER."

"Sorry, I'm, um, in the middle of something."

"Er, I hate to break up the lovefest, but we've got two life-flight helicopters coming in from a five-car pileup on I-40, plus we're busting at the seams with patients today. Can you come in?"

"Oh, all right. Yeah. Uh, can you get me some scrubs to change into?"

"Sure thing, Doc. And I'm sorry to bother you."

I hang up the phone and groan then bang my head on the hood of my car. This is just my luck. "I have to go. It's actually a five-car pileup. Some of the injured are coming in by Life Flight."

She touches my face. "Your ringtone is a lion?"

I shrug as I wrap my arms around her waist and tap her forehead with mine. She kisses the tip of my nose.

"Work is a lion because they always call at the most inopportune times, and it makes me growl." I show her my frequent caller list. "Mom's is her voice saying, 'Turn on, tune in, drop out.' Dad's is John 3:16. Tommy's is his voice saying, 'Risk, the game of world domination.' And my sister is nails on a chalkboard."

She giggles. "Your sister is nails on a chalkboard? That's awful."

My face hurts from the perma-smile. "You haven't met my sister."

"What is my ringtone?"

I bat my eyes and gaze far off. "Romeo, oh Romeo, wherefore art thou Romeo."

"I stepped right into that one, didn't I?"

"Yep."

She kisses me on the cheek. "Now go. See you tomorrow."

I kiss her again. I like this kissing tennis match we're playing, especially when the score is love-love. I have to leave, but not forever. It seems as though we are finally moving in the right direction together, so I'm going to do everything in my power to keep us moving forward. Somehow, I need her to trust me enough to get over her secret hurdle. And she needs to meet my parents. Plus, we need to finish that kissing match we started.

Chapter Twenty-Three
Darla

AFTER HE DRIVES AWAY, I scramble indoors and collapse on the couch. *What a day. He loves me!* If I ever had any doubt before, it's gone now. He said it. He showed it. I feel it.

And I am going to ruin it if I don't spill the beans. I was close to telling him when he started talking all about Doctors Without Borders. Sometimes, those docs are gone for months, if not years, at a time. That's the last thing Stella needs.

Another perfect chance to tell him he has a daughter, and I let it slip through my fingers. I could have said, "I love you too, and so does your daughter," but no, I didn't say anything. I let myself live in the moment, and that moment was awesome.

After I've watched the entire *Romeo and Juliet* movie that Theo gave me, I drag myself off the couch and toward the shower. I'm not sure why I bother. Five minutes in the Tennessee summer sun, and my shower-fresh feeling will be replaced with sticky, sweaty grossness. I throw on some clothes that won't stick to my skin in this sweltering, muggy heat and head out the door. If I tell him before Stella gets back, I'll have time to recover from his possible rejection. But if I wait until she returns, he might not be able to resist that beautiful face of hers. I am driving myself crazy. I need a counseling session with my favorite sassy therapist—Shelby. She always knows what to do.

I zoom across town to her condo. By the time I get there, my hair is already plastered to my sweaty face. But it's only Shelby; she won't mind. I rap on the door. No answer. I knock louder. I know she's here because her car is right outside her building. I text her, and she replies, telling me to use the spare key because she's getting dressed. I feel around under the mat to find the key and let myself in. Her condo is super classy. She hates all the modern art on the walls, but her mother insisted. But there are hints of Shelby's personality everywhere, from the herb garden on the kitchen windowsill to the autographed photo of the latest rock star she's cozying up to these days.

"Shelby?"

"Up here."

I run up the steps two at a time.

She stands in front of her bathroom mirror, wearing nothing but a towel. When she sees me, she shuts off the hair dryer and adjusts her towel. "What's up with you?"

I slide onto the counter and fidget with a bottle of perfume sitting next to the sink. "I've had the most wonderful, awful day."

"Not sure if that's good or bad."

I put the perfume bottle down before I spill the contents on myself. I don't think I can afford to buy her a replacement. "I need your advice."

She throws on a T-shirt and shimmies into a pair of shorts. She takes me by the arm and escorts me downstairs to her living room. After I sit down, she perches on the edge of the couch, facing me, waiting for me to spill.

"Oh, Shelby, he loves me." I love saying that. I want to say it over and over. I want to get a megaphone and shout it to everyone as I drive down the street.

She adjusts the clip in her hair. "Is this the wonderful or the awful part?"

I cover my eyes with my hands. "Both. It was the most perfect day. He's definitely a charmer. Took me places I hadn't been in a really long time."

She grins at me.

I smack her arm. "Not *that*." I sigh. "But almost *that*." If his stupid phone hadn't rung, we would have done *that*. *Stupid, stupid phone.* "He told me he loves me."

"That's good, right?"

I nod. "And it wasn't like an 'I want to get laid' I love you. It was a 'forever and ever' I love you."

She scrunches up her brow. "I'm still not following the awful part."

"When Theo finds out Stella is his daughter, I'm going to break his heart."

Shelby forces eye contact. "You have to tell him. Right now. Today."

"How?"

She throws her hands in the air. "I don't know. I think you're overanalyzing this. Say it, and see how he reacts."

"Tomorrow."

Shelby's face gets red. "No, no, no. You get your butt in your car and drive over to his apartment and tell him this minute."

"He got called to work a couple of hours ago for an accident on the highway."

She grabs me by the arm and escorts me to the front door. "He's probably home by now." She points to the door. "Go."

My whole body quivers. I don't know if I can take rejection again. I plead with my eyes. "Will you go with me?"

She stares at the ceiling and lets out a huge sigh. "If it means you'll tell him today, then yes."

I grab her in a big bear hug. "Thank you so much."

"Give me fifteen minutes to get ready." She stomps up the stairs. Over her shoulder, she says, "Everything will be fine."

"You can do this," Shelby says in the same voice she uses when trying to convince one of her clients to squat two hundred pounds.

I exhale and nod. "I have to do it."

After my third attempt at knocking, Shelby takes my hand and makes my knuckles rap on Theo's apartment door. No answer.

I take a step to leave. "He's not here. Let's go."

Shelby grabs my arm as I start walking away. "Maybe he's asleep. Give him a sec—"

"Can I help you?" A deep voice rumbles from behind us, stopping Shelby and I in our tracks. The smell of freshly baked chocolate chip cookies wafts out of Theo's apartment.

We rotate to see a carbon copy of Theo with the same dark-blond hair, the same light-green eyes, and the same facial features. But this guy is about a foot taller. His hair is going every which way, and he's not wearing a shirt, something Shelby doesn't miss. She purrs.

"We're here for Theo," she says.

"Not home yet." He motions toward the apartment with his head.

"Want to come in and wait for him?" He props the door open with his long arm.

"No," I almost yell at him.

"Yes," Shelby screams. She drags me under the guy's outstretched arm and inside the apartment. "I'm Shelby, and this is Darla."

His eyes get real big. "Oh. Make yourselves at home, although I'm not sure when he'll be back."

Shelby pushes me down on the couch and sits beside me.

"Let's go," I whisper to her. "I changed my mind."

She gives the guy a cheesy grin and speaks to me under her breath. "We're here. You're going to do this."

"I'm Tommy, by the way."

"Theo's brother?" I squeak. I can't tell Theo the news with his hulking brother here to witness it.

He grins at me. "Is that a problem?"

I stand and stare at Shelby. "I can't do this."

Shelby pushes me back down on the couch and strides over to Tommy. She holds out her hand. "Nice to meet you." She glances back at me, and her eyebrows shoot up. "This is a good thing." She rubs Tommy's arm.

His expression is priceless. It's as though he can't decide if he should let her continue or snatch his arm away.

Shelby squeezes his bicep. "You can... practice on him."

His deep voice rumbles with laughter. "Excuse me?"

I cover my face.

"You see, Tommy. Darla has something really, really important to tell Theo, and she's terrified at how he'll react. Could she practice her speech on you?" She gives him a hundred-watt smile.

He scratches his head, which releases Shelby's hold on him. "Uh... I guess. Sure."

Shelby claps. "Good." She waves an arm toward me. "Go for it. Spit it out."

I open my mouth, but nothing comes out.

She touches my shoulder. "You can do this," she says in her best Bela Karolyi voice.

Tommy leans against the wall, arms crossed over his bare chest. His expression appears as though he just opened the door and let two crazed females into his life.

"I can't tell him first. That would be a slap in the face."

"Tell me or don't. I don't care. I've got cookies in the oven." He takes a step toward the kitchen.

Shelby licks her lips. "Yum." She nudges me in the ribs.

"Well, you see…" I close my eyes and decide to blurt it out. Maybe if I say it to someone that looks like Theo, it will be almost as if I told Theo. Then when I do tell him, it will be a piece of cake. That twisted logic doesn't even sound good in my head, but what the heck. "We had sex in college, and Theo has a daughter."

I open my eyes, and Shelby smiles at me.

Tommy freezes mid-stride. He whirls around. His mouth is hanging open, and all the color is gone from his face. "Theo has a kid?" he whispers.

Shelby escorts him to the couch. He numbly points to the kitchen, and she pats him on the arm. "I'll switch off the oven." She runs into the kitchen, and she's back in record time.

That's when my tears start. I bury my head in my knees. Shelby and Tommy let me wear myself out with my tears while Shelby rubs my back the entire time.

A wave of nausea churns through my stomach. "Oh, Tommy. I'm so sorry." Whatever made me think I would feel better after I blurted it out, I'll never know. If possible, the guilty weight is even heavier now.

"Why won't you tell him?" he asks softly.

"I don't know how." I sit up and blink to keep the tears from blurring my vision. As lame as that sounds, it's the honest-to-God truth. There's not an instructional manual on how to tell someone he has a child and the baby mommy thought he knew all this time, so I have little to no guidance on the matter.

"We were together right before graduation. I promise I didn't even know I was pregnant until the end of summer. I was in complete denial. By that time, everyone had moved away. I didn't know what to do."

The verbal vomit spews all over the living room. It has been tucked away deep inside me for so long that it was bound to explode eventually. I tell them about the fun games Theo and I played and how he made me feel so special. I tell them how he made sure I made it out of the fire. Tears well up in my eyes again and spill over.

"Oh, Darla," Tommy says. "I can't believe this."

"At first, I didn't have a name to go on. He told me his name was Romeo."

Tommy's laughter fills the room. "That sounds like him."

"After that, he was with Mallory, my college roommate."

Tommy flinches. "Ew."

"All I had was his mother's name."

"Stella," he finishes for me.

I nod, and the runaway freight train of tears leaves the station again. Shelby rubs my back. Tommy takes me in his arms and holds me. This total stranger that is an exact copy of Theo consoles me.

"Shh, I believe you."

"And when he showed up a few weeks ago, I freaked out. He acted like he didn't know. I promise you, I emailed him time after time while I was still pregnant because I wanted to tell him, but I got nothing. The last time, I sent him a copy of the sonogram, and he wrote back telling me to stop emailing him. His exact words were 'leave me alone.'"

Tommy moans. He stands and paces the room; his hands run through his sweaty hair. Under his breath, he mumbles a string of curse words. "Uh… Darla… I don't know how to tell you this."

I throw my hands in the air. "Well, it can't be as shocking as my news. Spit it out."

His eyes are as round as saucers. Swallowing hard, he makes his Adam's apple bounce. His eyes ping-pong back and forth from me to Shelby, and a sigh escapes his lips. He stares up at the ceiling. "You sent those emails to me, not Theo."

"What?" Shelby and I both yell at the same time.

"How can that be?" I ask him. "I sent it to 'THEgamemasters@outlook.com.'"

He groans. "That was my address."

Shelby holds out her hands. "Wait, what? Mallory copied you on the email, but not Theo?"

"She didn't want him to see the shit she was sending to his family." He snorts. "Like one of us wasn't going to tell him."

My heart is in my shoes. I've kept him away from his daughter because of a stupid mistake. No wonder he's so clueless. I am the worst mother in the world.

"I had a friend that kept pranking me, and I thought they were from her. I never in my wildest imagination would have thought the emails were meant for Theo, especially with his diabetes and fertility issues." He sits down beside me. "I am so sorry. Because of me, he didn't know about his daughter." His voice cracks. He buries his head in his hands and tears stream down his cheeks. He wipes his face and stares at me with such grief that I don't even know what to say.

Shelby taps her finger to her lips. "You didn't start the email 'Dear Theo,' or 'Hey, Theo, it's me,' or anything like that?"

My arms flail in the air. "I thought I'd go with the cute 'Dear Romeo,' to spark a memory." I let out an exasperated groan. "Sometimes, I even amaze myself at how incredibly stupid I can be."

"I am so sorry," Tommy says again.

"It's not your fault. I thought he didn't want us. Now, every time I see him, it gives me another chance to tell him, and I can't say the words. He'll never forgive me."

"All this time, you've kept all this bottled up inside you." He sighs. "I need to ask you a question, and please don't be offended. Are you one hundred percent sure it's his?"

I knew this would come up at some point. I would ask the same thing if I were in his shoes. I nod. "Oh yeah. No doubt about it."

Shelby wipes a tear from my cheek.

Tommy grabs me again and holds me tight. With my face pressed against his body, I feel his heart beating out of his chest.

"He thinks he can't have kids."

"I know that too, and again, I missed a golden opportunity to tell him that doctors don't know everything. I let chance after chance slip right by."

"You have to tell him," he says.

"I know. But the time has to be right."

"There will never be a right time. You have to do it."

"You know him better than we do," Shelby chimes in. "What do you think he'll say?"

Tommy runs a hand through his hair. "I have no idea. I think he would understand the lack of communication."

I focus on my lap in shame. "I would hope so."

"But not telling him now, when you've had lots of chances? That might kill him." He focuses on the floor in front of him. Grief is written all over his clenched jaw muscles. "I don't know. You have to tell him before it gets worse."

"I will. I promise. But please don't tell him. It has to come from me."

He wipes the tears from my face. "No, I'm not getting in the middle of this one. I've messed up enough as it is."

"Thank you."

"Tell him," he says, his voice cracking.

I nod.

"Who all knows?"

"Shelby and Isaac. And they only know because they witnessed the all-out panic attack I had when I saw him for the first time about a week ago."

I snap my fingers. "Oh, I mentioned it to Stella's first-grade teacher, but I don't think that matters."

He pushes away from me then moans and collapses back on the couch. "If you tell me her teacher is Mrs. Silva, I will shit a brick."

"You know her?" I ask.

He wipes his face with his hands and groans. He stands to pace the floor again, smacking a couch cushion with his fist. "That would be our older sister."

I stand and pace the floor with him. With all the tears I've shed in the last ten minutes, coupled with the sweat dripping down my spine, I'm going to be dehydrated in two seconds flat. This could not get any more complicated. I know Nashville is a small big city, but this is crazy. I could not have purposefully created a more tangled snarl than what I'm in right now.

No wonder Jennifer was all messed up the last time I saw her. She figured it out. There's no telling how she'll react toward me the next time I see her, and I'm sure I'll be losing her friendship along with Theo.

"Oh my God. I named my daughter after your mother. Of course Jennifer's figured it out by now."

He whimpers. "So that's what her rambling text was about."

"What am I going to do?"

"I don't know except say something before she does. I'm telling you, they are tight, and if she's already put the pieces together, he'll find out, and it won't be from you. Since she's away on her trip, you might still have a little bit of time. I think she comes home this weekend."

I rock back and forth on the couch. "I think I'm going to throw up."

Shelby and Tommy share some nonverbal communication and step away from me. They give me a minute, and slowly, I am able to breathe again. This situation keeps getting worse.

I drag out my keys. "I have to go."

"Right now?" Shelby watches Tommy out of the corner of her eye. "I mean… he baked cookies."

Tommy chuckles.

"I'm going to the hospital to tell Theo. Right now."

She grimaces but gives me a thumbs-up. "You're right. Let's go."

When Shelby and I get to the front door, Tommy clears his throat. "Uh, Shelby? I can take you home if you want to stay for… cookies."

I cock an eyebrow.

Shelby stifles a squeak. "Sure."

She kisses me on the cheek and sends me on my way. I need to do this before I chicken out.

Monica, the ER nurse, waves at me as I pass through the security scanner. "How's your hand?"

I hold it up for her to inspect. "Much better, thanks. I'm down to a few butterfly bandages now."

Like the great nurse she is, she assesses my hand for redness and any other signs of infection. "Looks great."

"I'm looking for Theo."

"He's not here." She must have registered my surprise because she takes me by the shoulders. "He *was* here, but he left for a break."

I blew out a breath. I can't believe I was doubting him. "Do you think he went to the cafeteria?"

She chews on her lip. "I think so, but he's… not alone."

My audible gasp surprises even me. "Mallory?"

Her voice softens. "Yeah. She's become a permanent fixture when he's working." She glances around before she continues. "She even paid Carmen to call him in today. We didn't need him."

Well, that conniving little...

I have two choices. I can lie down and let things happen to me, or I can control the situation. After the things Theo said to me earlier today, I'm confident Mallory's visit isn't his doing. But there's only one way to find out for sure.

Since the cafeteria is open to everyone, I tell myself I'm not *really* spying. I bury my head behind a newspaper a few booths away from them. I don't think Theo is keeping things from me, but before I spill the beans, I want to make very sure things are over between them.

They sit with their backs to me; Mallory is practically sitting on his fricking lap. He chugs from a coffee cup and picks at the lid, while she talks nonstop. His mouth forms a tight line. She reaches out to cover his hand with hers, but he busies himself with more coffee chugging. The nerve of her, scooting even closer to him as if she's zoning in on her prey. She whispers something in his ear, and I'm going to need some Propranolol to lower my heart rate. He leans back and holds his palms out to her.

She flips her hair off her shoulder, scanning the room. Now that I'm certain he doesn't want her, I lay the paper down so she can see me. For a brief second, her eyes widen. Then she paints on a smirk and goes in for the kill.

She retrieves a small gift bag from her Louis Vuitton purse. While Theo dives into the bag, she side-eyes me. He laughs as he puts the item back in the bag. He places a hand on her shoulder, and I can't breathe. Without warning, Mallory kisses him on the lips, and it takes all my willpower not to climb over two tables and rip her hair out. He springs away from her and forces her to stand so he can get out of the booth. I've never seen a guy scrub his beard so much, and I'm loving it.

He races out of the cafeteria, away from me. Mallory shoves the gift bag back into her purse and storms off after him. Over her shoulder, she gives me a "this isn't over yet" sneer.

You got that right. She might have delayed my reveal right when I finally worked up the nerve, but this certainly isn't over.

Chapter Twenty-Four
Theo

I DON'T WANT TO BE A jerk, but Mallory will not leave me alone. The more I try to pry myself away from her, the tighter her grip becomes. She's like a human Burmese python. Today alone, I received a dozen texts from her. She wants to meet and talk, which means she wants to do the talking and none of the listening. I don't have time for this.

She said she wanted to give me my birthday present. I know what she usually "gets" me for my birthday, and I don't want that anymore. Thank goodness the present she got me was only a small Etch A Sketch game. I'm sure she made some excuse at the toy store about buying it for a ten-year-old. I have to give her points for trying to embrace my love of games, but it's too late, and I'm not so naïve as to think this was a genuine gesture.

We've had the "it's not working" talk-argument at least three times this week. It didn't sink in before the move back to Nashville, and it's not working now. I guess she thinks she'll wear me down eventually like she usually does. But this is not like the other times.

On the bright side, I received another message saying that my birthday plans for Darla awarded me three new letters to the puzzle. I don't know yet what letters to choose. If I choose correctly, this could break the puzzle wide open.

On my way to the doctor's lounge, the *click, click, click* of Mallory's heels on the tile floor don't hide the fact that she's following me. I know who it is before she touches my arm. Compared to Darla's touch, which makes me feel alive, Mallory's makes me feel as if I got pricked by a jellyfish. I roll my eyes and let out a heavy sigh.

"Oh, babe," she says. "Let's talk."

I close my eyes and do my best to steady my breaths. "Mal, why are you doing this to yourself?"

I march into the elevator, and of course, Mallory follows me. Boy, she doesn't even stop to take a breath. Her fingers fly across her phone, sending a text, while she still complains to me. She's a multitasker, that's for sure.

"I don't know why you won't go to the chancellor's dinner with me. Helllooo, it's the chancellor."

Please, God, help me find my happy place. I replay the afternoon with Darla in my mind. *Perfect day.* Yep, I found my happy place.

The elevator door begins to close, when a sweet voice says, "Hold the elevator."

I stick my foot in the doorway, and Darla rushes in. Well, this is going to be tons of fun.

"Thanks," Darla says. "Nine, please."

She leans against the other wall of the elevator as we start our ride upward; her eyes bore into mine. I feel as though I have a neon sign over my head, blinking "ex-girlfriend kissed me." I gulp. Of course, the elevator has to make a stop at every floor, extending this predicament as long as possible. *Awkward.* Mallory's eyes flick up over her phone at Darla.

"Darla." Mallory's voice is so high-pitched, it could break glass. "I've been so busy; I haven't had a chance to call you."

Darla focuses her attention on me, arching an eyebrow. "I'm sure you have been."

Shit. She knows.

Oh boy, this is going to be interesting. I feel sorry for the innocent souls that happen to catch the same elevator as this little love triangle. I jingle the change in my pocket and stare at the open and close buttons on the elevator wall. I try to will the mechanics of the elevator to miraculously zip up the shaft quicker. *Dang it.* My superpowers aren't working today.

Mallory must have gotten wind of my interest in Darla. That would certainly explain the full-court press she has put on me this week.

"Let's get together real soon," Mallory says.

Darla stares straight at Mallory, and I would love to know what she's thinking. "Absolutely."

Mallory zones back into her phone. When I glance back at Darla, she gives me a disapproving "mom" expression. I guess I deserve that. If we were alone in this elevator, I would be all over her. I sneak a peek at Mallory, who is giving me the stink eye. *Busted.* My best plan of attack is to fake confusion. I raise my hands to defend myself.

"Darla, have you met my fiancé, Theo?"

Darla busts out laughing. The jugular vein in Mallory's neck is about to explode.

"We've never been engaged," I say. "Besides, you broke up with me, remember?"

She sticks a bony finger in my face. "You tricked me into saying it, and you know it."

I shrug as I run a hand through my hair. If this elevator breaks down, I'm going to climb my way out of here. They both stare at me. Darla cocks her head. All of a sudden, the "in case of emergency" notice on the wall is very intriguing. A trickle of sweat slides down my back.

"He works out at the wellness center sometimes," Darla says to Mallory.

Thank you, you sweet thing. I owe you one big time.

"Oh," Mallory says. "Babe, why didn't you tell me? I would love to work out with you. We could do Pilates or Zumba together."

Darla snorts.

I have to think of something quick. "Well… it's always spur of the moment. You know how my schedule is."

"You working tonight?" Mallory's fake interest in Darla is so transparent, a blind man could see it.

"No, I'm headed upstairs." Darla holds out her cut hand. "I hurt my hand the last time I was working on nine. I wanted them to know I was going to live."

By the sourpuss scowl on Mallory's face, I'm not sure she has the same feeling as the ninth-floor staff. The elevator door opens, and Darla exits.

"Toodles, Darla," Mallory says.

She waves as she exits the elevator. "Toodles."

When the elevator stops on the tenth floor, I take Mallory by the arm and lead her to a vacant conference room. I close the door behind us. "Mallory, please stop."

She fidgets with her phone. "I miss you, that's all." She slumps down in a chair at the conference table, and I sit in one next to her. I take her hand in mine.

She gazes up at me. "It's Darla, isn't it?" Her voice is barely above a whisper.

"Yeah. We've both known it wasn't working between us. You haven't been happy with me, either."

She shrugs. Her phone buzzes, but for the first time I can remember, she doesn't answer it. "Do you love her?"

I nod. "I do. I'm sorry. I never wanted to hurt you. I'll always care for you, but Darla has my heart."

Her lip trembles. She takes a deep breath. "It doesn't have to be this way."

This girl is exhausting. I stare at the ceiling, trying to find the right words. "Yes, it does. I have to go." There's a girl on the ninth floor who deserves an explanation.

Mallory crosses her arms over her chest. "You'll be back, and I may or may not take you back." She gets up, spins on her heel, and stomps out of the conference room.

Since the elevators are notoriously slow, I take the stairs down to the ninth floor. I burst through the door and run right into Darla, almost knocking us both down. My arms wrap around her waist to steady her, but she pushes away from me.

"I was hoping I'd run into you," I say with a wink.

She rolls her eyes at my terrible pun and pushes the button to call for the elevator five times. I take her by the hand and guide her to the supply closet.

"Really? The supply closet? You need to read something other than medical romance novels."

I cage her in against the Pyxis medication inventory equipment. "She ambushed me."

Her jaw clenches. "That's your problem, not mine."

"I don't want her." Her expression softens, so I continue. "It doesn't matter what she says or what she tries. I love you."

Darla grabs me by the collar and yanks me down to plant a hard kiss on me. One kiss leads to another, until we are both starving for oxygen. I rest my forehead against hers, breathing in her breaths.

"I want to... never mind. Every time I get up the courage to tell you, something drives down my courage. You should get back to work."

We ride down the elevator together, hand in hand. I've never prayed so hard to keep Mallory from popping into the elevator again.

Darla mumbles to herself, making her even cuter.

I cock my head to the side. "You okay?"

"Yeah." She kisses me one more time on the lips. "See you soon."

She wraps her arms around my neck and gives me a squeeze. Then she pushes away from me and bolts down the hall.

That was odd. But I'll take her quirky oddness over Mallory's possessiveness every day of the week and twice on Sunday.

I review my latest text clue. I reply "S, L, B." Before I make it back to the clinic, my phone buzzes. The message reads:

> *You did not choose wisely.*

"Argh," I moan, stomping down the hallway and inadvertently startling an elderly lady heading toward me. "Sorry," I say.

Another text follows:

> *I know you worked all day long.*
> *But trust me, I won't do you wrong.*
> *A nighttime workout could make your mood lift.*
> *A little birdie says she has to work the night shift.*

If I ever meet the person sending these clues, I'm going to kick his or her butt. I drag myself into the fitness center, and even though it's only nine o'clock at night, I want nothing more than to have a date with my mattress. Tomorrow is going to be another long day at work. But I want to solve this puzzle, and so far, it's not spelling out anything that makes a bit of sense.

Chapter Twenty-Five
Theo

I HAVE TO ADMIT, THIS IS a great time to work out. Only two guys grunt out sets with free weights, and three others mindlessly jog on treadmills. At this time of night, I don't have to fight for a weight bench. I swipe into the fitness center, and Darla catches my eye. I wave, and she heads my way.

"Hey," I say. "Got called in too?"

I surprise myself by being able to eke out even one syllable. I get so goofy when I see her. When I'm around her, it gets hard to walk for various reasons. I want to grab her and forget there are people around. I take a few calming breaths and count to ten.

"I stopped by to get some work done after our lovely meet and greet with Mallory. Sue, the weekend exercise specialist, was green around the gills. I sent her home, so I'm locking up."

"My lucky day, I guess." *Liar.*

"Whatever you say, Dr. Edwards." Sounds like she didn't buy my lame excuse one bit. She's now able to read me like yesterday's news. "Do you want me to hold your kit?"

"Sure, thanks." I hand it to her. "About Mallory—"

"Don't worry about it. Now, go try to get a decent workout."

She points to the weights and shoos me away. I walk backward toward the bench, not wanting to break eye contact, when I trip over a weight that was left on the floor. I'm not very slick.

She covers her laughter with her hand and moves to the sea of treadmills. On the way, she picks up a folded piece of paper that was on the floor next to her feet. Without reading it, she slides it into the waistband of her yoga pants. She starts up a conversation with an elderly man huffing out a jog.

I bang out a few sets, but it's hard concentrating when she's wearing yoga pants that leave little to the imagination. I'm going to pass out if I don't breathe soon. She catches me staring at her and motions for me to follow her. I almost drop a dumbbell on my foot.

She practically skips down the hallway, past the dressing rooms and into a conference room. I follow like a puppy, hoping I know where this is heading.

She sits on the conference table and grabs my T-shirt to tug me closer to her. "I can only stay off the floor a few minutes, but wanted to see you. You need to get a handle on your... fiancé."

I slide her knees apart so I can get as close to her as humanly possible without being obscene. I mean, as much as I would like to take her blouse off, I don't think she would appreciate it if I got her fired. "Hush. I think I need a fitness assessment. Can you check my heart rate during strenuous exercise?"

She pulls my face to hers and kisses me. Oh, I'm a goner. As if I'm running on autopilot, I slide my hands around her waist.

"Not strenuous enough," I whisper.

She pushes me away. "Don't you ever think of anything else?"

"Not when I'm around you, but every now and then, I think about baseball."

"Thinking about Mallory right now?"

"Who is Mallory?"

Her bottom lip is getting a workout from the way she's nibbling on it. "You have some unresolved issues to deal with." She focuses on her hands. "So do I."

I tilt her chin up so she has to look me in the eye. "No issues on my part, I promise."

My feather-light kisses on her neck make her hum in my ear.

"So, nothing I say to you will make you leave me?"

I slide her hair off her shoulder so I can kiss that sensitive spot behind her ear. She responds by latching on to my shoulders.

"Nothing you say will change the way I feel about you." I slide my hands up her thighs, nearing her hip bones.

She stops my hands with hers. "Are you trying to get me fired?"

"Trying to show you I have no issues."

She gives me a quick peck on the lips and stares at me. "I'm ready to tell you. I've been trying to work up the nerve, then Mallory made me doubt if I should, but I'm ready."

Yes. Finally. A warmness overcomes me and spills out into what is probably the goofiest grin I've ever made. I love this woman. I hope once she tells me, she'll be able to feel the same way.

My phone buzzes, but I don't break eye contact with Darla.

"You see... please understand..."

My phone buzzes again. "Go on."

"The night at the party—"

My fricking phone buzzes for a third time.

She groans. "If you don't answer that, whoever it is will continue texting you until you reply."

Dammit. When I read the text, my chin hits the floor. The room closes in on me, and if I don't leave, I'm going to throw up all over Darla. I'm sure my blood pressure and my sugar levels are off the charts.

"You okay?"

"No." I cannot believe this. There must be some mistake.

"Work?"

I read the words on my phone display again. I squeeze my eyes shut and hope when I open them again, the text will be a fluke.

"I wish." I stumble away. "I need to go."

I gather up my kit and my keys and head outside. I read the text again.

We need to talk. We are pregnant. CU at your car, Mal.

I feel as if I'm swimming through Jell-O to get to my car. My feet won't move, and I don't really want them to. Mallory leans up against my car, still dressed in her professional business suit and high heels. She must keep late hours at the office. When she sees me coming, she stiffens and stands taller. Her blond hair whips across her face in the wind.

"Hey," I croak out. I don't know what's appropriate to say when someone tells you through a text that she's pregnant. I'm not sure if "congratulations" or "are you going to keep it" is the right thing to say. If I don't want to get smacked, I won't ask if it's mine. I don't feel like getting smacked tonight.

"Hey," she says and hugs me.

I loosely hug her back. I stuff my hands in my hoodie pockets to keep them from shaking. We don't say anything for eons.

"So…" I can't form more than one syllable.

I lean against my car and gaze up at the cloudless sky. I cannot believe this. I don't love her. She doesn't love me. It wasn't much more than passing time together. And we were always, always careful. It's virtually impossible for me to get her pregnant. This pregnancy is either the world's suckiest timing, not mine, or a sick, twisted lie.

"I don't know what to say," I finally admit.

She lights a cigarette, takes a puff, and hands it to me. I take it from her and almost suck in the noxious nicotine before I flick it away. She knows I hate smoking, and she shouldn't be smoking in her condition, anyway.

She huffs. *Typical.* "Say you'll give us another chance."

I close my eyes. Of course she wants me to give her another chance. That's the right thing to do. The boa constrictor around my heart squeezes out the answer she wants. That's what I know I should do. But I'm not sure I want to. I nod.

She exhales and wraps her arms around my waist, while my hopes of a life with Darla drift away in the warm summer breeze. I want kids so badly, I would suffer through a loveless life to be a father.

"How far along are you?"

"Um, not sure. About a month." She twists her necklace around her index finger, making the last joint of her finger beet red.

I nod. But in my mind, I'm doing the math. I've been back in Nashville for a month, and it has been longer than that since the last time we were intimate. Maybe she's further along than she thinks.

"But we haven't—"

"Maybe a bit longer. I'm not sure."

I brace myself for the coming wrath. "Have you been with—"

"Theo! How dare you ask me such a thing." She sniffles. "That's the meanest."

"You're right. I'm sorry. I thought we were being real careful. Condoms, birth control pills, you name it."

"Me too," she whispers.

"I need some time to process all of this. You know I will do what's right for the baby, but… I can't promise you anything more. Not yet."

She blinks at me as though she can't believe I didn't cave. She plasters on a thin-lipped smile. "Of course."

Mallory has the maternal instincts of a Tasmanian devil, so if this child stands half a chance of being nurtured, I have to be involved on some level.

There has to be a way to make this right and still be with Darla. And if not, I might go against my no-alcohol rule and pour myself a stiff drink or two.

Mallory kisses me on my cheek. "I'll call you later." She gets in her car and drives away.

I stand at my car, consumed by the silence. I'm going to be a father. This is the one thing I didn't think could ever happen. I should be thrilled, but I'm not.

A few people shuffle out of the fitness center, and Darla locks the door. That's why I can't be happy. Because she still holds the key to my soul, and I don't want it back. She notices me.

I try to get in my car and hide, but it's too late. From across the parking lot, she cocks her head to the side. No matter how I try to hide my pained expression, her maternal instincts must kick in, because she zones in on my emotions.

She rushes over to me. "Hey, I thought you had an emergency."

I nod. "It's being taken care of, for now."

"That's good."

She slides an arm around my waist, but for once, I'm not feeling frisky. I move her arm away from me. She holds her hands out in defense.

I lean over the roof of my car and rub my temples. Her baby-lotion scent wafts over me.

"Do you want to talk?" Darla asks.

We sit in my car for what feels like an eternity, neither of us saying a word. I swallow the massive amount of crap that has accumulated in my throat. I cannot believe I'm about to say this to her, but she deserves to know the truth. I would never try to keep anything like this from her.

"The text was from Mallory."

"Is she all right?"

I nod. "She's uh… she's pregnant."

I don't want to see her reaction, but I have to; I have to face her.

She stares out of the window on her side of the car. She bites her bottom lip, and a slight tear trickles down her cheek.

"Congratulations," she whispers and opens the door.

She gets out and rushes away. Seeing her run off kills me. I know, at this moment, I have lost her for good. No matter how much I love Darla, I have to do what is right for this baby.

If it is my baby.

Chapter Twenty-Six
Theo

*D*AWN IN NASHVILLE IS ONE of the prettiest scenes there is. When the sun rises over the Cumberland River, the entire downtown glows with shades of pink and orange. The blooming crepe myrtles in varying shades of pinks, reds, and purples line the sidewalks next to skyscrapers and honky-tonks. The AT&T building, known by locals as the Batman building, shimmers in the first light of day. Joggers line the streets, getting their miles in before the humidity makes the air too thick to move.

I haven't slept in days. In fact, I haven't left my apartment except to go to the hospital. But I'm so sick of staring at the same walls, and Tommy is tired of seeing me mope, that I had to get some fresh air—fresh air and good, strong coffee. My brother has taken up nail-biting, and I'm afraid to tell him too much because he has always been on team anti-Mallory. He doesn't need another reason to dislike her.

I need my sister. Jennifer is my rock when the going gets tough, but she's still away. Telling her about Mallory is not a conversation I want to have over the phone. I need a warm hug surrounding me, letting me know everything will be fine. And I'm definitely not getting my folks involved in this mess until I absolutely have to, so I'm on my own.

So much for fraternity brotherhood. I thought my frat brothers and I would stay in touch, but I can't think of a single person from college that I would want to talk to about this.

I'm still numb from the realization that I am going to be a father. If the mother had been anyone else, I would have been jumping for joy. If it had been Darla, we would celebrate the announcement and have my father marry us the next day. With Mallory, there is no passion; there is no "'til death do us part" feeling. I know it. She knows it.

Mallory isn't a completely bad person, but we were always going in two separate directions. When I needed to sleep after sixteen hours of being on service, she wanted to barhop. When I needed to study, she wanted to go to a concert. When I wanted to go to church, she wanted to go shopping. We're like oil and water, and the thought of being tied to her for the rest of my life raises my blood pressure to a dangerous level.

I drag myself down the street to the local coffee shop. I used to spend a lot of time here when I was in college. It has an eclectic vibe to it. Along with tons of Vanderbilt memorabilia, it also has autographed photos of famous people who have been customers here. They are secured underneath the acrylic table coverings so it doesn't matter if anyone spills a drink. I order two large coffees and find a table near the front—the Vince Gill table—when I see Isaac enter. I wave him over.

"Hey, I got your text. What's up?" He sits down, and I slide one cup of coffee toward him. "Thanks. You didn't have to do that."

"I need someone to talk to, someone not genetically linked to the issue at hand."

"Sure." He takes a swig. "You know Darla and I are tight, but anything you say to me won't go any further than here."

"I appreciate that. I guess you heard."

He clears his throat. I stare off to watch a couple saunter across the street, hand in hand, headed for the park. They act as though they don't have a care in the world. *Must be nice.*

"I don't love her," I finally say.

"Who?"

"Mallory. I don't love her. She doesn't love me. She likes the idea of me. I can't give her what she wants."

"What's that?"

"Prestige. A fancy house. Nannies. Tons of jewelry."

"Ahh." He takes a swig from his coffee. "She wants to be married to a doctor and all that that implies."

I nod. "It's not who I am." I take a gulp, not caring if it scalds my esophagus. This stuff sure is better than hospital cafeteria coffee. It costs a lot more too. I glance around the crowded coffee shop, making sure no one is paying attention to our conversation. "She's like an eight-track tape."

"You mean that thing before cassettes?" he asks.

I nod. "Yeah. My parents still have a tape deck in their stereo."

"I never understood why they called them eight-track tapes when they only had four tracks."

"Me either," I say. "But this is what happened when you listened to the tape too much. One track would bleed over to the next track, and neither track sounded good anymore."

He crinkles his nose. "I hated when that happened."

"She's not good for me, and even though she'll never admit it, I'm not good for her."

We sip our coffee for a moment before Isaac breaks the silence. "Tell her she has the wrong guy."

"I'm supposed to be infertile."

Isaac drops his coffee cup. The lid pops off, and we both jump up and do our best to soak up the spill with napkins from the dispenser. Hot liquid spreads all over the table and drips down the side.

A barista runs over to assist us. "Don't worry about it. I'll get it cleaned up and get you another cup."

"Sorry for the mess," Isaac says to her. He focuses back on me. "I don't want to be a jerk, but maybe it's not yours."

"The thought has crossed my mind. And she could be lying, but that would be an all-time low, even for her."

"You could demand a paternity test."

I lean back in my chair. "No."

The barista returns and hands Isaac another cup before leaning down to sop up the mess from the floor.

"That would make her seem like a slut and—"

"Dude, you broke up... how long ago? She could have been sleeping her way across the city; you don't know."

I clench my jaw. "She's not like that."

He sips his coffee. "People deal with rejection in many ways. Maybe there's no baby at all."

"Time will tell, I guess."

"Do you love her?"

"I already told you—"

"Darla," he says. "Do you love her?"

"Yeah," the barista says. "Do you?"

Isaac points to the barista as if to say, "What she said."

I take them both in. Isaac is usually a wisecracker, but right now, he's as serious as a melanoma. And the barista waits for my answer as if she's my new best friend.

"Since the day I first saw her. It's like I dissected my heart and handed it to her in the middle of microbiology class."

"Awww," the barista whines, clutching her chest as she leaves our table.

Isaac cringes. "A simple yes would have been good enough."

"Can I tell you something if you promise not to laugh?" I make sure the barista is long gone before I continue. We are not besties, no matter what she thinks.

"First, let me put my coffee down. I don't want a repeat performance." He holds up three fingers. "Scout's honor."

I lean in close to him. "She was my first."

His eyes get big, and he cocks one eyebrow up so far that it's hidden in his hairline. "Shut the front door."

"It's true." I can feel the heat rising up my neck and burning my face with a permanent flush. I probably look as though I have a gigantic port wine stain across my face. "Yep. Dr. Edwards was a frickin' virgin until that little darling paraded into the frat party our senior year."

He giggles. "Somehow, I find that hard to believe. But two young virgins going at it? That's… sweet."

"Well, I have a moral compass. It meant something to me."

"So where does that compass point you right now?"

I crunch my empty coffee cup. "I think it's broken."

He chuckles. "At least you got one. I fly by the seat of my thong."

I shudder at the mental picture.

"Listen, I can't tell you what to do. Nobody can. Obviously, I've never been in your situation. You have to do what you think you can live with. But you don't have to marry someone to fulfill your moral obligation to a child."

He's right. I know he's right, but I would feel like a deadbeat dad if I didn't marry her. That sounds like something out of a fifties sitcom, but I'm old-fashioned.

"The only advice I can give you is to not make any hasty decisions. Every time I do, it always comes back to nibble on my ass."

Too much information.

My thoughts go back to Darla. "How is she?"

He swallows hard. "Are you sure you want to know?"

"I have to know. She won't answer my calls. I even went to her house, but she switched off the front-porch light and wouldn't open the door."

His dark eyes fill with tears. "She's broken. I've never seen her so unreachable. Not even when she found out *she* was pregnant."

I cover my face with my hands. We were so close to having our happy ending, and I went and ruined it. I've ruined her. "Please take care of her for me."

"Of course. Shelby and I have been alternating staying with her at night. We don't want her to be alone right now. The little kiddo will be back first of next week, so that will help her get back to the land of the living."

Isaac focuses on the couple at a nearby table. "It was really, really hard for her to let you in, and now—"

"I know. I'm so sorry."

"I better get to work," he says.

"Yeah, me too."

We stand to leave. He gives me a big bear hug. It's not one of those bro hugs where a guy wants to show affection for someone he cares about without being too sappy. This is an all-out "I care for you and don't care who sees" hug.

I hug him back. God, I needed that. I needed to know that someone cares about what I am going through.

"Thanks," I croak as a tear flows down my cheek. I wipe it away before he can see it.

"Sure thing, brother." He saunters away, and I notice him brush a tear away too. I still don't know what to do, but I am certain I've ruined the best thing that will ever happen to me.

Chapter Twenty-Seven
Darla

M Y DAMN COMPUTER WON'T TYPE automatically. *Stupid, stupid computer.* I can't get past the bomb that was dropped on me three days ago. Tears pour out every moment I'm alone and sometimes when I'm around friends. My trash can overflows with snot rags. I don't remember the last time I ate. I think I took a shower this morning but can't swear that I actually put soap to skin. If it weren't for Isaac, my left shoe wouldn't match my right one today. I glance down to make sure I have on pants because I don't remember getting dressed this morning. My thoughts keep bouncing around in my head as if I'm in a pinball machine.

I thought I would be the one to ruin my relationship with Theo. And I never thought it would hurt so much. But it's definitely over now. *Kaput.* It's finished before it could even get started. I guess this would be the worst possible time to tell him about Stella. One more revelation would send him straight to the psych hospital.

I take out a little photo of Stella on her first day of school. She was so excited to carry her backpack filled with school supplies. I was able to hold my tears until I had dropped her off. After that, the floodgates opened.

I keep this photo in my wallet for when I need a pick-me-up. And today, I need a huge pick-me-up. I wish she were here with me so I could smother her with smooches. She would help me get through the pain without even knowing she was doing anything significant. Less than a week to go until she's home. I can make it. I know it's still super early on the West Coast, but I can't stand it any longer. I dial Diane's phone, and on the fourth ring, my sister answers.

"This better be important," she says. She switches the phone so we can FaceTime. Diane's eyes pop wide open. "You okay?"

"Having a bad day. Is Stella awake?"

She yawns. "No, but I think you need to see her face."

I nod and wipe a tear away. "I do."

"Hold on a sec." Diane slides out of the bed, and I see her husband in the background throw a pillow over his head. She meanders down the hallway, giving me a chance to wipe my tears and practice my faux happiness.

"Stella, Mommy's on the phone. She wants to say good morning." Diane moves the phone so I can see my sweet little girl all curled up in a ball. I miss my sweet girl so much.

Her eyes flutter open. "Hey," she says, her voice soft and sleepy.

"Hey, baby. Sorry I woke you up." Already, I feel a thousand percent better.

"K," she says, closing her eyes again.

Diane swivels the phone around until I see her face. "Sorry. It's five o'clock here. Are you sure you're okay?"

I nod, trying to convince myself. "Yeah. I was really missing her. That's all. Don't tell her I was upset. I don't want to mess up her fun." I sniffle, and my voice catches in my throat.

Diane doesn't seem convinced. "Call back in about three hours. She'll be up by that time."

I end the call and stare at the phone.

"Hey, cutie." Isaac leans up against my doorframe. "You look like hell."

"Nice to see you too." I slide the photo back into my wallet and toss it into my open purse.

He sits down on my desk. "I wish I could make it all better."

"Me too. But even my fairy godmother can't fix this."

He pouts. "It will get better."

I put my head down. Even Isaac, Mr. Chatty Cathy, cannot find the words to make me feel better.

"I really thought you two were meant to be together."

"Me too," I mumble.

He stands and looms over my desk. "I'm going to say this, and I might go to hell for it. I don't think there's a baby."

I let out a breath I've been holding for three days. "You have no idea how glad I am you feel that way." I lower my voice to barely above a whisper. "I felt awful for thinking it. Would she do that to get what she wants?"

He drums his fingers on my desk. "Only one way to find out."

He's right. I don't have to sit back and give up on something I want more than anything. It's time I grew a spine when it comes to Mallory. I bolt up so fast that my chair crashes into the wall behind me. "You're right. I'm tired of wallowing in my pity."

With renewed purpose, I pace back and forth in my office. "I've waited seven years to have him back in my life. I'm not going to concede so easily." I slam my fist on my desk, making Isaac jump back. "I'm going to her office, and we're going to have a little chat. One way or another, this ends today."

Isaac holds out his fist for me to bump. "And if she's telling the truth, can you handle it?"

If she really is pregnant with Theo's baby, I will have to be all right with it. I don't have to like it, but I will accept it.

"Ask me again in an hour."

Because I'm no dummy, I call in a favor to Brenda, the chancellor's assistant. I'm the only one the chancellor trusts to give him his immunizations, so Brenda and I have become buds over the years. Fortunately, she has access to Mallory's Outlook calendar and blocked off an hour at noon for a one-on-one with Mallory to discuss miscellaneous budgetary items. It pays to know people in high places.

Mallory's heels clicking on the ceramic tile floor give me a few seconds' warning before she bursts into Brenda's office.

When she sees me sitting at Brenda's desk, she skids to a halt. "Where's Bren?"

"Taking a break. I told her I would discuss the miscellaneous budget items with you." I motion for her to sit in the chair next to Brenda's desk.

She stares at me. Her arms are tightly crossed over her chest. It's as though she has aged ten years since the time I saw her in the elevator.

"I'm sure he told you," she finally spits out.

I nod, not taking my eyes off her. "I guess this is where I'm supposed to congratulate you?"

She twists her necklace around her index finger, and that nervous eye twitch she gets when she's lying has decided to show up. "That's real sweet of you."

I cross my arms over my chest. "That was sarcasm."

"What's it like?" she asks.

"Huh?"

She looks at me with panic in her eyes. "Being pregnant. What's it like?"

So, she thinks I'm going to give her prenatal advice. *Get on the Internet, for crying out loud. Buy a book.* I know we used to be friends, but this is a bit much.

"Well, it's exciting and scary and strange and ugly and beautiful. All of those things at the same time."

"Were you sick?"

"All the time." *Liar.* I was hardly sick at all, but she doesn't have to know that.

"How much did you gain?"

I wave her off. "Not much. Let's see... The last time I had the nerve to step on the scale, I'd gained fifty-five pounds."

She gulps. This is more fun than I thought it would be.

I reach over and pat her hand. "But don't worry about that. The stretch marks are in places most people will never see."

Her jaw drops.

I lean back in Brenda's chair. "I'll never understand why all the zits popped out. And my feet... they were so swollen. Near the ninth month, all I could wear were flip-flops."

Making her squirm reminds me of college. When I was in my maternal and child health rotation in nursing school, I would come back to the dorm and tell her everything I got to see and do. To me, it was fascinating and beautiful. To her, it was disgusting and an inconvenience.

Her necklace breaks in her clenched hand. *Come on, Mal. Confession time.*

"But totally worth all the changes," I say.

She drops her gaze to her broken necklace, and her hands tremble. She stares at the wall. A tear falls down her face. I slide a tissue box toward her. She yanks one out and dabs at her eyes.

"Who's your obstetrician?" I ask.

Her fingers continue to twist her broken necklace.

"If you haven't chosen one, I could make a call to Dr. Brown. He's wonderful. I've seen him for years. I could make a call for you to see if he can get you in." I pick up Brenda's phone and punch a few random numbers.

"No, no. That's not necessary." She clenches the broken pieces of her necklace in her white-knuckled hand.

"What's all this about? Why are you asking me these questions?"

She takes another tissue and wipes her perfect nose. "You love him, don't you?"

"As a matter of fact, I do. But it doesn't really matter, does it?"

"Of course it matters. All this time I've been with him, he hasn't been with me."

"You're not making any sense."

"What I mean is that he's been there, but a part of him was attached to someone else. I didn't know who that someone else was until he moved back here."

Interesting. Maybe all those nights when I was thinking about him, he was thinking about me too.

She blows her perfect nose and snatches another tissue. She leaves the balled-up, mucus-filled tissue on Brenda's desk. If this conversation goes on much longer, we're going to run out of snot rags.

"The first time I saw you two together, I knew," she says quietly. "I knew that he gave his heart to you a long time ago, and he doesn't want it back."

"I'm sure I don't know—"

"You had a picnic together not long after he moved back to Nashville. I was on my way to a meeting across campus. I saw you two. You were laughing and playing around. You looked like you belonged together. You two looked like you were... in love." She shakes her head, as though she's trying to rid herself of the memory. "And when we were in the elevator, I could see it in your eyes. In his eyes." She grabs another tissue.

I lean back in the chair. "It doesn't matter. He will do what's right. I'm sure he won't abandon you. At least you'll have Theo through it all. I didn't have him." I gasp when I realize what I said. "I mean... I, uh... never mind."

I cover my face with my hands. *Shit. Please tell me she didn't pick up on that.*

Mallory sucks in all the air in the room. "Oh my God." She covers her mouth.

I give myself a mental kick in the butt. Now, I've told everyone except Theo, including his ex-girlfriend. But with her loose lips, he'll know before his shift ends. I lean forward toward her. "Please don't tell him."

"You mean he doesn't know?"

"It's a really long and stupid and kind of funny story. In a nutshell, I didn't know his name at first. I didn't know what to do, and now that he's back here, I haven't had the guts to tell him. I don't know how. So please, I'm begging you, please do not tell him. It has to come from me. Even though you've figured out the perfect way to keep us apart, I am still going to tell him. You'll have to live with that." She doesn't have to know how wishy-washy I really am about the big reveal.

I reach across the ravine, commonly known as Brenda's desk, and take her hand in mine. She slouches back in her chair and trains her eyes on the ceiling.

The sound of Sleeping Beauty singing "Once Upon a Dream" comes through my cell phone—my clue that Stella is calling me. I hold up a finger to Mallory. When I slide my finger across my phone, I see my bright, beautiful daughter's face, all giggly and full of life.

"Hey, sweetie." The sight of her face makes me forget all the stress I'm under.

"Mommy, guess what!"

Mallory walks around Brenda's desk to stand next to me. She cranes her neck down so she can see who I'm talking to. It wasn't part of my plan, but this could be the straw that breaks the camel's back. She sucks in her breath when she sees Stella, the spitting image of Theo. Goofy is standing next to Stella.

"Goofy," she squeals, as though I couldn't have figured that out on my own.

I'm not that silly, but I love her enthusiasm. Goofy waves at the camera as he gives Stella a hug with his other overstuffed arm.

I wave back. "Hi, Goofy."

Diane swerves the phone around so I see her face. "Yep, you do kind of resemble Goofy."

"Ha ha. Very funny. Let me see my baby again before I convince Goofy to pee on your leg."

Diane swivels back to Goofy, who is signing an autograph for Stella. "Sorry, Darla. You've been trumped by a dog."

I giggle. "That's hard to beat."

Diane's face appears again. "Did your day get any better?"

I stare at Mallory and catch her swiping a tear off her cheek. "Yes, it did. Call me tonight, okay?"

"Of course. Ooo, I think I saw Minnie. Gotta run." And Diane is gone.

I'm not sure what to say to Mallory, who is still looming over me. Her eyes fill with tears. "Oh… Darla. She looks like—"

"I know."

"I am such a bitch," she says to herself, her eyes full of tears. "I'm not pregnant. I assumed he'd want me if he thought he was going to have a child. I know it was really stupid and teenagerish."

She confessed to me, and now, I can't breathe. She snatches one more tissue and wipes her eyes again.

"How long were you going to keep this charade up?"

"I didn't think that far ahead, okay? I've never been good at long-term plans."

Oh, Mallory. Act first, think later. She'll never learn. She gets up to leave, and I follow her to the door.

She cringes. "While I'm in the confessional booth, I might as well admit, I knew he was into you at that frat party. You were with him when the house caught on fire, weren't you?"

"Yeah."

"I'm really sorry for standing in the way. On purpose, I didn't tell you his name after the party. I wanted him for myself. I'm so sorry. You two deserve each other." She nodded to my phone still sitting on the desk. "And she's so beautiful."

My jaw drops, and so do my tears. "Thank you." My breath hitches. "But you realize my daughter hasn't had her father in her life because you were selfish."

"I know."

My voice quivers. "You hurt me, Mal. On purpose, you hurt me. Why?"

"I know. It was a terrible thing to do." She takes a deep breath. "I'm used to getting my way, and not once have I thought about how that impacts other people until now. I'm so sorry. I'm going to fix this. I promise."

I'm not sure I can find it in me to forgive and forget, but the short time I've been with Theo has taught me that's the right thing to do. *Dang, this is hard.*

"I believe you're sorry, but please don't tell him. I have to do it."

She gives me a kiss-kiss before I grab her in a hug. She leaves my heart filled with hope and a desk littered with soggy tissues. I never imagined that Goofy could bring out the best in such a crazy situation.

Chapter Twenty-Eight
Darla

AFTER THE VISIT WITH MALLORY, I talk Isaac into a late lunch at his favorite pizzeria. It doesn't take much to talk him into food, and I finally have an appetite again. I need the chaos of a lunch crowd and the chatter of waiters running through the maze of tables to drown out all the crap going on in my head. Plus, the smell of fresh-baked pizza dough is enough to rouse anyone from a coma.

"I knew it. I just knew it. She's as fake as a spray-on tan," Isaac says as he picks off the onions from his slice of pizza. He claims onions give him gas. *TMI.* "She didn't have the glow."

I roll my eyes. "Not everyone has the glow. I didn't."

"Did too. I knew from the beginning. I didn't know what it was at the time, but it showed on your face even before you knew it."

"Are you talking about the glow or the zits?"

He chuckles. "Why did she lie, and more importantly, why did she confess? To you, of all people." He slings an onion onto my pizza slice.

I shrug. "I think she really loves him."

"Oh, please." He takes a swig of his drink. "I don't buy that for one minute."

"She's used to getting her way. One time in college, she couldn't remember this guy's name, so she renamed him. For two years, he let her call him Trey because she said he looked more like a Trey."

Isaac chuckles.

"But I've spent so much time sharing the same space as her, I know the subtle tics she has when she's lying. The eye-twitch, necklace-twisting combo rats her out every time."

He shivers. "Girl, how did you survive?"

"She's not that bad once you get to know her."

Isaac stops focusing on me and focuses on something behind me. "Don't move," he says under his breath.

Not turning around takes all the willpower my body can generate. It's like trying not to pick at a scab. If it's there, I've got to pick and pick and pick until it's finally off. "What's going on?"

Isaac drinks from his cup and mumbles, "I think she's about to drop the bomb on him."

I snap my head around. Theo and Mallory sit at a table in the far corner of the restaurant.

"I told you not to look."

I hide my head behind the laminated menu. "When did they show up?"

"Somewhere between the glow and you two being roomies."

I pick up my purse and scan the room for the nearest exit. "I've got to get out of here."

"You totally owe me." He stands and lets out a big yawn, forming a human shield. He enables me to scoot unnoticed past two tables full of customers, the to-go counter, and out the side entrance. I run three blocks back to work. I do *not* want to watch what happens. It's a private matter. Although, I'm not going to lie, I am totally interested in what's going down.

Isaac finally drags his butt back to work. He always stretches out his lunch breaks as much as possible. He doesn't count the time it takes to get to and from a restaurant, nor does he count the time it takes for him to get his food.

When he gets back, he heads straight into my office. "You're welcome. You left me with the tab." He snaps his hands to his hips and taps a toe.

"Did he see me?"

"I don't think so."

"Good. Do you think she told him?"

He cackles. "Oh, definitely. But after his first few words, which were even new to me, I think it went okay. No chairs were thrown through windows, no pitchers of beer doused on heads. But fire-engine red is not a good facial color for him."

"He didn't take it well?"

Isaac rubs the back of his neck. "Every time she'd reach out to touch him, he'd jerk away like her touch burned his skin."

I hand him a ten-dollar bill for my lunch, and he bats it away. He knows I'll offer, and I know he won't take it.

"So, what happened?"

"Well, Miss Nosy Nelly, he sat there for a few minutes with his head in his hands. Then he kissed her on the cheek and left."

"Did he see you?"

"Uh-huh."

I pop him on the shoulder.

"Ow! What was I supposed to do? I had to pay for my, excuse me, *our* lunches. He waved. I waved. He looked like death warmed over. Then he left. That's it."

I stare up at the ceiling and blow hair out of my eyes. "Now what?"

"All I know is she did the right thing. Can you?"

I growl at him, but he's right. All these secrets are making my blood pressure skyrocket. And Stella will be home soon. But every time I'm with Theo, I cannot make my mouth say the words he needs to hear. I am such an idiot. I'll tell him at the barbecue tomorrow. That will give him a little break from crazy revelations, and hopefully, he won't put me in the same category as Mallory. The last thing I want to do is trap him.

Later that afternoon, I get a text from Isaac. For crying out loud, we're only twenty-five feet away from each other. That's taking modern technology a bit too far. Then I read the text:

He's here.

I open my office door to see Theo sitting at the front desk of the wellness center with Isaac. Theo looks so defeated, like a six-year-old that has dropped his ice cream cone. His dress shirt is all wrinkled, and his tie hangs loose. He strides to me in only two large lumbering steps and wraps his arms around my waist. I wrap my arms around his neck and inhale the scent of disinfectant and laundry detergent. Only a doctor could rock that combination. I breathe him in as he holds me close.

"She lied to me," he mutters, barely above a whisper.

"I'm so sorry. I don't know what else to say."

"You don't have to say anything. Just don't leave me."

"Never." I lean back, and he rests his forehead on mine. "Does this mean I'm still invited to the barbecue?"

He kisses me on the cheek. "Absolutely." He hugs me again. "Please don't ever lie to me."

I hold him tightly for a moment. Then I take his face in my hands and kiss his perfect lips. Muscle memory kicks in as I take in the dark circles under his eyes.

"You look like you haven't slept in days."

He shrugs.

"Go get some sleep. I'll see you soon."

He lingers a few minutes, holding me in his arms, before he kisses me on my forehead and leaves.

I have never lied to him. I have left huge gaping holes in the truth that are so big he could drive a semitruck through them. But I have never told him something that was not true. I wonder if I could get off on a technicality.

I hum a tune while I dust the dining room. Thinking of Theo makes my spirits soar and my step a little lighter. The last few weeks have been awesome, aside from the little disagreement we had on our date and the hiccup with Mallory. We've spent time together, and I've gotten to know him. He's the person I knew he would be—funny, intelligent, kind, gentle.

A few more days, and Stella will be home. Then I won't be able to keep them apart. I hope they are drawn to each other and that my shortcomings won't ruin everything.

My cell phone rings, and I see Shelby is calling.

"Hey, you," she says. "So, today's the cookout. Are you ready?"

I nod, even though I know she can't see me. I run a hand over the four gift bags sitting on my dining room table. "Yep. I've got my plan, and I hope he's so distracted by my creativity that he won't be too mad." This could go extremely well, or I may never be invited back to another family gathering. Telling him there is a gamble, but time is running out. I hope I get extra points for making it a game.

"He'll love it. Can't wait to see his reaction."

I stop, duster in midair. "What?"

"Don't be mad, but when we were at Theo's, I kinda, sorta slipped Tommy my number."

I gasp. "Shelby, you sly dog."

"We're not dating or anything like that. I haven't even seen him since that day. Only a few texts. Anyway, he invited me to the cookout. I can cancel if you think it will be weird."

I plop down in a dining room chair. "No. You shouldn't do that on my account. Do you like him?"

"I don't know. He's cute and smart as a whip. And damn, can that boy bake, but he's still got two years left of graduate school in Boston."

Wow. Shelby sure does work fast, but I hope she doesn't forget all about Tommy when the next guy shows her attention. She gets a lot of attention, but she deserves a nice guy, someone who doesn't crave the spotlight, like the last train wreck. Tommy might be exactly what Shelby needs.

"Tommy says Jennifer is home from her vacation today. You have got to tell him before she does."

"I know. I have to do it today."

"Listen, I have to go. I'll see you later, but I do think your gift idea will help soften the blow."

I exhale. "Let's hope so."

I lay the phone down on the table and proceed with my chores. Next on my list is the laundry. I've hardly had to do any since Stella has been out of town. While the machine fills up with water, I sort the darks from the lights. A pair of yoga pants is wadded into a ball, so I flop them out by the waistband. A folded piece of paper floats to the ground. I had forgotten that Theo dropped that a few days ago while I was working the night shift at the fitness center. That was about the time all hell broke loose, and I guess I forgot to throw it away.

I pick up the piece of paper and unfold it. It's a printout of clues and a Hangman puzzle. *No. This cannot be happening.* Every time we hung out, he was rewarded with clues to a puzzle.

Tears well up. I am such an idiot. I feel so humiliated, so used, so played for a fool. All the time we spent together wasn't real—the picnic, the late-night workout, the birthday plans, everything. *Oh God, no.* Please don't tell me everything he said and did was to win a stupid game.

I rack my brain, trying to figure out who would have sent these clues to him. I need to confront Shelby and Isaac to see if they had anything to do with this. Or perhaps it was Tommy and his sister. They seem to understand his love of games. Shelby is the first to be on the witness stand. She loves this kind of cutesy stuff, and she knew my schedule. But if Jennifer put the truth together like Tommy thinks, she could have done it. But she wouldn't have known about my work schedule. Isaac would have known that part, but he's not very creative. I call Shelby, but it goes straight to voice mail. *Dammit. I'm such a fool.*

All those times when Theo happened to be right there at the right time, knowing my weaknesses, was too coincidental. He went right along with the game.

And now I have to meet his mother. I have to put on a smiley face and pretend I don't know. Now, I'm not the only one that has some explaining to do.

Chapter Twenty-Nine
Darla

THE POTTED ORCHID WOBBLES AS I balance it on my hip while shoving my keys into my jeans pocket. The handles of the four gift bags dangle from the elbow of my other arm.

I have put some serious thought into how I am going to announce my secret, but now, with the stupid Hangman clues I found, I feel all messed up inside. To think that Theo may have been playing me like a fiddle this whole time ticks me off, and I have half a mind to forget all about telling him.

But he's Stella's father.

Standing outside of the address Theo gave me makes me nauseated. My keys rattle as I try to shove them into my pocket. I should have faked a stomach virus. I could say that my car broke down. I could say that I got lost.

But I'm here now. It's time to face the music. He has as much explaining to do as I do. And when I get my hands on the person who sent him those messages, they'll wish they never messed in my love life. I run all this through my mind and still cannot come up with a logical answer to who it might be.

Before I can knock, Theo opens the door. His face lights up. Right now, I would like to knock that smirk off his face.

He scans down to my full arms. "Wow. Let me help you with this."

"Thanks." I hand over the plant when he reduces the distance between us. He leans down to kiss me, but I jerk my face away from him, and his lips land on my ear.

He stares at me with confusion. "What's up?"

Don't play dumb with me.

He eyes the gift bags on my arm. "What's in the bags?"

I can't help but grin. "Oh, a few things for the birthday boy." *But I might exchange them for switches if he tries to weasel out of knowing about this stupid Hangman game.*

He groans. "I told you I had everything I need."

Here goes nothing. "Can I talk to you a minute in private?"

"Sure." He escorts me through the house he grew up in.

Photos documenting four children in various stages of life cover both walls of the main hallway. My eyes zone in on the baby pictures. One in particular is a carbon copy of Stella when she was a baby.

We step into the kitchen, which smells like apple pie and love.

"Mom, this is Darla."

His mother, I'm assuming Stella, turns around. Sure enough, she looks like the intelligent, educated hippie that Theo described. A braid of long grayish-blond hair lies down her back. She wears a long skirt with flip-flops. Theo looks so much like his mother, I could have picked her out in a crowd. Any other day, I would have loved this woman. Today, the introductions only postpone my confrontation with Theo.

She pulls me into a giant hug then leans back and stares at me. I am staring into the eyes of my daughter's grandmother, and this lady doesn't even know it. My throat clamps shut, and I force down the desire to cry. There's so much love in this house that my Stella should have known since she was born. At this point, I don't care about the Hangman game. My daughter is part of this family, and because of stupid mistakes and misunderstandings, she was left out of all this love.

I swallow my emotions and bite my lip to keep from crying. Maybe coming here wasn't a good idea. I should have told Theo in private and definitely way before now. Yep, I should have faked the stomach virus.

"I've heard so much about you."

I can't help but smile. "Not sure that's a good thing."

She squeezes my shoulders. "It's all good. Now you two go out back and chillax. Roman's out there firing up the grill."

I point at the plant Theo holds. "This is for you."

She takes the plant from Theo, and her eyes twinkle. "You didn't have to do that."

"I wanted to thank you for inviting me."

She pats my cheek. Oh dear, I already like this lady. I hope I don't hurt her son. She might fling the plant at me ten minutes from now. The best I can hope for is that she'll be thrilled she has a grandchild and that it will lessen the shock Theo will probably feel when he realizes what I've been keeping from him.

"Is there anything I can do to help?" Even as I ask, I know I'm stalling.

"Nope. Today, you're a guest. Next time, you're family."

I'm not sure if there will be a next time. Theo takes my hand and leads me to the back door.

"Nice to meet you," I throw over my shoulder.

We step out onto the deck, which shows the wear and tear of four rowdy children. I imagine Theo and Tommy tossing a football back here or Jennifer lounging in the hammock, reading a romance novel. The backyard is so picturesque. I bet there were lots of family game nights on the big picnic table and lots of laughter.

Theo's dad mans the grill. His apron reads, "I'm a holy smoker." He waves the smoke away from his face.

"Dad, this is Darla."

The Reverend shakes my hand, and the corners of his eyes crinkle when he grins. "Nice to finally meet you. Relax and enjoy the quiet while it lasts."

Truer words were never spoken. I give Theo the evil eye as he points me toward a lounge chair.

"Did your mom say your dad's name was Roman?"

"I was wondering if you caught that."

"Yes, I did… Romeo."

He lies down on the lounge chair, and I perch on the edge, ready to scram if I need to. Theo's dad waves at us through the smoke at the grill, and Theo waves back.

"So, what's up? You seem really nervous."

"I am, a little. But first…" I hand him the yellow bag. "Happy birthday."

He takes the bag from me. "You shouldn't have."

I snatch the bag away from him. "Okay, I'll return it."

He grabs it back from me and tears into the bag, tissue paper flying all over the backyard. He cocks his head to the side as he pulls out the game.

"It's the game Operation," I explain. "You know, in case you need some practice."

He cracks a wide grin. I hand him the blue bag, and he doesn't waste time with protests. He drags out the game Sorry.

He laughs. "I love this game."

"I figured you might be 'sorry' you ever met me."

He leans over and kisses me on the cheek. "Not a chance."

I clear my throat and hand him the green bag.

He cocks one eyebrow as he pulls out the next game. "Twister?"

My face heats up, and I'm sure my neck is completely covered with a blotchy blush. "Maybe we can play that one… just you and me." I cover my mouth. I have never been so forward with a guy. At this point, I have nothing to lose.

He winks at me. "You bet."

I let out a deep breath. Here goes nothing. I pat my jeans pocket to make sure my keys are still there in case I have to make a quick getaway. I can do this. It's now or never. I'm glad Theo's father is nearby but out of earshot. At least I have someone close in case I need backup. Maybe Theo will be so impressed with how clever I am, he won't be too mad about the bomb I'm about to drop on him.

I practically throw the pink bag at him as I bite my lip in anticipation.

He takes out the dry-erase board and markers. "Uh… I'm not getting this one."

I take it from him and draw the Hangman scaffold. "I didn't think you wanted lipstick, so dry-erase markers were the next best thing."

He beams. "I love it. Best gift ever."

"Let's play a game." I draw sixteen lines, one for each letter of the sentence "You have a daughter."

He rubs his hands together in anticipation. This may be the last moment he likes me, but the truth has to come out. No more stalling.

"'Sup, bro?" Tommy asks Theo, making me drop the dry-erase board in the grass. Shelby stands next to him, her fingers threaded through his. Tommy's timing sucks.

"We were enjoying some peace and quiet until you showed up," Theo says with obvious annoyance.

"That's my job." Tommy stands straighter and stares at me.

Shelby tugs him toward a swing in the corner of the yard. "Tommy, you need to finish telling me about that 3-D printer thingy."

"Huh? Oh... yeah."

He swings an arm over her shoulders, and they slip away from us. Shelby had better not go too far, because she's next in the hot seat.

Then, in an instant, the moment is lost. Jennifer enters the backyard.

Dang it.

Theo pats my arm. "I'll be right back." He rushes over to Jennifer and gives her a big hug. Shelby has an "oh shit" expression on her face. Jennifer gapes at me then at Theo. I take one step toward them, when my phone rings.

I go to hit ignore but answer when I see it's my sister. "Hey, Diane, what's up?"

Diane sounds as if she has recently finished running a marathon. My sister doesn't exercise at all. Maybe Stella has instilled some good habits in her. She sure could use some.

"Darla, don't panic," she says.

I stop dead still.

"I wasn't until you said that. Is Stella all right?" My words end in a high-pitched shrill, causing everyone in the backyard to stare at me.

Shelby and Jennifer rush up to me with Theo following closely.

He studies me. "What's going on?"

"Stella's sick," Diane says. "She was fine one minute, then all of a sudden... It's real bad."

I drop my cell phone.

Shelby takes me by the shoulders. "Talk to me," Shelby yells. "What is going on?"

I know she screams more words at me, but I feel as if I'm underwater. I see her mouth moving, but her voice is muffled. The ground tilts, and suddenly, it's a lot closer to my head. The cool grass cushions my fall. I blink a few times, feeling as though I have driven through the high elevation of Monteagle, when all of a sudden, my ears pop and I am able to hear again. Unfortunately, everything seems all too clear now.

Shelby is yelling into my phone. Theo has his fingers around my wrist, counting my pulse. Tommy tosses him a blood pressure cuff and stethoscope. He stuffs the earpieces into his ears and wraps the cuff around my arm.

Jennifer strokes my back. "It's going to be okay," she says, her eyes holding my gaze.

"We've got to get Darla to the pediatric hospital," Shelby says. "They're airlifting Stella from the airport."

Theo rips the stethoscope from his ears. "What happened?"

Shelby nibbles on a fingernail. "I don't know. Diane was hysterical. Something about Stella cutting her foot a few days ago, but it got worse, so they decided to come home early. She was limping this morning but became unresponsive on the plane."

"Get me out of here," I mumble as I try to stand.

Theo grabs my arms and yanks me up. "Come on, let's go."

I blink a few more times and nod. We rush out of the house, and Theo throws me into the backseat of somebody's car. He climbs in next to me, and Shelby scrambles into the front seat.

Jennifer, in her calm, teacher-like voice, points Tommy toward his car. "Go, I'll be right behind you."

Tommy slides behind the wheel next to Shelby and peels away from his family's home.

Theo pulls me into a hug and wipes a tear off my face. "Are you cold?"

I didn't realize I was shivering. Theo runs a hand through my hair, and I sob until the front of his shirt is soaked.

"So much to tell you," I whisper brokenly.

He kisses my cheek. "Focus on your baby right now."

I nod. I don't think I have the energy to explain or the ability to form complete sentences, anyway. Shelby and Tommy debate about the quickest route to the hospital.

"No, there's construction on that road," Shelby says. "It's a snail's pace. Take Woodlawn instead."

The car makes a sharp turn and suddenly picks up speed again. It feels as though we are going in circles. My baby could be dead.

Please, please, Stella, please be all right.

"Come on! Would you move if you're going to?" Tommy yells at the car in front of him. Then he speeds up. "'Bout time."

The car comes to a screeching halt. Theo drags me out of the car, toward the automatic doors of the emergency room. We rush up to the front desk, while Tommy and Shelby speed off in search of a parking place.

"I'm Dr. Edwards. This is Darla Battle. Her daughter is being airlifted here from the airport."

The clerk checks the radio communication. "Life Flight is on its way. Have a seat here, miss."

Theo sits me down in the chair next to the desk.

I stare at the clerk as she continues talking. I know she's speaking English, but I have no idea what she's saying. I plead with my eyes for Theo's help.

"Darla, she needs Stella's history."

I blink. "Yeah. Uh, it's…"

"Was she born at this hospital?" he asks.

"Yes."

"Check the electronic medical record," he tells the clerk.

"That makes things easier. Is she allergic to anything?"

"Uh… no."

The clerk taps at her keyboard. "Is she taking any medications?"

"No." My voice hitches. Theo's warm hand rests on the small of my back.

"Blood type?"

"She's B positive."

"Okay, we'll probably need you to donate blood, just in case."

"Uh, okay. Wait. I'm AB negative." I sigh and bury my head in my hands. I can't even help my own child. "I can give blood for your bank, but it won't help her. She'll reject my blood type."

I peer up at Theo. I know without asking what his blood type is going to be.

"I'm B positive," he says. "But I'm not supposed to donate blood. Diabetes."

"Hmm," the clerk says, writing all our answers down. "We may need you to donate anyway, depending on our supply."

Tommy and Shelby rush into the emergency room, and Shelby wraps me in a hug. "Is she here yet?"

Tommy squeezes Theo's shoulder.

"Tommy, she's got B positive blood," I say. "If necessary, would you donate blood?"

"Of course."

"The helicopter's landing now," the clerk says. "Come with me."

We all follow on her heels.

She stops. "Only immediate family."

I desperately seek out Tommy's expression. He gives me an encouraging nod.

Shelby gives me a kiss on the cheek. "It's going to be all right. You know what you have to do."

I take Theo's hand and tug him forward with me. "Come on."

He scrunches his forehead. "She said family only."

After I swallow the frog in my throat, I say what I've needed to say for a very long time. This isn't how I wanted to tell him, but I don't have any other choice. The secret ends now.

"You *are* family. You are Stella's father."

Chapter Thirty
Theo

HOLY MOTHER OF GOD. THIRTY seconds ago, I was helping someone I love deal with a medical emergency. It's what I'm good at—staying calm during a crisis. But thirty seconds ago, I wasn't a father, and it wasn't *my* medical emergency. Now I couldn't even remember how to add fractions if anyone asked me.

She said Stella is mine. I have a child. We have a child. The blood drains from my head, and I feel as though I'm going to pass out if I don't tell myself to breathe. I'm only able to meander down the emergency room hall because Darla leads me by the hand.

A gurney whizzes down the hallway toward the emergency room and vanishes behind a privacy curtain. From the viselike grip Darla has on my arm, I know it was Stella who was whisked past us.

A tall woman rushes up to us and wraps her arms around Darla's neck. "Oh God, I'm so sorry. I don't know how this happened."

Darla hugs her back and wipes tears from the woman's face.

Darla's sister, Diane, wipes her nose with her sleeve. "I was so scared. I don't know how you deal with trying to be brave. I tried to stay calm. I promise I tried."

"It's okay," Darla says. "I hope it will be okay."

Her sister glowers at me. "Who is this?"

I see fear in Darla's eyes as she shifts her focus from me to the woman. "Diane, this is Theo."

Her eyes stare a hole through me. "You seem familiar."

The airport. *Holy crap.* The little girl at the airport. The same little girl in Jennifer's class. She's Darla's. She's my... I stumble backward, putting my hands out to steady me. I crash into a wheelchair parked behind me in the hallway.

"This can't be happening," I mumble. "I saw her with Stella at the airport."

"Oh God," Darla says under her breath.

"And Jennifer was her teacher, wasn't she?" I ask.

Darla nods without meeting my eyes. I pivot and lean against the wall. Jennifer knew. She knew, and she didn't tell me. The deer-in-the-headlights expression she had when I mentioned Darla's name, the stranger-than-usual phone conversation... everything makes sense now.

"Who is this?" Diane asks again.

Darla clears her throat. "Theo is Stella's father."

Diane throws daggers at me with her eyes. "I thought you didn't know who the father was."

Darla bites her trembling lip. "Not exactly."

Diane marches over to me and slaps me across the face, hard. Damn, that hurt. "You horrible son of a—"

"Stop it," Darla yells, moving between us.

"Stella Battle's parents?" a man calls out.

Darla and I push past Diane and rush toward the man. He's wearing a yellow gown over his scrubs, booties over his shoes, and a mask hangs around his neck. It all screams, "full contact precautions." They think whatever Stella has is infectious. *Shit.*

"I'm Dr. Michaels. Dr. Edwards, right?"

I nod. "Theo."

"I'm a pediatric infectious disease specialist. They called me in to take care of your daughter. We're getting little Stella settled right now."

My daughter. I have a daughter.

"What happened?" Darla asks.

"From the appearance of the affected area on her left foot, we're looking at a serious infection."

Darla sniffles again. "How?"

"Her aunt told the flight nurse they went on a pontoon boat ride, and when Stella jumped onto the shore, she fell and cut her foot on a rock. The brackish water must have been the perfect breeding ground for bacteria. I think we're dealing with an aggressive infection, hence the protective gear."

I can hardly form complete sentences at this point. I'm lucky I even know my own name. I think it's Theo. "What kind of bacteria?"

"We're doing cultures of blood, tissue, and saliva to determine exactly what. Once we know that, we can focus on her best treatment."

"But it could take days to get the cultures back," I say.

He nods. "I know, but I have my suspicions, so we'll start antibiotics as soon as we've collected all of the samples. We'll need to get her to surgery to clean out the wound and debride if necessary."

Darla gapes at me, wide-eyed. "He thinks there's dead tissue."

"What do you think it is?" I ask him.

He stares at both of us and sighs. "I'd bet money on necrotizing fasciitis."

I have lost all ability to breathe. Flesh-eating bacteria. *No! This cannot be happening.*

Darla whimpers into her hands.

I shake my head so hard, I think it's going to fall off. "That's impossible."

"Rare, but not impossible. This is the third case at this hospital alone this summer, but she's the youngest patient I've seen."

Darla sniffles. "But chances are it's something more common, easier to treat, right?"

"I hope to God I'm wrong. But I need you to prepare for the worst."

"Which is?" I ask.

I don't want to know, but I need to know. I have a strong feeling I know what he's going to say, but the words have to come from him. This isn't a nasty boo-boo that needs a kiss and a good dousing of antiseptic to make it all better.

He clears his throat before he continues. "Organ failure, amputations, possibly even death."

Darla backs up to me and spins around. "I think I'm going to be sick." She runs to the nearest bathroom.

I wipe my face with my hands. I think I'm going to lose my lunch too. "Is your wife going to be all right?"

I take a slow, deep breath. "We're not married."

"Oh, sorry. Anyway, we have to stay one step ahead of the organism, and that may mean losing limbs. It's awful to think about your little girl without a leg, but it might save her life."

I hold my hands out in front of me. "I don't want to go there yet." I turn my back on him and try to breathe.

"If it's Strep A, we've got a treatment for it. But we have to stay on top of it. It's pesky, but not very virulent as long as the body doesn't try too hard to fight against the treatment."

I wheel around and cock my head to the side. "What do you mean?"

Darla bursts out of the bathroom, wiping her mouth with her sleeve. Her face has a greenish tint to it. "Can I see her? Please, I need to see her."

He sighs. "One at a time, though. It's very crowded in there, and you'll have to suit up. We're trying to get her in to surgery soon. So get in and out before we intubate her."

Darla's lip quivers. There are so many unspoken words behind her sad eyes. I know she'll have to tell me everything, but not right now.

"You go first," she says. "I guess I owe you that much."

"Are you sure?" I ask.

Her lip quivers. "Go before I change my mind."

I nod and slip away with the doctor. He helps my trembling hands get inside the armholes of the protective gear. One leg at a time, I hobble into the suit, and he fastens the Velcro strips for me. "It sure is different being on this side of the bed, isn't it?"

I nod.

He opens Stella's door, and we enter the beehive of activity surrounding this little bitty human that I created. A nurse taps information into a computer next to the bed. Everyone in the room is rushing about, doing their jobs like they are supposed to do. But to me, it looks as though they aren't paying her any attention. Stella lies there with no one holding her hand or whispering to her not to be scared.

My little girl so sick, it about kills me. Her eyes are closed. Beads of sweat cover her forehead. I want to pick her up and rock her until she's all better.

I can't believe I didn't put the pieces of the puzzle together. She's got my crazy hair, my nose. She's a female version of me when I was in the first grade. She looks exactly like me in every way possible. I should have been able to zone in on that fact and pick her out in the crowd. But I saw her in Jennifer's class and at the airport, and it didn't register because this is supposed to be impossible. I've always been told I would never be able to father a child, but I did, and she's the most beautiful person I've ever seen. I can't let anything happen to her.

Stella's left leg's has Betadine spread all over it, all prepped for surgery. Her left foot is three times the size of her right foot—swollen and cherry red. The edema extends up her calf, almost to her knee. Either it doesn't hurt, she doesn't feel the pain anymore, or she's the bravest person I know.

The nurse taps Stella's arm, and her eyes flutter open.

I blink away the last few tears and try to put on a brave face for her. "Hey, there. Do you remember me?" Probably not, considering the only part of my face not covered are my eyes.

Even though she's in pain, her eyes twinkle with recognition. "How's your sugar?"

Her sweet voice makes me chuckle. "It's pretty good. How are you?"

"My leg hurts."

"Dr. Michaels is going to help your leg."

Her eyes well up with tears. One trickles down her sweet little cheek. "I'm scared."

I sit beside her and take her little hand in mine. Even through my gloves, I can feel her soft skin. "Me too. It's okay to be scared. You do everything the doctor tells you to do, all right?"

Her breath hitches, and another tear escapes from her eye. I wipe it away.

"Where's my mommy?"

"She's right outside."

More tears fall. "I want my mommy."

I nod and stand. "I'll go get her." I lean in and kiss her forehead.

I kissed my little girl. On my deathbed, I want this moment to flash through my mind. Not because she's so sick and could die, but because it's the first time I got to kiss my daughter. I didn't get to see her take her first breath or her first step. I wasn't around when she spoke her first word, which I am very sure was "mama." I didn't even get to change one foul-smelling, dirty diaper. I have none of those memories. This is my moment, and I will never forget this moment no matter how long I live.

When I go to leave, she says, "I got chocolate ice cream." How she can be so scared and still think of something as trivial as ice cream, I'll never know.

I smile back at her, knowing good and well that she can't see it behind my surgical mask. "And when you're feeling better, we'll both get chocolate. Deal?"

She nods. "Deal."

I head back into the hallway. Darla waits right outside the door for her turn. Her eyes plead with me to tell her that Dr. Michaels is overexaggerating the severity of the situation.

As the nurse helps me out of my gear, I tell Darla, "She is beautiful."

She bites her bottom lip and heads into the room.

The nurse balls up my gown and disposes of it in the hazardous waste container. "I could tell you were her daddy a mile away. She's the spitting image of you."

"Yeah, she is."

I slide down the wall and crouch on the floor. My hands cover my face, and I shed more tears than I knew I was capable of producing. I've already developed such a strong connection to my daughter. These feelings are supposed to be reserved for a person I've spent years caring about, possibly decades. But here I am, and after one hour, I have a connection stronger than I have ever felt before. It's almost as if my soul knew about her all along.

Chapter Thirty-One

Darla

SEEING MY LITTLE GIRL BEING whisked away to surgery is more than I can handle. Her voice echoes in my mind, screaming, "Don't leave me, Mommy. Don't leave me." I feel as though I'm living a nightmare in which my feet won't move and everything is just out of my grasp. And as soon as I think I reach what I want, it's suddenly out of my grasp again. I have never felt so helpless in all my life. The control freak in me can't control this. Not one single thing is within my control right now.

I stand in the empty emergency room bay, all alone with my thoughts. The family-only section of the emergency room is lonely, and I don't know where Tommy and Shelby went. I have no one. The sterile room filled with medical equipment is quiet, but I'm screaming on the inside. My mind is like a pinball machine again. I cannot land on one emotion long enough to do anything about it.

A cleaning lady slips into the deathly quiet bay. "Ma'am?"

Her voice makes me jump.

"I need to disinfect the room. Can I help you out of your gown?"

"Uh, yeah. Thanks."

She gingerly helps me out of the gear and places everything in the hazardous waste container. "Dr. Michaels knows what he's doing. He'll take good care of her."

I nod.

She pats my arm. "Let's get you to the waiting room where the rest of your family is."

She leads me out into the hallway where Theo is curled up against the wall. I slide down next to him and lean my head against his shoulder.

He doesn't reach out for me. We cry together in silence. His breaths are labored, and a moan escapes his lips. I have broken him. In the span of one hour, he has found out he has a daughter *and* that she might die. He will never be able to forgive me, not that I'm worthy of forgiveness.

"It's my fault," I whisper. "Everything is my fault."

"It's not—"

"Excuse me, Dr. Edwards?"

We gaze up to see a nurse standing over us.

Theo clears his throat. "Yes?"

"I'm Sharon, one of the ER nurses. Dr. Michaels told me you have the same blood type as Stella."

He nods. "Stella." He says her name as if he's trying it on for size.

"I know you're a diabetic, but he would really like you to donate blood for her. We need the least amount of reasons for her body to reject treatment. With you having the same blood type and being her father—"

"You can have every ounce of my blood."

Sharon motions with her head. "Come with me. We'll have to monitor you closely afterwards."

"I don't care." He rises to his feet and holds out his hand to help me up. "I'll meet you in the waiting room as soon as I can."

I throw my arms around his neck. "Thank you."

His arms hang by his side.

I step back and watch him leave with the nurse. He glances back at me once more before they round the corner.

I stumble around until I find Tommy, Shelby, and Diane sitting in the corner of the busy emergency waiting room. All three jump up when they see me enter.

Shelby wraps her arm around my shoulder. "Let's go."

Together, we make our way to the surgical waiting room for the longest night of my life.

I sit curled up in a chair, wrapped in Isaac's arms. He made it to the hospital almost before Shelby could get off the phone with him. Even though he's not the person I wish was holding me, Isaac cares for me and for Stella in a way that I need right now.

Theo has been gone for two hours. Tommy sits with his elbows resting on his thighs, head in his hands. Shelby sits between him and me, a comforting hand on each of our backs. Diane leans up against the wall, her breath hitching.

My eyes follow a little girl bouncing down the hallway. She holds her daddy's hand and clutches a smiley face balloon in her tiny fist. I may never get the chance to give my baby another balloon. I still have the deflated one from the day she was born. It was a pink teddy bear. I kept each balloon she got for every birthday. They range from unicorns to teddy bears to super heroes. They're among the mementos I have stashed away in Stella's boo-hoo box. Every time I rummage through it, I boo-hoo. If I had it with me today, I would ruin every item in the box with my tsunami of tears. Stella has made my life worth living, and if I could trade places with her, I would do it in a heartbeat, without even flinching. She does not deserve to be so sick, so close to death.

"She's going to be fine," Isaac says, his breath catching in his throat. "She has to be fine."

He holds me tighter. I feel his tears land on my forehead. As much as I'm hurting, it also hurts to see him so distraught. He's always the happy one, no matter what. Not today.

He has gone beyond the call of duty when it comes to Stella. He sat through Princesses on Ice. He has watched every animated movie we own with her a thousand times, although truth be told, I think he enjoyed them as much as she did, if not more. He searched high and low for the perfect puppy for her. I'll never forget the expression on her face when he brought that little ball of fur into the house. Stella and Yeti were fast friends. She was so happy, which made Isaac happy.

If something made her happy, Isaac was all over it, even if it meant letting her plaster makeup all over his face. I can still see her applying one color of eye shadow after another to his eyes along with eyeliner that looked as though it were applied using a fat kindergarten-style crayon. She used her artistic skills on me next. We looked like two hookers when she got finished with us. Stella was so proud.

I fish out my phone and fumble through the photos I have stored until I find one from that day. I show it to Isaac. He giggles, and tears flow down his cheeks. He giggles more and holds me tighter.

"God, what I wouldn't give to have her do that again," he says.

I wipe my face on my sleeve. "All that was missing was some six-inch pumps, and you'd have been ready for a nice stroll down Second Avenue."

"Not funny," he says, but he can't fight the grin on his face anymore.

I wipe his tears. Without him, I would be so lost right now, especially since I scanned past the selfies Theo and I took on our birthday excursions. Isaac leans over and sees them before I can shove my phone deep into my pocket.

Diane paces the floor, chatting up a storm on her phone. Everyone in the busy room has to listen to her conversation with her husband. She fidgets with her wedding ring, and her hand works its way to her necklace. I grab her arm and force her into the chair next to me. She throws her phone in her purse and wraps her arms around me.

She squeezes me around the waist. "It's going to be fine."

"She's all I have." I choke on my words, and my breath hitches.

"You have us too, right, Isaac?" Diane asks.

"Yes, you do," he says. "And we'll get through this together."

They envelop me in a burrito-style hug. I soak Diane's blouse with tears. There's no way I could do this without them. Shelby enters with a cardboard drink holder and four steaming-hot coffees. She shoos Isaac over so she can sit by me and show some love. Diane and Isaac grab coffee cups. Shelby holds one out to me, but I wave her off.

Jennifer, a man I assume is her husband, and a college-aged girl rush into the waiting room. I can only assume she's the baby sister I haven't met yet. Reverend and Mrs. Edwards follow right behind them. They huddle together, and The Reverend leads them in a prayer—a prayer for my little girl, a prayer for Theo, a prayer that probably does not include me. Not that it should. After they finish praying, they continue to stick close to one another. The youngest girl sits in Mrs. Edwards's lap as though she's five years old instead of college-aged. She wraps her arms around her mother's neck. Theo's mother kisses her baby girl on the cheek.

Jennifer's husband hugs her. He runs a hand up and down her back. It's such a sweet, simple gesture, but I would give anything to have someone comfort me like that right now. They share a hushed conversation. Jennifer buries her head in his chest. He strokes her hair as he continues to whisper to her. I gaze over at this classic Americana painting of the Edwards family and wish I had this loving family to cling to. I guess I never will.

I'm such a coward. I cannot even go talk to them. They appear as devastated as I feel. Their child and grandchild are hurting. It's a double whammy. Add them to the list of people that will never forgive me.

Jennifer catches my eye from across the room. She pats her husband on the shoulder before she strolls up to me. "Can we talk?"

I know I deserve a serious tongue-lashing, but I don't think I have the strength to defend myself right now. She does deserve to hear my side of the story, so I follow her out of the waiting room, and we head down the hallway.

"I know I owe you an explanation. I didn't know you were his sister. All this happened so suddenly. I didn't know what to do."

She grabs me in a hug, and I hug her back, so thankful that she has crossed the Edwards-Battle barrier. I know I am not worthy of her compassion, but I need it so badly right now. I know it's Stella who's in danger, but she's my life. When she hurts, I hurt.

"I don't care, okay? None of that matters. Hey, don't blame me that I'm good at putting two and two together."

I laugh and cry at the same time. "I was so scared you'd tell him before I—"

"Not my place. There, there. None of this is your fault."

"Yes, it is. I let her go against my better judgment. I knew I should have kept her with me." My words come out all choppy between my short breaths. "As long as she's with me, she's fine."

I've always kept Stella close. Ever since I came to the conclusion that I was going to raise her on my own, I've had to be two parents. I had to be the good cop and the bad cop, and the only way I knew how to do that was to keep as close an eye on her as humanly possible at all times. The first day of kindergarten was agonizing. Giving up control to let her do a simple rite of passage like starting school was hard enough. I'm still shocked I let her go across the country with Diane. That didn't end well.

"It was a freak accident," Jennifer says. "It could have happened anywhere. And it doesn't matter now. Trust the doctors. Trust God."

"I'm trying," I say through another round of tears.

She hugs me again like a sister would. "Where's that crazy brother of mine?"

"He went to donate blood, but it's been a while. I hope he's okay."

She takes a step backward. "He shouldn't be giving blood." She frowns. "But I guess I would too if it were my child."

"When the dust settles, if the dust settles, he's going to hate me."

She wipes another tear from my cheek. "One day at a time, Darla. Let's get through tonight."

Theo enters the room, as pale as a ghost, holding a bottle of orange juice.

Jennifer grabs him in a hug. "How much did they take?"

"Only a pint. I tried to get them to take more, but they wouldn't."

She slides his hair off his forehead. "Did they check your sugar?"

He rolls his eyes. "Yes, Mother. That's what took so long. It tanked, and my heart rate was off the charts. The bloodletting along with the stress is making it hard to regulate."

In my tunnel vision over Stella, I forgot about Theo's health.

"But I'm okay now." He looks at me for the first time. "Any news?"

I shake my head. "Nothing yet. Thank you, Theo."

He takes another gulp of his orange juice. "Dad and Tommy have B positive blood too. If the doctors need more, I'm sure they will be willing to help out."

I lean in to hug him, but he backs up and puts his hands out defensively. He juts his chin up and stiffens his spine. "I can't do this right now. I don't want to talk to you."

I guess I should have expected this reaction, but it still stings. Even though I didn't plan for the truth to come out like this, I guess I naively assumed it might bring us together.

"Theo," Jennifer says.

He stares at her. "You knew. You knew, and you didn't tell me." He sneers at me. Through his clenched jaw, he says, "I only want to be in the same room with you when we're discussing Stella's care plan. You got it?"

I bite my lip to keep it from quivering. "Got it."

He storms away toward the waiting room. Jennifer puts her arm around him, but he snatches it away. I give them a head start back into the waiting room before I slip back into my seat next to Isaac.

"Focus on Stella," Isaac says. "Focus."

Theo finds a place to sit next to his mother. His little sister moves from their mother's lap. She sits next to him and holds his hand. His mother wraps her arms around him, and he crumbles in to her. From across the room, I see his entire body tremble from exhaustion, from stress, from such deep sorrow. His little sister rests her head on his shoulder and strokes his hand.

"Focus," I reply to Isaac.

Chapter Thirty-Two
Theo

I HUDDLE BETWEEN MY PARENTS, IMPATIENTLY waiting for news—waiting to see if my little girl has lost her leg or even worse... if she has lost her life. My mother plays with my hair like she has done a thousand times before. Any time I was ever upset as a child and even as an adult, her fingers would softly comb through my hair, giving me the peace I need. My mother has always been there for me, from skinned knees to diabetes scares, and even through the rare girlfriend breakups. She always knows what to do and say, and she knows when no words are necessary, like now.

My father holds my hand, and I can feel him silently pray for everyone involved—for Stella, for me, and even for Darla. It's hard for me to pray for Darla right now. I guess I wasn't cut out for the ministry like Dad. He treats everyone with equal compassion like the Bible teaches. I can't forgive her like I know I should. She has had plenty of chances to tell me about Stella, and she chose to keep my child from me.

I can't even talk to Jennifer right now. We've never had a divide like this before, and it's killing me. She rests her head on Tommy's shoulder, and they speak in hushed tones. Her eyes plead for me to talk to her.

My voice breaks through the silence. "I'm sorry for all this."

Mom squeezes my shoulder. "We're family. We get through things together."

"Yeah, but I know this is a lot to digest all at once. I promise you, I didn't know she was mine. I wouldn't have kept that from you."

"We know, dear."

"Don't be disappointed in me."

My mother squeezes my shoulder. "This is a blessing. You have a child, Theo. It's nothing short of a miracle."

"Your mother's right," Dad says.

"It doesn't feel like a miracle right now."

Jennifer wipes her face of tears. "Theo…"

I peek over at Darla on the other side of the room. She has her knees tucked under her chin, and she turns her head, resting her cheek on them. She seems so devastated, so alone.

"It will," Dad says.

My mother squeezes my shoulder again. "I have a granddaughter, and she's named after me." She kisses me on the cheek.

I grin. I only now realize that. Tommy nudges my foot with his shoe. He winks at me. I think back to the one night I had with Darla. We didn't share our real names, but somehow, I must have mentioned my mother in a conversation. It warms my cold heart. Stella is named after my mother. Knowing this, it's wrong for me to stay mad at Darla. I shouldn't, but I still am.

Dr. Michaels enters the waiting room. I stand. Darla stands. This is the moment of truth. I can't read his face. Doctors learn early on the art of a poker face. We can't let our emotions get the best of us, especially when a family is facing critical news about their child. I've been there many times. If the doctor isn't calm, the parents freak out. This isn't helping me at all today. *Oh, please tell me my daughter made it through the surgery. Please.*

Darla and I meet him halfway across the room.

"She's stable."

I exhale. I think I've been holding my breath ever since she was wheeled into surgery. Darla whimpers and grabs on to my arm. My parents must be saints to have managed all the childhood injuries and illnesses of four kids all these years.

"We made three incisions, one on her foot and two on her calf. We cleaned out the infection as best we could but left all three incisions open because we will probably have to go back in."

"Why?" Darla asks before I can.

"That's how this infection works. We think we've got it cleaned out, but if one microbe is left, it starts destroying again. We may have to go in multiple times."

"What's next?" I ask, not really wanting to know.

"Every day is a new challenge. She'll need to stay sedated and intubated. I need to be honest with you; she is not out of the woods yet. I'd like to talk to you about an unorthodox treatment."

Darla's eyes are full of hope. "What do you mean?"

"It's a theory. I don't have scientific evidence, and no clinical trials have ever been done. But the theory is that with high-dose antibiotics, which is standard protocol for infections like this, the immune system kicks in to do its job but creates a severe inflammatory response, causing more damage to surrounding tissue. Sometimes IV steroids suppress the immune system only enough to avoid the inflammation and let the body get rid of the infection one hundred percent."

"So, she's still fighting?" Darla's hope-filled words ask what I was thinking.

"Yes, but before we put her under, her vitals were already becoming unstable, and she's started having hot and cold sweats. We don't have the luxury to wait and see."

Darla and I lock eyes. It's as if we can read each other's minds.

"Do it," we both say without a second thought.

"I can't guarantee that it will work, and it's very risky."

"Do it," we both say again.

It's not much, but I'm thankful Darla and I didn't argue over the course of action for Stella. It's nice to have some common ground, even though it's not enough to make a difference in how I feel about her right now. At least we can come together for Stella.

The doctor nods. "I should get the culture back tomorrow. If it's Strep A, I'll order the steroids and continue with aggressive antibiotics."

"Can we see her?" Darla asks, reading my mind again.

"Remember, she's sedated and won't be able to talk to you. And you can only stay for a few minutes. Two visitors at a time. I'll let you know when you can go in."

"You go first," I say to Darla.

She shakes her head. "We see her together."

I'm not sure if I'm ready to be on team Darla, but maybe a united front is what Stella needs right now. "Okay."

Dr. Michaels leaves, and we are left staring at each other. I stand there like a bump on a log with my hands stuffed in my pockets. She checks her watch, glances up at me, and back down at the floor.

Darla and I tiptoe into Stella's ICU room. The nurse waves us in. Lots of beeps pierce the otherwise quiet, sterile environment. The nurse checks Stella's vitals and records her urinary output. She examines each toe and finger.

"Come on in," the nurse says to us. "She's sedated, so she won't respond to you. Don't let that scare you. She needs rest, so don't stay long. Stay clear of her leg too."

I put my hands on Darla's shoulders and guide her closer to Stella's face, which is covered in beads of sweat. Her sweet cheeks have a deep-red tint to them, and oh, how I wish I could kiss them and wake her up like Sleeping Beauty. I slide a sweaty curl away from her neck. God, she's burning up.

"Stella Bella, it's Mommy. I'm here. You rest and get better, okay?" Darla's voice cracks.

I rub her shoulder.

"I love you, baby. Please get better. Please." She kisses Stella's hand and cheek. "Please be strong and get better. I'm right outside that door, so don't be scared. I love you so much." Darla gives me a sad expression before she focuses back on Stella. "Stella, your daddy's here. You need to get well so you can tell him all about you. He needs to know how special you are."

My heart melts. Even though Darla knows how hurt and mad I am at her, she knows exactly what Stella needs right now. It's all about Stella. That's what Darla told me once. Nothing else matters.

Darla motions for me to come closer. "Talk to her," she whispers as she wipes the tears from her eyes. She knows as well as I do that Stella won't respond to us, but there's enough evidence to confirm that patients remember what people say when they're unconscious.

I wipe the snot and tears off my face and sit on the bed next to her. Darla places Stella's hand in mine, and I wrap my fingers around hers.

"Hey, kiddo."

Darla smiles.

"It's me. We've met a few times, and I knew you were special for a reason. I didn't know why at the time. I'm your... I'm your..."

I look at Darla. She motions with her head for me to continue.

"I'm your daddy. And I would love nothing better than for you to get well so we can get that chocolate ice cream we talked about. Okay? So please be brave and strong. I love you, sweet girl."

I lean down and kiss her cheek.

Darla kisses her again. "I'll be back soon. You rest."

We leave her room. Darla's eyes are full of emotion. Another tear trickles down her face. As I'm about to wipe it away, she does it herself. She doesn't need me, not even to wipe her tears off her face. She never has. I ignore Darla and continue down the hallway toward the waiting room. Her sobs don't even make me glance back. I don't even slow down as I storm away from her.

Chapter Thirty-Three
Darla

THE WAITING ROOM IS MY new home away from home. I haven't left in the three days since Stella was airlifted here. She made it through the first surgery. No telling how many more she has to go. She still has all her fingers and toes, and she's still fighting for her life. If it weren't for the tube down her throat and IVs in her arms, I would think she was in a deep sleep. I try pretending that she's all better and that in a few days, she'll be back to her old chipper self, riding her pink, heart-covered bicycle up and down the driveway. But I wake up to live the nightmare another day.

A piece of me died two days ago when the doctor confirmed that Stella does indeed have flesh-eating bacteria. He cultured group A Strep from her wounds, and today, he started her on corticosteroids along with target antibiotics. Maybe today will be better, and she won't need any more surgeries.

I convince Diane to catch a flight back to California. When she's not in control, she makes my life miserable. I can't handle that right now, and with Isaac and Shelby here, I have enough mothering. She means well, but I need her to go home for now. She would stay as long as I wanted, but right now, it's best if she tries to get back to her normal life.

I would like Theo to do some comforting, but he's in the far corner, staring at his shoes, as usual.

Diane pivots around to face me before she leaves the waiting room. "I can stay. Say the word."

"No. You go home. No one knows how long this is going to last. I may need you later."

"You say the word, and I'll be here as fast as the plane can get me here."

She wraps me in a big hug. We've never been touchy-feely sisters, but I need this right now. "I'm so sorry."

"Stop saying that. You have nothing to be sorry for."

"Well, one thing's for sure. The next time I take Stella anywhere, you're going too."

"Is that a promise?"

"Me too?" Isaac asks.

She rolls her eyes. "California is not big enough for your personality." She kisses me on the cheek and wipes my tears. "And it won't be too long from now either. You have to believe that."

I nod and bite my lip to keep another round of tears from flowing.

"I hope things work out with you and Theo," she whispers in my ear.

"Me too. We have to try for Stella's sake."

She gives Isaac and me a final hug and Shelby an air-kiss before she leaves. Next, I need to tackle trying to get Shelby to go home. There's nothing more she can do here but climb the walls, and I'm sure she'll start getting on my nerves soon. If it weren't for Yeti, Isaac would be here day and night.

I escort Shelby and Isaac out of the waiting room. "You two need to go too."

"I feel like you don't need me anymore," Isaac pouts.

I hug him. "I need you most of all. We're not doing anything here except waiting. You need to go back to work and wait there."

"Okay, but you'll call me with every update, right?"

"Of course I will. Thanks for the clean clothes. Will you bring me another change of clothes and my toothbrush? My teeth feel fuzzy."

"Ick. Too much information. Kiss kiss."

I hug him again, but he avoids my funky breath.

Shelby kisses me on the cheek. "We'll be back later this afternoon. Please call if you need anything. Promise?" She gives me another squeeze and leaves.

The Reverend and Mrs. Edwards exit Stella's room with tears in their eyes. Theo jumps up to meet them halfway. His arm brushes against mine. Mrs. Edwards hugs Theo before she focuses on me. We haven't had a moment together since this whole nightmare started, so I don't know where

I stand with her. This could be her chance to slap me or chew me out for what I've done to her son.

Instead, she pulls me into a hug. "I love my little Stella. She's an exact duplicate of this one when he was that age." She jerks her thumb toward Theo. "How did you know my name?"

I move away and wipe my eyes. Theo shrugs.

"Well, when I met Theo, he had broken his insulin pump, and he mentioned that Stella was going to be mad at him. It was the only connection I had to him." I stare at him. "He told me his name was Romeo."

Mrs. Edwards pokes him in the ribs.

He rolls his eyes. "Hey, to be fair, she told me her name was Juliet."

His mother howls with laughter. She touches my cheek before leading me away from Theo. "He loves you," she whispers in my ear. "He's hurt right now. Give him time."

I nod, and she kisses me again.

Reverend Edwards brings Theo and me close. He puts my hand in Theo's. It's as if I'm holding a cold, dead fish. What once felt like energy at the slightest touch has transformed into lifeless flesh. His sad eyes focus on his shoes.

The Reverend puts one hand on top of my head and his other hand on top of Theo's. He bows his head and says a silent prayer. I feel a peace overcome me that I cannot explain. It's as though I know Stella is going to be okay. Or if not, I know I will be able to handle whatever happens. He kisses me on the cheek and hugs Theo.

"Call me if there is any change. I'll be back tonight."

"Thanks, Dad," Theo says.

And with that, all his family and all my friends leave the hospital. Theo and I stare at each other. It's easy to avoid one another when there's a crowd, when other people initiate conversations and try to keep us occupied and keep us from having to spend any time together. But now, with everyone gone, he cannot avoid me.

"When's the last time you ate?" I ask.

He shrugs. "I don't remember. I'm not hungry." He starts to leave.

"When's the last time you checked your sugar?"

He glances at me over his shoulder. "I don't need another mother. Leave me alone."

He exits the waiting room. I follow him. Perhaps he doesn't need me, but I need him. He makes his way out of the building into the open courtyard. He sits in the sun on a park bench and rests his head against the wall. His eyes are mostly closed, a posture that clearly signals, "do not disturb."

In the nearest restroom, I change out of my three-day-old grungy clothes into clean ones. I'm still grubby, but at least with clean clothes and some deodorant, I won't offend as many people. As I fold up my dirty jeans, the slip of paper from the Hangman game falls out of the pocket. I had almost forgotten about that. It's not the most important issue right now with everything else happening, so I pick it up and shove it in the pocket of my clean pants. I roll up the dirty clothes, cram them into my bag, and head out the door to see if Theo is still outside. He hasn't moved. He appears either dead or asleep. If he feels anything like I do, he cannot sleep and wishes he were dead.

I stride up to him. My footsteps scraping across the bricks announce my arrival. He peels one eye open.

"Can we talk? This is the first moment we've had alone, and I need to explain—"

"Nope."

"Theo, please. Let's talk."

"I said no."

I sit next to him at the picnic table. "Please let me say this."

He abruptly stands, startling me. He grabs my arm and ushers me to a more secluded place in the courtyard. He peers around to see how much of an audience we have before speaking. "Me first. How could you?"

"Theo, I—"

"How could you keep something like this from me? When were you going to tell me? When she got married? Never?" His voice cracks, and his hands tremble. He paces around in a circle. "I need food." He marches toward a door to the hospital. "I bet you can't even guarantee she's mine."

Oh, he did not *say that.* I rush toward him and push him onto the nearest park bench. I don't care how many people overhear our conversation.

"Now you shut up. I know without a doubt that she's yours. And you do too, you, you..." I can't think of anything bad enough to call him. Minding my every word around a child has deleted the curse words from my vocabulary faster than the southern sun could have zapped my energy. "You doodie head."

He cocks his head to the side. "What?"

"You're a jerk." I storm away.

"Oh, I'm the jerk. I'm not the one who kept a child a secret for almost *seven years.*"

I get back in his face. "We graduated. I didn't know I was pregnant until late that summer. What was I supposed to do, Romeo?" I put my hands on my hips. "And for the record, I thought I did tell you, but you didn't waste any time before hooking up with someone else, did you? It sounds to me like you used me for a good time."

His mouth drops open. "Oh, so that was your justification? That you *thought* I was a player? I had to be. Why else would I be attracted to you? Do you have no confidence in yourself?"

He crosses his arms. His eyes are narrowed to angry slits. I've never seen this side of him. I think he could tear my head off if he had the energy. I throw the Hangman paper at him. He unfolds it and groans.

"So, I was only another game, right?" I ask.

He lets out a guffaw. "Games are supposed to be fun."

I reel back. Even he seems shocked at his choice of words. All this time, I thought he loved me. He said he loved me, but now he's telling me that his time with me was nothing more than a chore, like doing the dishes or cleaning out the gutters. And the saddest part is that I believed every word he said—everything from "do you believe in love at first sight" to the "love is patient, love is kind" stuff.

I wait for a physician to pass us and get out of earshot. "How many points would you have scored if we had slept together this week?"

"We'll never know." He stares off and swallows hard. "It was letters, not points, by the way."

"Well, excuse me."

"It doesn't 'excuse' you from not telling me."

I turn to leave. Under my breath, I mumble, "You should have stayed at Johns Hopkins."

He grabs my arm. "What did you say?"

I shake him off. "Nothing. Never mind."

I'm almost to the door that leads back into the hospital, when he grabs me by the arm.

He swings me around. "No, no, no. I never told you I was at Johns Hopkins. How did you know?"

I scan the ground.

He squeezes my shoulders. "Answer me, dammit."

"Okay. I knew where you were. I was about six months pregnant. Mallory emailed me a picture. She said you were *the one*. She was going to marry a doctor. I didn't know what to do."

He backpedals. "You bitch. You didn't want me to know anything about my own kid."

"It wasn't like that. Let me finish."

"You didn't tell me on purpose." He laughs a terrible, evil chortle. "And you told my sister, for Christ's sake."

I close my eyes, count to ten, and take a calming breath. "It's not like that."

He sneers at me. "Did you tell Tommy?"

I stare at him and swallow.

"Jesus. You told Tommy? You had the guts to tell Tommy but not me."

"Let me explain."

"Whatever."

"I'm not trying to justify anything. I'm telling you the truth. Do you think I wanted to go through having a child by myself? I had nobody! I had no one to help me through nighttime feedings, and fevers, and ear infections. And I had no one there to share the big moments with—when she smiled the first time, or rolled over, or took her first step, or when I had to leave her on her first day of school."

I can't believe I have the courage to say these things. He stares off, taking it.

I can't stop the tears. "I had nobody. So don't tell me anything about not having confidence, because I didn't have time to care about that."

He sits down on the bench and buries his face in his hands. Deep, guttural sobs bubble up from his chest.

"And you know what else? You can think I'm selfish, evil, and that I deserve a lonely, shallow, pathetic life. I think those things too, and much worse, but you have no idea what I've been through the last seven years. So hate me if you want."

From my wallet, I remove the picture of Stella on her first day of school and drop it in his lap. "But don't take it out on her. She deserves to have you in her life. So for her sake, do the right thing, at least until she's well. After that, you can go back to hating me."

"Please leave." His voice is so hoarse, I can barely understand his words.

When I get to the door of the hospital, I look back at him sitting on the park bench. His head hangs low as he stares at her picture, overcome with sorrow. I wipe my face and rush back into the ICU waiting room.

Chapter Thirty-Four
Theo

THE NURSE WIPES MY ARM with an alcohol pad and sticks the needle in my vein for the third donation in less than a week. I feel no pain. She hands me the stress ball to squeeze so the blood will continue to flow from my arm into the collection bag. Every time I do this, I am one step closer to passing out.

Within five minutes, sweat already trickles down my face and into my ear.

She places her hand on my forehead. "How are you feeling?"

I shiver. "C-c-c-cold."

"I need another blanket over here and an Accu-Chek Machine, please."

Staff hustle around me, while my eyes go in and out of focus. A wave of nausea comes over me. I shake my head and attempt to sit up. The room spins.

"Whoa. Lie back, sir."

My teeth chatter. "Stella. Gotta... Stella."

The nurse wraps a blanket around me and places a heated towel over my head. I can't stop my entire body from shivering.

A physician stands over me. "I'm Dr. Crutchfield. We're going to admit you to the hospital for observation."

"No. C-c-c-can't."

"Your body can't handle this anymore. If we don't intervene, you might go into organ failure."

Rigors keep me from lying still. "Don't care."

"I do. You're the patient now."

He raises the bedrails and instructs patient transport to move me to the fifth floor.

"Darla."

"We'll let her know where you'll be."

"No. Don't. She's got t-t-too much going on."

They wheel me into the elevator. The nurse pricks my finger, while another checks my blood pressure.

"BP is eighty over forty. Glucose is forty-two."

The doctor and I make eye contact. "Give him Glucagon, one milligram IV."

"Yes, sir."

"No." I push the nearest person back. "Leave me alone."

"You know your low blood sugar keeps you from thinking clearly. Lie still."

They wheel my bed into a room, and I take another swing, this time hitting the doctor in the side.

"Theo, we want to help you. Your brother's here."

Tommy stands in the doorway.

I don't care if he's concerned. He needs to go. "Get out of here."

He steps closer to my bed. "Hey now, let them take care of you."

I rip the blood pressure cuff off my arm. "There's nothing wrong with me. Get the hell out of my way."

Tommy's strong arms slam me back down on the bed, pinning me in place. "Yep, your sugar's too low. It's the only time you're an asshole."

I struggle beneath his grip without any success. "Wish I could say the same for you, you lousy piece of—"

"Now, now. I'll let you get in a few jabs later, but right now..." He rams his forearm across my chest and takes my chin in his other hand, forcing me to eyeball him. "Theo." He lowers his voice. "You're sick, brother. Let them take care of you."

A tear trickles down my face. "Stella."

"She's in good hands. You get better, because you'll do nobody any good dead."

A pin pricks my arm, and a warm solution fills my vein.

"Breathe."

"Can't. You're on my chest."

He chuckles and releases his grip on me. He runs his hands through his hair.

"Mom."

"She's on the way."

I breathe a sigh of relief. No matter how old I am, I'll always feel better if my mother is with me when I'm sick.

"When's the last time you had some food?"

I close my eyes. The thought of food makes my stomach flip over. "I don't know, and please don't use the F word. I might puke all over you."

The nurse wraps the blood pressure cuff on my arm again and pumps it up. She releases the air and takes the stethoscope out of her ears. "Pressure is one hundred over sixty. Pulse is ninety."

"Is that good or bad?" Tommy asks me.

"Better."

"Glucose is sixty."

Tommy sighs. "I know that's better." He collapses into a chair next to my bed. "That hasn't happened in years. I hate it when that happens."

My heart isn't racing anymore, and it's becoming easier to breathe. I'm actually able to form sentences again. Thank God Glucagon kicks in within minutes.

"I don't know what your problem is. This is fun... not."

He pops open a bottle of orange juice and takes a swig. "At least you're getting your sense of humor back."

I hold out my hand. "Give me that."

He holds the orange juice just out of reach. I lean over to get it, and he moves it out of my reach. "Tommy, give it. I'm tethered to the IV pole. Come on."

"Say please."

"Tommy, give him the OJ," Mom says, standing in the doorway.

He has to juggle the bottle to keep from dropping it. "Oh, hi, Mom." He hands me the bottle.

She leans down and kisses my forehead. "Cold and clammy."

I close my eyes and finish the rhyme she taught me when I was little. "Need some candy. Hot and dry—"

"Sugar too high," Tommy says. "And my work here is done. Now, I have to be the hero and donate some blood for your sorry ass." He pops me on the leg and winks at me.

Mom gives him the evil eye.

He holds his hands out in front of him. "I'm kidding." He scoots out of the room before Mom pushes him out.

Mom swipes my hair out of my eyes and wags her finger at me. "No more blood donations."

"But—"

"But nothing. Tommy and your dad will donate if she needs it. Your body can't handle it anymore. And I won't let you."

I can't meet her gaze. She's right, but it makes me feel helpless. "It's the only thing I can do."

She cups my cheeks in her hands. "I'll never forget when you were first diagnosed. You were so sick, and we didn't know what was going on. I thought you were going to die." She swallows hard. "When the doctors figured it out, I was ready to donate my pancreas so you would be all right."

My mother is a saint. I hit the jackpot when it came to getting the best mother in the world. I know she would do anything for me and for the rest of us. Maybe that's what being a mother is.

"Don't tell Darla."

She leans back and sits beside me on the bed. She holds my cold, clammy hand. "She'd want to know. I try to stay out of all you kids' love lives, but Darla is a keeper. I know you two have some things to work out, but I can tell by the way you watch her every move... You never looked at Mallory that way. You need each other right now, and she needs to know what's going on with you."

"She's got enough to worry about." *And I'm still pissed at her.* The nerve of her getting all in my face about that stupid game when she admitted she knew I was at Johns Hopkins all this time. She could have told me about Stella at any point, but she chose not to.

"Son, she can handle it, and you're going to be here at least overnight. Maybe she can stay up here with you tonight."

"That's not a good idea. Besides, she won't go more than two feet from that waiting room until Stella is better."

Mom pulls my blanket up to my neck. "You're probably right about that. Like I said, she's a keeper." She gives me a kiss on the cheek and makes herself comfortable in the chair next to my bed.

A nurse comes in and hands me a hospital gown to change into. I guess I'm not going anywhere tonight. Careful not to rip the IV out of my arm, the nurse helps me out of my T-shirt. I unzip my jeans and wriggle out of them. The Hangman game and Stella's picture slide out of the pocket and land on the floor. The nurse hands them to me. I can't help but beam at the cute face staring back at me. Both of us have to get better so we can get to know each other.

I place the picture on the bedside table and unfold the Hangman game. I stare at the last word of the puzzle, blinking to focus my eyes on the letters. I'm pretty sure the puzzle is supposed to read, "you have a daughter," but whoever sent this to me must suck at spelling because the letters I've been awarded don't come close to spelling the word "daughter." The word has the right amount of letters, and it starts with the letter d, but the other letters don't spell out anything. I rack my brain, trying to figure out who sent this to me now that I know Darla didn't. Whoever it was meant well. He or she wanted to make sure I didn't miss another opportunity with Darla, and that someone knew the best way to get me motivated was a good old-fashioned game. And it worked.

My money is on Tommy. He had to be working with someone who had the inside scoop on Darla's schedule, but this smells like something he would do, especially if he knew about Stella. That doesn't put him back on my friend list, but maybe it shows he might have felt a tad bit guilty for knowing something so important and not telling me.

Not that it matters anymore. Darla kept Stella from me all these years, and now she has the nerve to be mad at me over a stupid game, one I thought she was sending me in the first place. We can have this pissing match as much as we want, but it doesn't change the fact that Stella may die.

I'll do everything in my power to keep that from happening.

Chapter Thirty-Five

Darla

I WATCH AS STELLA IS WHEELED away from me again for her third surgery to clean out any visible signs of infection in the wound. As I stand in her empty ICU room, I notice a drawing taped to the wall by her bed. It's a picture of a girl with a dog, and the caption reads, "git wel soon, Camille." I clutch my chest. Her school buddy drew a picture for her. It's such a sweet gesture from one child to another. What I wouldn't give for one more crayon drawing on the living room wall or another silly picture plastered to my already overloaded refrigerator door.

Dr. Michaels tells us that another surgery is necessary to save her life. I know there is going to be a time in which he will tell me he had to amputate her leg or that she didn't make it. She's too young to have to deal with something so scary and tragic. She's completely unconscious, not moving at all, and it terrifies me.

I have settled into the mundane routine of sitting in the waiting room, waiting for eight in the morning, two in the afternoon, and eight in the evening. These are the times when I can put my eyes on her and convince myself she has made it through another six hours.

At night, it's like a big deathly quiet sleepover for all the families of ICU patients. Sleeping bags litter the floor, and couches and chairs become makeshift beds. One by one, we take turns at the bathroom sink, taking sponge baths. We don't talk, and we don't make eye contact, because if we do, one of us will break, and then all of us will break. None of us can afford to crumble. We rotate charging our cell phones in the only two outlets in the entire room. I will definitely write a strongly worded letter to the head of ICU about how to make it easier on families who have to live here. A fricking coffeepot and a few more outlets wouldn't hurt anything.

No matter how many blankets I use to pad the worn-out cushions, the scratchy couches aren't made any softer. My second-hand sofa at home is in ten times better shape. The snack machine still has a bag of chips hanging from the third row, which prevents any other salty treat from dropping. I don't know how many people have tried to free that stupid bag that taunts us all. I guess our lives are like that one-and-a-half-ounce bag of trans fat. We're all hanging in midair, hoping someone will be strong enough to help us.

Theo and I never speak. When he's around, he huddles in a corner of the room, as far away from me as humanly possible. His dark, vacant eyes tell me everything I need to know. He hates me, and there's nothing I can do about it. I've hurt him more than one man can handle. That is, when he's around.

Last night, he didn't show up at all. He didn't scoot in to the visitation at the last minute, nor did he sleep in the waiting room. He was completely AWOL. As mad as I am about the game, it pales in comparison to how angry I am that he seems to have forgotten about our daughter. There are no words to describe the frustration I feel toward him right now.

During the days, we have a steady stream of friends and family that try to keep us company, try to keep us fed, and try to keep our hopes up. Diane calls for updates on cue after every visitation time. Shelby usually stops by after work.

Reverend and Mrs. Edwards come by in the middle of the day. They are both so kind to me even though they don't have to be. It seems as though every member of their church filters in and out, offering food, a shoulder to cry on, and prayers—lots of prayers. They don't even know me, but they treat me like family, as if we've been connected for years instead of days. I wish they were my family. I've never known people who have so much compassion for others, for someone they've never met. I devastated a member of their church family, and they still treat me with love and kindness.

Tommy stays the night when Theo doesn't, which is so sweet of him. He's cordial, but I can tell he's messed up about all of this. Jennifer and her little sister Heather are in and out. Jennifer makes me get out into the sunshine even if it's just for a "snig," as she would say. Many times, she has offered to talk to Theo again for me, but it's no use. I love her for wanting to, but she doesn't need to be the peacemaker.

I've learned that Heather is the spitfire of the family. She says exactly what's on her mind and makes no apologies. She's absolutely adorable, and I can see so much of Stella in her, from her spunky attitude to her long dark-blond hair. Oh boy, am I in for a world of trouble when my daughter gets older. *Please God, let her get older.* Bring on the teenage years. And I'll find a way to get her that pony she keeps asking for. Whatever she wants, I'll figure out how to get it for her.

Isaac stops by in the mornings before work. This morning, I sit by him while Stella's in surgery. He's all fidgety, even more so than usual. He taps his foot and drums his fingers on the end table until I cover his hand with mine.

"You're more nervous than I am. What's up?"

"Oh, nothing. When's Shelby stopping by?"

"I think she said she would stop by after work like usual. You'll see her before I will. Why don't you ask her yourself?"

He shrugs. "I guess I could."

"Calm down. I need peaceful vibes around me."

He crosses his legs in the chair and does a deep breathing yoga pose. "Ah. All better."

"Why don't we go down the hallway before you drive everyone crazy? But not too far in case…"

"Sure, that'd be good. Where's Theo?" he asks as we head out the door.

I shrug. "He's gone a lot. I guess he's not cut out for this part of parenting. It's easy when things go smoothly. Nothing about this is easy."

He rubs my shoulders.

I moan. "Thanks, buddy."

"Do you two talk?"

"Hardly at all. His usual sleeping hangout is over in the far corner. He comes in, gets a blanket, and lies down. The only time we interact is during visiting times, and he's missed a few of those this week, which really pisses me off. When he does show up, he puts on a brave face for Stella, but when we leave her room, he goes his way, and I go mine."

Isaac hugs me. "Have you tried to talk to him again?"

"He's made it clear he doesn't want me near him."

He frowns. "I thought he'd come around."

"Me too, but he hates me. Right now, I am dog-tired. Speaking of dogs, how is Yeti?"

"That fleabag hates me," Isaac says.

I giggle. "It's your own fault. You've stepped on him a thousand times."

"Well, you shouldn't feed the hand that bites you, or something like that."

If there is a way for Isaac to mutilate the English language, he will. "What?"

"Fortunately, Yeti looooves my new boyfriend."

"New boyfriend? When did this happen?"

He gives me a wry smile. "I don't tell you everything. Anyway, it's like some furry bromance they're having. 'Isn't Yeti a sweetie pie? I love my whittle Yeti. Yes, I do, yes I do!'"

"Jealous much?"

"It's disgusting. That dog has practically licked the hide off his face. He needs to learn how to hold his licker."

I grin. Isaac is good comedic relief in an otherwise sober and dreadful environment. The boring hallway with the standard-issue hospital artwork even seems less drab with him in it.

"Don't be surprised if instead of having Yeti waiting for you when you get home, it's me."

I pat him on the back. "Poor baby. But you don't know how much I appreciate everything you're doing for me and Stella. You're taking care of everything, from watering my plants—"

"Oops," he says.

I poke him in the ribs. "Regardless of the plants, you're letting me focus on Stella. And the cookies are delicious. I hope you don't mind me sharing with some of the other families stuck here in ICU purgatory."

"Not at all. Next time, I'll bring more." He stops to stretch. "Several fitness members have asked how you and Theo are doing. It appears that you two have lots of friends."

I nod. "There's a steady stream of dudes in scrubs that stay and chat for a few minutes even if he's not around. I'm guessing one of them is covering for Theo, not that I would know."

"Anybody else show up?"

I laugh. "What is up with you?"

He picks up his pace. "Nothing."

I grab his arm. "You know something. Tell me."

He glances at his watch. "Oh, it's getting late. Shelby's going to have my ass if I'm late again." He pecks me on the cheek. "Toodles. I'll stop by later." He backpedals away from me in a rush, but not before he blows me a kiss. He bumps into Theo and gives him a hug.

It's terrible that I feel the tiniest bit jealous. Isaac is my friend. I don't have many people in my corner, and I'm very protective of Isaac. He and Theo share a moment, and before Isaac leaves, he points to a person coming off the elevator.

And out of the blue, Mallory strolls in. I don't know whom she is here to comfort or if she's here to gloat. No matter what the reason, she's here now. Theo and I both stare at her, not knowing what to think of her appearance. She waves at Theo but continues toward his family. She gives Mrs. Edwards a kiss on the cheek. It's not a kiss-kiss that she would give her friends; it's a sweet, respectful kiss.

Mrs. Edwards hugs her and whispers in her ear. Mallory shrugs and gives her another kiss on the cheek. The reaction from Theo's mother is a far cry from Jennifer's stiff spine and thin-lipped smile. Mallory quickly moves past Jennifer and on to Theo. They share a private conversation. She does most of the talking, and I'm not sure how I feel about that. My argument with Theo may have sent him scampering right back into her arms. He nods as he focuses on his sneakers. She kisses him on the cheek and gives him a hug before making her way over to me. I can't even say hello before she's wrapping her arms around me.

"Oh, Darla, I'm so sorry."

"Thanks."

We move to the corner of the room to have a little bit of privacy. She sits next to me and holds my hand. "What can I do?"

"What?"

"I saw Isaac at the fitness center, and he thought it would be a good idea for me to stop by. I hope that's okay."

"Hmm."

"I'll sit with you. I'll bring you food. Whatever you need."

"I'm confused. Isaac?" I ask, keeping my eyes trained on Theo.

He hangs his head low, but from time to time, he surveys us through the hair that has fallen over his eyes.

"Yeah, he cares so much for you and your little girl. I'm not here to cause problems. I'm here because at one point, we were friends." She lets out a nervous laugh. "After Isaac gave me a serious tongue-lashing about what I did, he convinced me that I needed to show you my support. And he was right."

My sleep-deprived, food-restricted body leans into hers, and she cradles me, letting me weep. This is what I need. Right now, even with the torture of my baby being so sick, I feel as if a weight has been lifted off my shoulders. At least one person doesn't hate me. It's not the person I would have preferred, but I'll take it at the moment.

"Theo has always been in love with you," she says.

"Past tense. He hates me. Can you blame him?"

She rubs my shoulder. "Give him time."

I sit up in my chair and wipe my eyes with the back of my hand. I stare into her pretty blue eyes. "What if she doesn't make it?"

"If there is one thing I've learned by being around the Edwards bunch these last few years, it's that they have tremendous faith. Draw strength from it. It will help you." She motions with her head toward Theo. "And he's a good guy. You deserve him."

Wow. I never thought those words would come from her. She kisses my cheek and promises she'll be back later today. At the door, she waves good-bye to me. I glance over at Theo, who witnessed everything. He has a "what the heck" expression on his face.

My thoughts exactly.

———— ✦ ————

Stella makes it through surgery with both legs intact. Dr. Michaels says there was more necrotic tissue that needed to be removed, but he thinks the combination of steroids and antibiotics have halted the spread of infection. Hopefully, her cultures from today will be negative for any more growth.

Working in a hospital, I know how expensive even one day can be. Even with my health insurance, I cannot imagine how much this will cost me. The price of being airlifted to the hospital will probably make me hyperventilate. But I'll take out a second or third mortgage on my house if it means getting Stella the care she needs.

Theo's parents are here again. His mother has to be one of the kindest people on Earth. When she visits, she insists we all sit together. Even if Theo is not around, she holds me as though I'm one of her flock. She lets me rest my head on her shoulder and cry my eyes out. Once, during one of my crying jags, Theo bolted out the door, unable to handle it all.

Mrs. Edwards never questions me, never judges me, and always comforts me. I hope Theo realizes how fortunate he is to have two healthy, living parents that adore him. By the way that he treats them, I'm sure he does.

Today, Mrs. Edwards sits between Theo and me. She wraps one arm around me and the other around him. She plays with our hair. It reminds me of what my mom used to do when I was little. She faintly sings gospel songs, barely above a whisper. I rest my head on her shoulder and am about to close my eyes when Shelby enters the waiting room.

"Hey, any news?" she asks, yanking me up to stand.

"Nothing new."

She escorts me away from the Edwards family so we can chat in private. She glances over at Theo. "So is Mr. Jerk Face still moping around?"

"Wow, he's gone from Dr. Hotness to Mr. Jerk Face."

Shelby giggles. "My, the mighty have fallen." Her face gets solemn again. She wipes the hair from my face. "I'm really disappointed in him. I thought he'd snap out of it by now."

I shrug. "Some things aren't meant to be."

She pouts. "But you still love him, don't you?"

My eyes wander around to find Theo. He quickly shifts his eyes toward me as he stumbles out of the room again and heads straight into the men's room.

"What do you think?"

Chapter Thirty-Six

Theo

FINALLY, I HAVE THE PLACE to myself. The last family left me alone on the second pew—alone with my thoughts and fears. The ornate stained-glass windows depict the life of Christ, making me feel welcome. The large cross above the altar beckons me to kneel and cast my burdens on my God. The candles flicker softly in the dimly lit chapel. If I listen carefully, maybe God will tell me in simple words what I'm supposed to do. So far, the noise in my head occludes any divine messages.

My baby is so sick, and I am unable to do anything about it. It goes against my code as a physician to give up. Even more so, it goes against my code as a father, even though this is all new to me. I don't have a clue what to do. I feel as though I'm failing her; I'm failing everyone.

A shadow falls across my shoulder. Isaac tiptoes up the aisle. He lights a candle, kneels at the altar railing, and folds his hands in a silent prayer. When he stands, our eyes meet. He sits down beside me. We sit in silence for what seems like an eternity. I guess we both are hoping for some divine intervention.

I feel an arm go around my shoulder. I cannot stop myself from laying my head on his shoulder. The tears begin, and I am having trouble breathing. Isaac holds me.

"I can't lose my girl."

"You won't," he says.

I wipe my face and sit back up. He pats my shoulder with one hand and wipes the tears off his face with the other.

"I never thought I'd have a daughter. I dreamed about it but never thought it would happen. And now—"

"I know. And you're going to have lots of years with her."

My shoulders slump. "I don't know, man. I always thought I had unwavering faith, but I don't know anymore." I lean over to rest my forehead on the back of the pew in front of me.

He pats my back. "You have to be strong."

"She has to make it, or I don't think I will."

He sits up taller. "Listen to me." Candlelight flickers on his dark, tear-stained face. "I know you and Darla aren't in a good place right now. But if things go south—"

I snap my head toward him.

He puts his hands up in defense. "I'm not saying I think they will, but if they do, you have to be strong for Darla." His voice cracks. I can see the pain he's been holding in during this terrible time. He's devastated too. He loves Stella, and I'm so thankful she's had him in her life.

He clears his throat before continuing. "She's a mommy. Please be strong for her. I'm begging you. She can't be left hanging. Not right now."

I bury my face in my hands. He sniffles. I know what he's saying is what needs to be said, but it hurts so much. I don't know if I have anything left to comfort anyone else.

He stands to leave. "Your faith is still there. You're trying too hard." He takes out a tissue and dabs at his eyes.

"Thank you," I whisper.

"Peace, brother."

Isaac leaves, and I'm all alone again in this beautiful chapel. *Thank you, Lord. I needed that.*

———— ◦◦◦ ————

I drag myself back to the dark, quiet waiting room. Most of the families have already settled in for the night. The ones that are still awake speak in hushed tones so as not to disrupt the ones that are faking sleep. I tiptoe over to the cabinet, take out a blanket and pillow, and head back to my designated corner. It's so dark that I can't see Darla, but I know she's in her usual spot on the loveseat across the room.

Several people exit the bathroom, causing a blinding sliver of light to filter through the drab environment. Darla flips over and shades her eyes with her pillow. I should go to her. She's not asleep. But I'd better not. If

I go over there, I would probably screw up again. Maybe I'll try to talk to her tomorrow after I've had some sleep. I unfold the blanket, place it on the floor, and prop the pillow up against the wall. My bones are so rigid from sleeping in this position. I feel like an old man with my stiff, creaky back and knees. I groan as I try to find a comfortable position on the floor. I wedge myself into the corner so I won't fall. I'm so weak that I don't think I could keep myself from sliding over into a heap on the floor if I start heading in that direction. I'm so damn tired.

The last time I had the nerve to check out my reflection in the mirror, I couldn't believe that was me staring back. Dark circles reside under my puffy eyes, and my skin is a sickly, sallow color. My physical appearance shows exactly how I feel on the inside: empty, dead, and lost.

I check my phone for any text messages. A few coworkers have left messages asking about Stella and letting me know that they are thinking of me. Before I shut down my phone for the night, my thumb hovers over the photo album app. I finally have the nerve to check out the last few photos I added. They are of the birthday celebration. I swipe through them, landing on the last photo we took at the ice cream parlor. We were so happy that day. Life fell apart so quickly not long after.

I close my eyes and pretend I'm in my apartment, hoping I can convince myself that I'm in a soft comfy bed down the hall from my healthy daughter and that this is all a terrible nightmare. So far, I haven't been able to convince myself.

Out of the still darkness, one sniffle after another breaks the silence. That's a pretty typical sound at night. Nighttime is when at least one mother breaks down. She can be strong during the day when she puts on her brave face, but at night, the truth comes out. Fortunately, the sobs are usually followed by someone trying to comfort her. This quite often makes the sadness worse before it makes it better.

Tonight, there aren't any encouraging words, only an occasional sniffle. In the dead quiet, someone hiccups. *Sniffle, sniffle, hiccup, hiccup.* Jesus. It's Darla crying, and she has no one to tell her it's all going to be okay.

She flops her blanket off. In the shadows, her silhouette sits up, and her hands rake through her hair. She stands and shuffles toward the bathroom. When the sliver of light breaks through the waiting room, I see Darla slip inside.

Shit. I know I should be the one to comfort her, but I don't think I can. At this point, I'll probably say the wrong thing and make her feel worse than she already does.

Crap. I get my selfish butt off the floor, one sore knee at a time, and creep over to the bathroom. I slip inside, trying to keep the light from disturbing those attempting to sleep. I stand with my back to the door, not sure what to do now that I'm here. I peek under the stall doors and see her body curled up in the back stall. More hiccups. More sobs. Her breath catches in her throat. My breath catches in mine. She needs someone to hold her. She needs me to hold her, but my stupid feet won't move. This should be automatic. I should rush over to her and tell her I'm here for her. I can support her, and she can support me. That's how it works.

I want to. I really do. But I can't. It's as if my feet are glued to the floor. As much as Darla is hurting, I'm hurting too. I don't know if I have it in me to fake a comforting hug.

The door behind me bumps me out of the way. A lady gasps. I put my finger to my mouth as I slip out the door. This lady will help her. They can help each other. I don't know if it's because of pride or pain, but I can't do it. I don't know if I will ever be able to do it. I don't care. I don't. I really don't. God, I feel like a pathetic loser.

Chapter Thirty-Seven
Darla

ANOTHER AGONIZINGLY LONG DAY. STELLA made it through another surgery and is now resting in her room. I'm so sick of the doctor saying he doesn't know when she'll start responding to the treatment. His stock "only time will tell" answer pisses me off. Her leg doesn't appear as cherry-red today, in my opinion, but I try not to focus on anything except her pretty little face. I'm so proud of how strong her little body has been, but even the strongest have limits to what they can handle. She's so much like her daddy—so mild-mannered on the outside, but tough as nails on the inside.

I can't imagine how empty my life would be without my sweet Stella. I feel so empty thinking about the possibility of losing her. She's my life. I don't remember even living before she was born. She gave my life purpose.

Theo thumbs through Stella's chart, taking in every note, every lab, every medication dosage. He scribbles a dose calculation on a napkin to double-check what has been prescribed. "Her urine creatinine is a little elevated today."

The nurse practitioner should be used to his micromanagement of her care by now, but I would be ready to smack him if I were the nurse on duty.

She focuses on the lab results. "I'll make sure the doctor knows. It's such a slight change, he probably won't think it's significant."

"It's significant to me," Theo says. "In addition to her bacterial infection, she has a family history of type one diabetes, so I would appreciate it if you would pass this... *insignificant* finding on to the doctor."

She clears her throat. "I'll let him know."

"Thank you," I say, trying to intervene before Theo bites her head off again.

Theo hands her the chart back and acts as though I'm not even in the room. The bell chimes over the intercom, signaling visitation time is over.

I give my unconscious Stella one last kiss. "Sleep well, baby girl. I'll be back later."

Theo kisses her cheek and follows me out the door and down the hallway toward the waiting room. Six more hours of "wait and see." Theo passes all the sofas and continues down the hallway toward the hospital exit. We can't keep doing this. It has to end now.

"Theo, wait up."

He stops but doesn't turn to face me. He stares at the ceiling tiles as if they will give him the patience to deal with me.

"I need to talk to you."

"Not now. Yes, I've checked my sugar, and no, I haven't had anything to eat, so please leave me alone." He storms away.

"Theo, go home," I call after him.

That shocks him out of his funk. He changes direction so fast, I almost run into him. Pain, sadness, and fatigue are spread all over his face, making him seem ten years older. He watches several staff members pass before he says anything.

"Why? Don't like sharing her?"

Ouch. I'm trying to do the right thing now. I stand in front of him so I don't have to yell at the top of my lungs. Although, that might make me feel better.

"It's obvious you begrudge being here, so leave. I'm tired of tiptoeing around you. I've said I'm sorry until I'm blue in the face. I'm done. Start acting like an adult."

He stuffs his hands into his jeans pockets and bites his quivering lip.

"Go home, get some sleep, and for God's sake, eat something. You're Mr. Asshole when you haven't eaten."

He sneers at me. "At least I have an excuse." He walks backward. "I'm outta here. You happy?" He begins to leave but not before he gives me one more stare down. He shakes his head and continues his exit. If he takes my bitchy advice, he might come back rested and with a brain full of glucose. I know I should take my own advice, but it doesn't work that way for moms.

His image grows smaller with every footstep. I know I should run after him, tell him I'm sorry and that I didn't mean to be so cruel. My damn feet must be stuck in the tile floor, because I can't even move out of the way for the staff members entering and exiting the building.

Darla, you sealed your fate and possibly Stella's too.

Right when I get situated again in the waiting room, Theo's sisters and brother enter. Jennifer scans the area and puts her hands on her hips. Tommy shrugs. The youngest, Heather, sees me. She breaks from the Edwards pack, comes to my couch, and sits beside me.

"We haven't had a chance to talk."

If I didn't know better, I would think I was shaking a twenty-year-old Stella's hand. She has the same messy blond hair, the same green eyes, and the same cute dimple when she tries not to grin.

"You're staring at me."

I blink. "I'm sorry. It's just that…"

"I know. My niece looks exactly like me. I've been told that about a thousand times in the last few weeks." She giggles. "I can't get over the fact that I have a niece."

"I'm so sorry how this all came down."

She waves off my comment. "Don't worry about it. I was beginning to think my brother never made mistakes." She sucks in a breath. "I didn't mean it like that."

I nudge her with my shoulder. "It's fine."

"What I mean is that Theo follows the rules, even with games."

She makes me chuckle. "I don't know about that."

Heather laughs, and that familiar dimple pops out. "At least he followed his heart one time."

I swallow, and my eyes fill with tears. "You're a good person."

She squeezes my hand. "So is he."

Jennifer and Tommy join us. Now, it's one big Edwards reunion, but it reminds me of lyrics from a *Sesame Street* song: "One of these things is not like the others."

Jennifer sits on the other side of me. "Where is he?"

I groan. "I sort of lost my temper and made him leave until he got something to eat and changed his attitude."

Tommy perches on the edge of the sofa, forcing Heather to scooch closer to me. Thank goodness she's tiny, or all of us would never fit on this couch.

"'Bout damn time." Tommy clears his throat. "I know you said you didn't want us to get involved, but your way isn't working very well. Would you mind if we tried the Edwards approach?"

My pent-up emotions get the best of me. Tears pour out of my eyes, and I sob into my hands. "Please, do whatever you can. I can't take this rift between us anymore."

Tommy snaps his fingers. "I guess it's settled. Sis and Sis, let's go. We have an intervention to conduct."

Chapter Thirty-Eight
Theo

THE WINDOWS OF MY APARTMENT rattle from the force of me slamming the door behind me. She has some nerve, telling me I need to go away. If I didn't leave, I was going to say something I would live to regret. If I had the energy, I would slam the door three more times for good measure. But all I can manage is to throw my keys across the room. They hit a pile of crap on my dining room table. If I don't pick them up now, I'll never remember what I did with them.

I move some junk mail out of the way that Mom must have put there for me. Underneath the pile are the board games that Darla gave me for my birthday. I must have left them at my parents' house when we rushed out of there to get to the hospital that fateful day, and Mom dropped them off here for me. One at a time, I open the boxes to smell the fresh cardboard smell of a new game waiting to be played. All the plastic game pieces are still in their plastic bags. The Twister mat has that familiar plastic smell and hasn't been overcome with stinky feet yet. When I move the last box, the dry-erase board sits facing up, its unanswered Hangman puzzle staring at me, taunting me. I run my finger through the drawing, smearing it until it's completely illegible. *Don't care.*

The bright light from the floor lamp is too cheerful for me, so I switch it off before I slouch down on my couch. It's more comfortable than I remember. But compared to the hard waiting room floor, anything would feel like a Tempur-Pedic mattress.

I'm too wired to sleep but too tired to eat. Darla should have told me. I'm a reasonable guy. I could have handled the truth. Well, my handling of the truth has been quite crappy now that I think about it. It's exactly the reaction she was afraid I would have, and it's exactly why she didn't know how to tell me. But still, she told everyone else *but* me. That's what hurts the most. I was the least important person to her. I would bet she told the clerk at the grocery store or maybe the dude that changes the oil in her car. It wouldn't surprise me if the librarian and the mailman probably knew from the get-go.

Thinking back over the past few weeks, I realize she did try to tell me about her really big secret. And like the hypocrite I am, I assured her she could tell me when she was ready. I went back on my word about always trusting her and believing in her. And I sucked at the "not keeping a record of wrongdoings" or the "rejoicing in the truth" part of the scripture that I preached to her. I let her down a thousand times worse than she could ever hurt me.

I lie down with my hands across my face. This is actually the first time since I found out about Stella that I've had the chance to contemplate everything that has happened. I'm a father. *I. Am. A. Father.* I have a daughter, and she is so sick, so sick she might die. No, I can't let myself think that right now. I will not let her die. As long as I'm alive, I will fight to keep her alive.

A key rattles in the lock of my apartment. I groan. I should never have given Tommy a key. The door opens. Jennifer, Heather, and Tommy rush in, flipping on the lights, which burn my retinas.

I don't even give them the courtesy of making eye contact. "Get out of here."

Jennifer sits beside me on the couch.

"What are *all* of you doing here? Don't y'all have your own lives?"

Tommy sits in the recliner by the sofa. "Come on, Theo. We don't have to be here. We want to. We're family."

"How did you know I was here?" I ask Jennifer, who's sitting next to my feet.

"We stopped by the hospital. Darla told us she shooed you away."

"Figures."

Tommy moves to the coffee table. I snap a glare his way. He's way too close for comfort.

"I said get out of here."

"Theo, shut up," Jennifer says.

Heather heads for the kitchen and makes herself at home. Little sisters are notorious for the "what's yours is mine" mentality.

"No more," Jennifer says, wearing her big-sister attitude. That's never a good sign. "Tommy's here because he cares about you."

I scowl. "Even you don't believe that. I bet Tommy had a field day when he found out."

My brother grimaces and opens his mouth to speak.

Jennifer motions for Tommy to stay silent before he can say anything. "You don't mean that," she tells me. "Stop being so *sortatious*."

Tommy takes a deep breath. "Theo, she came over here the day you took her ice-skating to tell you, but you hadn't come home from work yet. It took her a while, but she finally worked up the nerve to practice her speech on me."

"You've got to be kidding me."

He flails his arms around. "I didn't know what to do. She promised me she would tell you. In fact, she said she was heading straight over to the hospital to tell you. I thought it was best coming from her."

That was the day Mallory showed up at work, begging me for another chance. No wonder Darla was there. She had finally worked up the courage to tell me, and Mallory ruined the moment.

"If you could have seen the torment she was going through—"

"She kept it from me on purpose." I stare at the ceiling. "First, Mallory lies to me and then this." I clench my fists.

"It's not the same, and you know it," Jennifer says. "And for the record, I didn't know squat until you stopped by my class that day."

Heather enters the living room with beers for everyone but hands me a bottle of water. She tears open a bag of chips, and the three of them grab handfuls as though this is any other family night at the Edwards household.

"What are you so mad about, anyway?" Heather asks me, or at least I think that's what she said. Her mouth is so jammed full of chips, I'm not even sure she was speaking English.

"What do you think?" I reply.

"I mean, are you mad that you have a kid, or are you mad that other people figured it out before you?"

I close my eyes to block out this unwanted intervention.

Heather keeps pushing. "I'm being serious. I don't know the backstory, so help me out. Are you mad that you have a kid?"

I can't believe I'm having this conversation with my little sister. "Of course not."

"Okay, are you mad that Stella's hers?" Heather asks.

"Definitely not," Tommy answers for me.

I stare at them. I couldn't disagree, even if I had the strength.

"Are you mad you didn't know for so long?"

I move to a sitting position. "I don't know. I mean, yes. I mean, maybe. But I've been here a month, and she still didn't tell me on purpose. Who does that?"

"She has no self-esteem, Theo," Jennifer says. "She tried to tell you."

I snort. "She tried to tell *him*." I point at Tommy.

Jennifer lets out a sigh. "Before that. Long before that. I'm talking about when she was pregnant. She sent you emails telling you about the baby."

My head snaps to attention. I'm completely awake now. My eyes feel as if they're about to bug out of their sockets. "I never got any emails. I think I would have remembered that."

Tommy stands and paces the room. He stuffs his hands into his jeans pockets. "Uh, no, you didn't get them... I did."

I jump up, ready to punch my brother in the face, but Jennifer grabs my arm to hold me back.

I clench my fists. "What are you saying?"

"I'm saying she thought she sent them to you. Do you remember a long time ago when I was getting a bunch of crazy emails? A friend of mine was pulling a joke on me, and I thought Darla's emails were part of that, so I deleted them. And I might have told her to leave me alone. I guess she was doing what she thought you wanted."

My mouth drops open.

"I'm so sorry, man. Darla didn't even realize it until the day she was practicing her speech on me. She didn't want you to be mad at me so she made me promise not to say anything to you until she had a chance to clear the air." He reaches out and squeezes my shoulder.

I sink back down onto the couch and cover my face with my arm. Tommy sits on the coffee table in front of me. His words swim around in my brain, nauseating me. Darla really did try to tell me. My heart aches when I think of how abandoned she must have felt when she thought I didn't want her or the baby. I can't think like that right now. "But even so, that doesn't justify not telling me now."

"She's not a mean person," Jennifer says. "Forgiveness, Theo. Forgiveness."

"Well, it's your fault," Heather says to me.

We all stare at her. "And how is that?" I ask.

She chomps down on another chip. "Condoms, dude. Didn't Mom teach you better?"

Tommy laughs under his breath, and I punch him on the shoulder. "Ow!"

"Heather, that's not nice," Jennifer says through a stifled grin.

Heather giggles. "I didn't mean for it to be funny. What were you thinking? That you'd be immune to having babies?"

"Jeez, Heather, I didn't plan for this. And yes, I did think I was immune, thank you very much."

They all know what the doctors have told me. They all know how hard it has been for me to watch other people my age get married and have kids, knowing I was told I would never have that.

I sigh and sit up. "It was not my normal practice, okay? I don't sleep around. She was special."

"*Is* special," they say in unison.

"Whatever. If I had known, I would have done the right thing. I wasn't... I'm not a love 'em and leave 'em kind of person."

Heather smirks at me. "Then explain to me why you're leaving now."

Tommy fist-bumps her.

Damn. The baby of the family is now the wise one. That's a hard pill to swallow.

Jennifer smiles at me. "Love is patient, love is kind. It does not envy, it does not boast, it is not proud."

Tommy continues. "It does not dishonor others, it is not self-seeking, it is not easily angered, it keeps no record of wrongs."

Thanks a lot, Tommy. I'm going to remember this when some girl finally cracks his armor. It's only a matter of time, and I'm going to make him eat his words.

Heather clears her throat. "Love does not delight in evil but rejoices with the truth. It always protects, always trusts, always hopes, always perseveres."

Oh, now my baby sister has to gang up on me too. I thought we were buds.

"Love never fails," they all say together.

Ugh. The problem with having a pastor for a father is that every member of the family can whip out scripture at any time to suit their specific argument. But this passage hits too close to home. They're right, and they know it. *Damn it.*

I rise from the couch and growl at them. "I need to take a shower and get back to the hospital. Let yourselves out."

They have the nerve to do a round of high fives as I head down the hallway toward the bathroom.

"Assholes," I mumble to myself.

Chapter Thirty-Nine
Darla

ONLY THREE HOURS, FORTY-NINE MINUTES, and thirteen seconds until I get to visit my Stella again. I've tried using the "I work here" card and the "I'm a nurse" card over and over to try to get in more often, but the ICU staff never cracks. Even the pouty lip doesn't work. They go strictly by the book. So I only get to see her three times a day like everyone else. At least the doctor hasn't rushed her back to surgery again. I'm going to put that in the win column of the Get Stella Better game. While I wait for the next visitation session, I obsess over every little detail of the waiting room.

There are seventy-two ceiling tiles. I know because I've counted them ten times today. The stain on the wall by the water fountain drives me crazy. I think I'm starting to see the image of Mother Teresa in it. It's either her or one of those cartoon characters that Stella likes to watch on Saturday mornings. And there is not enough toilet paper in the ladies' room to make it through the night.

One family left, and two more moved in here today. Each parent has the same glassy-eyed appearance, as if they have been hung out to dry. We don't talk. We don't share stories. We nod, and in that silent gesture, we empathize with one another. Isaac, Shelby, and Theo's family left for the day, leaving me alone with too many thoughts.

I slip off my shoes and lie on the plaid loveseat, wearing my worn-out gray university sweatshirt that's torn so much around the collar, I should probably be using it as a dusting cloth. This loveseat has been my bed since the beginning of this black hole of despair. The magazine I'm reading is six months old and dog-eared from all the readers it has had since it was left here by some other poor soul. Actually, I bet no one has read one complete article. I know I haven't. I stare at the pictures and flip from one page to the next. Even the perfume sample still dangles from one of the staples.

A thump behind my head interrupts my literature time. I lean my head back to see where the noise came from. It's Theo. He has a shy expression on his clean-shaven face. He's wearing his old T-shirt that has "Don't trust atoms. They make up everything." printed on the front. He came back. It only took him a few hours, but he's back, and the resting angry face has been washed away.

"Hey," I say.

He sits down next to me. "Hey."

"You shaved. It looks good. Not that the beard didn't. You seem... younger." Without his beard, he looks more like how he did in college. "I like the shirt too."

He surveys the shirt and grins. I wonder if he's thinking about the night I wore it, because that's where my mind went.

"I've been doing some thinking," he says.

This is the most he has talked to me in weeks. I put my magazine down, not caring about the article "How to Tell if Your Man is Lying," anyway. Apparently, if he swallows while talking, he's lying.

"I'm very stressed out and about a quart low on blood."

"What?"

"Never mind that. The thing is I'm still very hurt and angry. I don't know if I'll ever get over being hurt and angry." He doesn't swallow.

Uh-oh. I bite my lip. There's going to be a permanent indentation where my teeth have been sawing my lip in half. I was hoping he was going to forgive and forget, but it doesn't feel as if he's headed in that direction.

He continues. "But we have to work together if we want Stella to get healthy again. She needs to feel that we're a team." He leans back and slides my feet into his lap. As if on autopilot, he rubs the soles of my bare feet.

Mmm, that feels heavenly.

"And we're not doing her any good moping around, crying our eyes out every second of the day or snapping at each other. She wouldn't want that, would she?"

"No, she wouldn't," I reply. "She would want us to laugh."

His head bobs up and down like a little kid, like my... like *our* Stella.

"That's what I was thinking." He slings my feet off his lap and drags his duffel bag over to him.

"Are you moving in?" Lord, how I wish he would.

He cracks a faint smirk. "I hope not." He takes out the first item. "Operation." He tosses me the game. I almost fall off the couch, trying to catch it. "Maybe Dr. Michaels could use some practice."

"I hope not."

Next, he plops the game of Sorry in my lap. "We are going to get that word out of our systems tonight." He exhales. "I'm sorry I hurt you about the Hangman game. I really thought you were the culprit. I never in a million years would want to hurt you. And you have nothing to be sorry about. No more sorries. Got it?"

Gulp. "Got it." God, I love him.

His eyebrows dance. "Now, as much as I wanted to, I didn't bring the Twister game. I thought that might be a little racy for the waiting room."

I haven't seen his jovial side in a while. "Good thinking."

"But..." His eyes get really big. I can only imagine what Christmas morning is like with him. "I did bring the dry-erase board." He drags it out and shows me that he rewrote my puzzle, but with all the letters filled in.

I give him a high five. "Seems like you've gotten better at Hangman."

He fakes a shocked expression. "Not really. You never could make it difficult. Oh, and one more thing." He stands up and jerks his shirt up with one hand. With the other, he tugs the waistband of his jeans down. "Do you see what this is?"

Perhaps he should lay off the caffeine. "I don't know what I'm supposed to be seeing."

He gets a hangdog expression. "You don't see it?"

"Uh, I see your pump and some very bony ribs. How much weight have you lost lately?"

The beginning of a smile tips up the side of his mouth. "Not important right now." He points to his underwear.

"You have on clean underwear, I hope?"

He motions for me to continue.

"Okay, they are tagless?"

"No. I mean yes, but that's not the point. These, my dear, are my big-girl panties."

I bust out laughing. "What?"

"You told me to act like an adult. So, I'm showing you I've put on my big-girl panties, and I'm going to try. I can't promise anything because, well, you know me. I don't *adult* very well. I haven't had much practice."

I slap my thigh. "That is hysterical."

He stares at me. I stare at him. I think we're both afraid to speak, afraid that anything we say may get in the way of the progress we've made in the last five minutes.

"I'm not mad anymore. I know you didn't keep her from me on purpose," he says. "Give me some time to adjust, please?"

Whew. I can live with that. "Okay."

He clears his throat. "So, pick your poison. What will it be first?"

"Hmm." I survey all the goodies. "Sorry. I'm ready to pulverize you in a good ole game of Sorry."

He opens the box and drops the game board on the coffee table. "In your dreams, Juliet."

"Bring it, Romeo."

If I didn't know better, I would think we were back in that fraternity house bathroom, keeping score of our winnings on the mirror with lipstick. We had so much fun playing games. It was then that I knew I loved him. It was the night I lost him. It was the moment we made Stella. It was... perfect. I don't know if I can ever get back that feeling, but right now, I'm loving the fact that he's not ignoring me. That's a huge step forward.

For two hours, we battle it out over the Sorry board. We accumulate an audience of ICU families watching us duke it out. As expected, most of them cheer for me. *Ha! Take that Dr. Edwards.* Theo loans the Operation game and the dry-erase board out to other families, and it's nice to pass the time mindlessly and laugh. I forgot how much he could make me laugh.

He taps my game piece off the space it was on. He doesn't even try to stifle a chuckle.

"Do you really think you're going to get away with sending my game piece back home again?" I ask after he sends it back to the home space for the fifth time. "I don't think so."

"Sorreeeee," he screeches.

I throw a Goldfish cracker at him. Of course, he catches it in his mouth. *Show off.*

An alarm sounds over the intercom, making me jump so high that I practically hit the ceiling.

"*Code Red, Code Red, Pediatric ICU, Third Floor. Code Red, Code Red. Pediatric ICU, Third Floor.*"

Theo and I stop what we're doing and stare at each other.

"Oh God, no." He jumps up, knocking the game board off and sending the pieces flying everywhere. He runs to the ICU entrance with me not far behind. In fact, every person in the ICU rushes that way with a crash cart.

"Coming through, please move," the code team barks at us as four physicians rush past us into the ICU.

Theo runs after them, holding my hand, not caring about the rules or the ward clerk yelling at us to leave. We frantically scan around to see which room the code team enters. *Oh, God, please not Stella's.* It may be selfish to pray that the emergency is for someone else's kid and not my own. I should feel guilty, but I don't.

"No," Theo says, his voice breaking. He rushes to Stella's door right behind the doctors.

Jill, Stella's nurse, blocks his way.

"I've got to get in there," he says.

"Sir, you can't go in there right now."

"That's my daughter!"

"I'm sorry. Not now." She pushes us backward, toward the ICU entrance.

"What's happening?" I scream at her.

"Stay back," she says. "You can't go in there right now."

But I can see past her into the room. I can see the doctors surrounding Stella.

"Everyone, clear," one of the physicians orders to the others.

Oh my God, her heart has stopped. My little girl's heart has stopped. This can't be happening.

"Stand clear. Shock."

A loud, cringe-worthy thump comes from my baby's body.

Theo takes me by the shoulders and swings me around so I can't see what's happening. He covers my ears with his hands. There is so much noise and yelling that I don't even notice my own screams.

Theo buries my head in his chest, and the pressure of his hands over my ears increases. I know the doctors have shocked her a second time.

He releases me and uncovers my ears. "They got a pulse," he whispers to me. "Her heart's beating again."

Jill grabs us and pushes us out of the ICU. "You have to leave now! As soon as I can, I will come get you."

We are thrown back into the waiting room. All the other families are dead quiet as we stand in the middle of the room. I rush away from everyone to a corner. I rock back and forth, tapping my forehead against the wall. My whole body trembles. We almost lost her. Our baby almost died. This isn't supposed to be happening. Our baby needs lots of costumes and play jewelry around her neck and a princess crown on her head, not tubes and monitors, and especially not shock paddles. This is all wrong. She's supposed to be splashing around in a swimming pool or riding a pony. This isn't natural.

Theo wraps his arms around me. "Come here," he whispers.

I lose it. It doesn't matter if he hates me. I need him right now. I need someone to be strong for me because I can't be strong anymore. My tears soak his shirt, and the noises I make are those only a mother can make.

He strokes my hair as he cries too. "I know. Shh. She's okay. They got her back. Try to breathe."

I push away from him. *Breathe in, breathe out. Inhale, exhale, hiccup.* "I'm sorry."

"I thought we were done saying that word."

I rest my head on his chest again. "I'll never stop trying to apologize to you."

He kisses me on the forehead.

"Miss Battle, Dr. Edwards?" the ward clerk asks from the waiting room entrance. "You can come in now. Sorry about that, but they needed space to work." The nurse ushers us into Stella's room.

Dr. Michaels is there, consulting with the code team. He waves us over and wipes his sweaty brow. He cracks a grin, the first I've seen from him in weeks. "We had a little scare, but this is one tough girl. We got her back."

I rush to Stella's side and kiss her face a dozen times.

Theo sighs. "What happened?"

"Your little girl has turned a corner."

Thank you, God.

"Her kidneys kicked into high gear all of a sudden. Urinary output skyrocketed. Her heart didn't stop, but she became arrhythmic when her blood pressure dropped suddenly. Cardioversion was the only thing we could do quickly to keep her from arresting. We did a quick check, and her electrolytes were out of whack, so I've increased her fluids and potassium to replenish what she peed out."

He straightens Stella's sheet before he feels her forehead with the palm of his hand. "I was going to wait until visiting hours to update you, but I might as well do it now."

I grab Theo's hand. This cannot be good. Dr. Michaels's "updates" send me down the rabbit hole of despair every single time. Theo squeezes my hand.

"We've had two days without any spikes in temperature and no signs of necrosis. I'd like to take her back to surgery tonight to make sure there is no additional tissue damage. If not, I'll close her incisions and start weaning her off the ventilator. How does that sound?"

"So, she's getting better?" Theo asks with hope in his voice.

"No, but she's not getting worse. I think we can get her up and moving around again and see what happens from there."

I could kiss Dr. Michaels right now. Stella has been stuck at one stage for so long, I didn't think this was ever going to happen. If my life depended on it, I couldn't wipe the smile off my face.

Theo grins at me. "That sounds great," he says to the doctor. "Do you need me to—"

"No, Theo. You've done enough. I think you two should get some sleep. Taking her back to surgery tonight means that you won't get to see her during the evening visitation. But in the morning, she might be awake."

"And you think I'm going to be able to sleep now?" I ask.

Dr. Michaels laughs. "Well, at least try. Now go on. Go to the cafeteria or something. Get out of that waiting room. I'm sure the walls feel like they're closing in on you."

Theo grins down at me. "Come on, let them work. Suddenly, I'm hungry."

"Me too."

We give our unconscious—but one step closer to being well—daughter one more kiss for good measure before we leave... together.

Chapter Forty
Theo

A T THIS HOUR OF THE day, we almost have the whole cafeteria to ourselves. A few people mingle around before they go back to visit with family members, but it's not jam-packed like it is during lunch times. In complete silence, Darla and I sit in a booth, eating. Even hospital food tastes delicious tonight. For the first time in forever, I'm able to actually breathe. Getting oxygen and glucose to my brain helps my mood. I believe our little girl is getting better. *Thank you. Thank you. Thank you.*

"Theo, do you think she's going to make it?" Darla pleads with her eyes for me to give her some medical wisdom.

I put down my fork and wipe my face with a napkin. "Honestly, I don't know, but I feel like she is. I completely feel it. I can't explain it. God has given me a peace about this whole situation."

She lets out a breath. "I feel it too. Maybe it's wishful thinking, but maybe it's divine intervention. I don't know." She scoops up another forkful of rice and stuffs it in her mouth. "This is usually nasty-tasting, but it's good today."

I shovel food in as fast as I can. I'm so weak from lack of food, lack of sleep, and from giving blood that my fork won't hold still as I lift it to my mouth. I could sleep for a week if my brain would shut off for a second.

"What did you mean by being a quart low?" she asks.

Crap. I was hoping she didn't pick up on that. "That's a phrase for when you give blood, that's all." I dare not make eye contact, because she's getting way too good at reading my mind.

She puts her hand on mine before I can lift the fork again. *Shit. She doesn't buy it.*

"How many times?"

"How many times, what?" I ask.

She stares at me, and I cannot will my eyes away from her gaze.

I clear my throat. "Three times," I mumble.

"Three times?" She sits back in the booth. "In a little over a week, you donated three times? Are you crazy?"

"Shh. Yes, I'm crazy. Crazy in love with our little girl, and if you had her blood type, you would have done the same thing. Don't tell me you wouldn't have." I point my fork at her. A piece of my sesame chicken drops off my fork and onto her plate.

She picks it up and eats it. "That's where you were. I thought you couldn't take the responsibility of being a parent, when all along..." She wipes tears from her eyes.

"Yeah." I nod. "I had to bribe them to take my blood the last time, and they had to admit me because my sugar tanked. After that, Tommy had to donate blood to give to me. It was like a round-robin of donations. Crap, I guess I owe him one now."

Her mouth drops. "Why didn't you tell me?"

I reach over the table and slide a strand of hair behind her ear. "Because you had enough on your plate, and I was fine. You didn't need two babies to worry about. And before you get mad at Tommy, I made him promise not to say anything."

"I know this is all new to you, but you're already a very good daddy."

My fork clatters onto the table. That's the highest compliment anyone could ever give me. And hearing it from Darla is like winning an award for best actor. "You think so?"

"Yeah, you're playing catch-up quite nicely."

I sit up straighter. "I'm good, ain't I?"

She rolls her eyes. "And modest too. Some things never change. I have to say, you make pretty babies."

I shrug. "*We* make pretty babies."

Silence surrounds us again. The elephant is still in the room, and I can feel the tension creep up my spine. By the way she bites on her lip, Darla must feel it too.

"You probably had recently started medical school when I found out I was pregnant. Mallory sent me that card by email."

I lean back in the booth and focus on the ceiling. She has to let it out, and I love her, so I have to accept her reasoning, whether it makes sense to me or not.

"She announced to everyone you were the love of her life. Finally, I had a real name. Do you know how many Romeos there are in this world?"

I almost laugh.

"So, one of the email recipients was THEgamemaker@outlook.com. It had to be you, so I sent an email to it. Nothing."

"I know."

Her eyes bug out of their sockets. "What?"

I lean forward. "After you shooed me away earlier, my family converged on me for an intervention. I think it would have been more fun if I was a crack addict. Tommy told me what happened."

"I thought you didn't want us. I thought you wanted Mallory."

My jaw drops. I slump in my chair and let out a deep groan.

"After that, I didn't know what to do. I felt so... lost." Her eyes tell me everything I need to know. She didn't hide Stella from me, and she didn't do anything out of spite. She really didn't know what to do. And most importantly, I know she tried.

"And when you came back, I thought you already knew, so I didn't say anything. When it was obvious you were clueless, you had been back a while. I tried to tell you, but I panicked because I was afraid of how you would take it. Then, everything kind of snowballed out of control." She stares off and takes a deep breath. "I guess I lost that round, huh?"

"You will be penalized one hundred points."

She leans back in her chair and breathes a sigh of relief. Her mouth tilts up in a small smile. "Wow. You're serious. Shouldn't Tommy and Mallory get penalized too?"

"Oh, you leave Tommy to me."

"And Mallory? She knew I was into you at the party, and she deliberately kept you to herself for seven years."

I look down at my food. "I think she's penitent, but it's too late. No physician at work will give her the time of day."

"She's not a bad person. I think she's too... assertive."

Ain't that the truth?

I throw my hands in the air. I could have had the girl of my dreams and my daughter all this time. Even though I'm upset about missing out on so much, I know Tommy didn't do anything to hurt me. Neither did Jennifer or Darla. I just wish she would have told me all of this back on the first day of orientation. Now that I know everything, I understand why she was so confused, mad, and stressed. She thought I was an arrogant jerk that didn't want our baby. It all makes perfect sense now.

"Talk about not getting the memo," I say.

She giggles. Boy, it has been a long time since I heard that sweet laugh of hers. I sit back and take a deep breath. I feel as though I have run a marathon. I sit up straight again and lean across the table. "Now let me ask *you* something. How often have you left that waiting room?"

"Other than to pee or change clothes, not much."

I point at her. "See, that's a good mommy."

She shrugs, and we're enveloped in silence again. I feel as if that elephant is sitting on my chest.

"I told Stella," she finally says.

"What?" I ask, fork dangling in midair.

She blushes. "I wanted to tell her before she was sedated. So before she went into surgery the first time, I told her you were her daddy."

"How did she take it?"

"She said 'yes' and fist-bumped me."

I grin. "That's my girl."

"Your girl?"

"*Our* girl."

We eat in silence for a bit, but I have to ask. Not knowing is eating me up. I missed so much. "What was it like being pregnant with Stella?"

She beams with pride. She scrolls past our birthday photos on her phone then stops on one picture and hands me the phone. "Diane took this right before I went to the hospital to deliver."

It's as though I'm staring at an angel. Darla looks the same, except she has the cutest bulging belly and this glow about her that I cannot describe. If I wasn't in love with her before, this picture would have sealed the deal. She's carrying our child. She didn't have to, but she did.

"Oh, Darla, you're so beautiful. So happy."

"Happy and scared. Terrified, actually. Here's something you'll find more interesting." She swipes a few more pictures out of the way. "Here's the first picture of your daughter."

The tears stream down my face again. I can't stop them. "I'm so sorry I missed—"

"Nope. We don't use that word anymore. It's not your fault, remember?"

I wipe my face dry. There's one more item we need to clear up, and I would rather do it in private, not in front of the entire cafeteria staff and the few nurses currently on break.

I slide out of the booth. "Let's go outside for a stroll. When's the last time you got some fresh air?"

"Jennifer dragged me outside for about five minutes a few days ago, but I felt guilty, so I headed back in."

I take her hand. "Let me show you my favorite spot to de-stress when I'm working nights."

We take the elevator to the top floor of the hospital and walk out onto the rooftop patio. All the seats around the potted plants are vacant. Moths fly around the luminous black lanterns strung from pole to pole. Raised flower beds line the space between each set of benches, and the fragrance from summer-blooming shrubs fills the air. At this time of night, it's very peaceful up here. There's hardly a sound except for an occasional car driving down the road and the low hum of air conditioner units. We're the only ones here. Everyone else who knows about this place is more than likely at home by now.

I lead Darla to the middle of the patio, where the strings of lanterns meet in a peak. "What do you think?"

She spins in circles. "I didn't know this even existed. It's so quiet, and you can see the whole city from here." She has never looked sexier.

"Do you remember when I mentioned I wanted to do Doctors Without Borders?"

Her eyes stay fixed on her sneakers as she nods.

"I still want to do that, but Dr. Frank from the ER goes every year for a week or two and takes his entire family. Maybe someday, I'll do that, but I had another idea. After you cut your hand, it got me thinking."

She waves her hand in my face. "It wasn't that big of a deal. It's all better now."

I kiss the small line where the tuna can cut her hand.

She wraps her fingers around mine and gives my hand a squeeze. "An urgent care center could have fixed it up if one was open that time of night."

"Exactly. There needs to be an urgent care center open twenty-four, seven. It could free up the ER to focus on sucking chest wounds and cardiac emergencies."

"What if it had a flat rate for each visit? That way, people who don't have doctors can afford preventive care too."

I love this woman. She has a heart of gold. "I'd need a nurse who... knows what's going on. You could wear that ridiculous T-shirt of yours if you want. You know, the one about talking to a nurse because she'll know what's going on."

She rewards me with an eye roll.

"What do you say? Want to work with me?"

"Heck yeah."

I give her a wink. "I've got a proposal written up for Dr. Frank to review. We'll see what he says."

She gives me a kiss on the cheek. "I think it's brilliant."

Heat rushes up my neck. I take her by the hand, lead her to the balcony edge, and lean against the half wall that surrounds the entire patio space. It reminds me of a castle turret in King Arthur days.

I clear my throat. If I don't say this now, I'll forever be kicking myself in the butt for not making things right. "I know that the S word is supposed to be removed from our vocabulary, but I have to apologize for something."

"No, you don't."

I take both of her trembling hands in mine and draw her close to me so I can see her face. "I promised you that I would be patient and kind and not hold a grudge. I assured you I wouldn't freak out, and that's exactly what I did."

She shifts her weight from one foot to the other, and her lip quivers. *Shit.*

"What I did was a complete misunderstanding. But you left me alone when I needed you the most. I needed you to be my strength."

"I am so sorry. I don't think I could have hurt you any more than I did. That's not the real me. There were so many times I wanted to hold you until you cried yourself to sleep, but I was too hurt and stubborn. It's not a valid excuse." I rub her shoulders. "I promise you I will never let you down again. Please forgive me."

She sniffles. "I wish I had told you sooner. I wish so many things. She's the only thing that kept me going for so many years. She's been my little ray of sunshine." Sadness crosses her face.

"Stella is a gift. And I don't want to lose another minute being angry with you about our precious gift that's fighting for her life downstairs. I love you, Darla. Please say I haven't pushed you away."

She sobs into her hands. I can't tell what she's thinking. I don't know if the things we've said to one another have made it too impossible for us to fix our relationship. My apology may be too late.

She lunges for me and wraps her arms around my neck so tightly that I'm afraid I'll collapse from lack of energy and oxygen. But I hold on to her as if my life depends on it.

"I love you too," she whispers against my neck.

Adrenaline kicks in, and I'm not in the least bit tired anymore. I stroke her hair as we stand there, wrapped in each other's arms.

"Oh, and one more thing," I murmur in her ear. "That Hangman game *was* fun. It was a lot of fun."

She laughs.

I step back from her and remove the crumpled piece of paper from my front jeans pocket. "I've got to know. Who do you think sent me all these clues?" I show her the Hangman printout.

"I have no idea who did this."

"Good, because I think whoever wrote this has a serious case of dyslexia. It says 'you have a,' and after that, the next word is all jumbled. I'm assuming it's supposed to spell out 'daughter.'"

We both study the clues.

Darla gasps and growls. "Isaac is dyslexic. He promised to stay out of it. He's going in the naughty chair."

"Leave him be. He put a fire under my butt to do something. I certainly didn't need to wait around for another frat party."

She rolls her eyes. "Ha-ha. Wait a second." She snatches the puzzle from me and reads the clues again. "He might have designed the puzzle, but there's no way he knew about all this and where I'd be. I think he had a partner in crime."

"Maybe Shelby?"

"She said she didn't know anything about this. She's gonna get it if it was her."

"Doesn't matter." I take her face in my hands and kiss her lips, softly at first. She wraps her arms around my waist, and one hand slides under my shirt. When my tongue finds hers, I come alive again.

I break away long enough to whisper, "You know, there's over five hundred beds in this hospital. What do you want to bet that there's at least one that's not being used?" I wiggle my eyebrows.

She pops me on the shoulder. "You're awful. Tell me that doctors do not do that."

I shrug and hold my hands up in defense. "All I know is that there's a list in the residents' lounge that shows where the empty beds are every night. I'm speculating what it's for." I'm sure my dimple has made an appearance.

"No, absolutely not." Even though she protests, she has a goofy grin plastered on her face.

"Actually, I walked in on two doctors one night. It almost blinded me."

She giggles. "That is totally unprofessional, and I cannot believe adults would do things like that."

I pin her against the half wall of the patio and nuzzle her neck. "And rumor has it there's an entire research unit that shuts down on the weekends. Today is Saturday, right?"

"What if Dr. Michaels needs to update us on Stella?"

I pat my back pocket. "I've got my phone, and he can also page me if he needs to reach us. You'd be surprised how fast I can get dressed when I have to."

She nibbles on the inside of her mouth then pushes me aside. "I want to see that list right now."

"Oh, so you're interested in knowing where the vacancies are. Nice."

She rolls her eyes. "As if. I don't believe you."

"I could go home and get the Twister game if you want."

She takes my hand and leads me away from the wall. We stand side by side, my fingers laced between hers, as we wait on the elevator door to open. The *ping* interrupts the quiet, and we step inside, standing against opposite walls. I push the button for the fifth floor, the closed research unit, and I wink at her.

As soon as the doors close, she is all over me. *Excellent!*

I fish out my wallet, remove my ID badge, and wave it in front of her face. "See, if you were a big-shot doctor like me, you could swipe into any unit in this hospital. Even the closed research unit."

She rolls her eyes. I swipe my badge into the wall-mounted access system, but nothing happens. I swipe again. Nothing.

Darla giggles. "It might help if you flip it over."

I stick my tongue out at her, like all big-shot doctors would do. When I swipe again, this time with my badge turned the correct way, the light changes to green and the door to the dark unit opens.

"Kind of creepy," Darla says. "Are we going to get killed making out, like in all those slasher movies?"

I take her hand, and we scamper down the hallway to the last room on the right. I figure the farther away we are from the nursing station, the better. As soon as we're inside the room, I close the door behind us and pin her against it. The streetlights filtering in through the window give us enough brightness that we can see well enough not to run into the equipment all over the room.

While I kiss her neck, she busies herself with the hem of my T-shirt. I break away from her skin long enough to slide my shirt over my head. Darla throws it across the room, and it lands on the blood pressure machine.

She places featherlight touches on my chest, her fingers trailing down my stomach until she rests her hands on my waist. I can barely control my breathing. She pushes me backward, toward the bed, until I bump into the footboard. With one quick snap of her wrist, she snatches the privacy curtain, and it skitters closed around the bed.

I motion with my finger for her to come to me, which she does without hesitation. As soon as she's close enough, I grab her by the sweatshirt and yank it over her head, trapping one of my hands inside it. I trail kisses down her neck toward those perfect breasts, but I can't touch them the way I want while my one hand still clings on to the sweatshirt like it's attached with Velcro. With one last-ditch effort, I pitch the sweatshirt off my hand so I can devour her breasts.

She inhales sharply when I kiss the soft skin right above her bra. The sweatshirt drops to the floor, and together, we collapse onto the bed. Darla lands on top of me. I roll us both over until she is beneath me, and my hands fumble around, searching for her bra hook. I find it and strip her bra off quickly. Darla moans, and her hands roam through my hair as I get reacquainted with her body. When my mouth makes its descent to her stomach, she covers herself with her hands.

I peer up at her. "What's wrong?"

Her teeth sink into her bottom lip. "It's… well, uh… when I lost my baby weight, things never went back to normal. The skin is kind of loose."

I kiss her hands, and she finally gets the courage to move them. I don't see loose skin. All I see is a beautiful stomach that used to hold my precious baby. I kiss it and imagine what it would have been like to feel my baby kicking inside Darla's abdomen. I love this woman more and more every second.

Darla fumbles with something next to her. The head of the bed rises to a fifteen-degree level. My eyebrows shoot up.

She holds up the remote that controls the bed. "I guess there *are* benefits to a hospital bed."

I crawl my way back up her body. "Now you're talking. Don't hit that call button. We don't need a code team rushing in."

She cracks up and takes my face in her hands. "That would be our luck, wouldn't it?"

"I love you, Darla. I always have."

She gets a wicked, non-Darla-like expression in her eyes. "Prove it."

My hand slides down and unzips her jeans. "You read my mind."

Chapter Forty-One
Darla

I COULD STAY WRAPPED IN THEO'S arms forever, but the mommy guilt kicks in. I should be in the waiting room in case Stella needs me.

Theo props himself up on his elbow and leans in to give me another kiss. "In case there's a fire, my name is Theo Edwards. And you are…"

He makes me laugh. "Darla, and we have a child. So if there is a fire, let's please go get her together before we run out of here."

"Absolutely. Together forever." He points at me. "And no more important information by email."

I hold up my index, middle, and ring fingers. "Scout's honor."

He cringes.

"What's wrong?"

He buries his face in my chest. "I, uh, I need to do a better job of stashing condoms in my wallet."

And we have now come full circle. I laugh, making his head bounce on my chest. "Dr. Edwards, you should know better." If we got pregnant again, I would think we won the jackpot.

"Excuse me, but I don't make a habit of having… S-E-X at work. I'm shocked I even have my wallet with me."

His phone buzzes, making us both snap out of our sex-induced haze. He grabs it off the bedside table. "It's Dr. Michaels."

My lungs stop. I clutch the sheet and pray that everything's okay.

"This is Theo," he says into his phone. He bites his lip and listens intently. All of a sudden, his eyes get big, and he gives me a thumbs-up.

Finally, I can breathe again.

"Thank you. Yes. We'll see you first thing in the morning." He hangs up the phone and grabs me in a big hug. "She's out of surgery, off the vent, and breathing on her own. Everything's good. She should be awake in the morning for us to visit with her."

When I think I have no tears left, I produce about a gallon more. My breath catches in my throat. Theo rubs my back to help calm me. I bury my face in his chest.

He takes a deep breath. "As much as I want to stay here all night, I left my diabetic kit in the waiting room. I need to check my blood sugar."

"Of course." I wipe my eyes and sit up. When I do, my hand lands on the call button. It lets out a loud *beep.*

I gasp.

Theo flies out of the bed, his legs tangled in the sheet. "We gotta go."

I jump up but can't find my clothes. His T-shirt is still on the blood pressure machine, so I snatch it and throw it on.

"Hey, what am I supposed to wear?"

I shrug and point to my sweatshirt on the floor by the door. "Wear that." I throw on my jeans and stuff my bra and panties in the front pocket.

Theo jumps into his pants, not wasting time trying to find his underwear. He yelps when he zips up his jeans. He should have slowed down for that. He throws on my sweatshirt, inside out, picks up his sneakers, and peers into the hall.

"Let's go."

I grab my purse and shoes and let him lead me toward the elevator. A security guard rounds the corner at the other end of the hallway as we safely scoot into the elevator. I balance on one foot at a time while I put on my shoes. Theo doesn't even bother. We face each other and bust out laughing.

As soon as the elevator deposits us in front of the ICU waiting room, Theo puts a finger to his lips, signaling me to stay quiet. Our baby is getting better, but so many other families are still in anguish. I have to be respectful to them. We tiptoe into the dark room. Theo grabs his kit from his usual corner and a blanket from the cabinet. I lead him to my designated loveseat. He wraps a blanket around us, giving us a tiny bit of privacy. Theo places a chaste kiss on my lips before he unzips his kit and checks his sugar. After he has given himself his insulin, he tugs me onto his lap. Theo's hand slides up my thigh, making me giggle.

"Shh, you're going to wake up the other parents," he whispers. With the other hand, he thumb wrestles me. Even in his weakened state, he can still whip my butt at thumb wrestling.

"You're part of the problem," I say. "I cannot believe we *did* that."

"I can. I'll never be able to go into room S5104 again without smiling." He nibbles on my ear and presses my thumb down. Of course, he would be thinking of thumb wrestling. No fair. I'm distracted.

"And no protection... again," I say.

"You are such a tramp, Nurse Battle. What am I going to do with you?"

"Me?"

"Shh. Yeah, you. First of all, Stella was conceived at a frat party. What if you're pregnant again? This time, it was in a hospital bed—S5104 in case you forgot—while this baby's big sister is in surgery? Our kids are going to be so messed up."

Thinking of having a house full of little Theos converts me into a giggly schoolgirl. "All my fault, right?"

His hand creeps up my side under my "Don't trust atoms" T-shirt that he was wearing an hour ago. He's so adorable, wearing my inside-out sweatshirt. I wonder if anyone else noticed.

"Yep. That's my story."

"Her sister? So you're convinced that I'm pregnant *and* that it's a girl?"

"Uh-huh." He kisses my neck. "I've got a name picked out too."

"Thanks for consulting me. Is this payback for not being involved in the baby naming the first time around?"

He slides me onto my back on the loveseat. "Um, something like that. I'm kind of partial to Juliet."

I giggle. "Uh, no."

"Lady Macbeth?"

"Stop it. I like the name Grace."

"Perfect. Can our third child be conceived in the old-fashioned way? In the backseat of a—*oof*."

I've cut off his sentence by goosing him in the ribs. I tickle him until he slides to the floor with a thump.

"Are you all right?"

He gives me the thumbs-up. "I'm good. Uh-oh. I think I broke my pump again."

"Ooooh, Stella's going to be mad at you."

"I liked it better when they hated each other," one of the dads says from across the room. An *oof* comes from him. Moms have to stick together.

The next morning, we line up outside the entrance to the ICU, waiting for visiting hours to commence. Theo holds me close, and his fingers draw little circles on my back.

His family bursts into the waiting room. When they see Theo and me cozied up together, his mother raises her hands in the air. Her tears of joy are no match for Jennifer's. She envelops Theo in a huge, all-consuming hug. Tommy wraps an arm around me and gives my shoulder a squeeze.

Isaac and Shelby enter, and when Isaac sees me shaking my head, he backpedals. I grab each of them by an arm and sit them down onto a couch away from Theo's family. Theo stands by my side.

"How could you?" I ask.

Isaac curls into a ball. "I don't know what you're talking about."

I stuff my hand into Theo's front jeans pocket.

"Down, girl," Theo says. "Not here."

"Oh, hush." I retrieve the Hangman puzzle and throw the wadded piece of paper at Isaac. "Don't try to deny it, Mr. Dyslexic."

He cringes. "Oopsies, but it was her idea." He points at Shelby.

She gasps. "That is not... well... it's not completely true."

I take a step forward, but Theo holds me back.

Shelby stands and takes my hands in hers. "We were joking around and thought there had to be a playful way to get you two together." She grins at Theo. "I didn't know Isaac actually did anything." She bats her eyes at me and sighs. "Fine, I may have slipped him some useful information from time to time." She points at Isaac. "Thanks a lot for getting me in trouble."

She turns back to me. "I can't believe I'm going to say this, but don't be mad at him, or me for that matter. We love you and Stella. In Isaac's crazy way, he wanted you to be happy."

I peek over Shelby's shoulder to see Isaac's sad puppy-dog face.

Theo sticks his hand out to help Isaac off the couch. He gives Isaac a back slap and a hug. "Thanks, brother."

If Theo isn't mad at him, I certainly can't be. He's my best friend, and even if he deserves for me to be a bit angry at him, I can't do it. I bury my head in his chest and wrap my arms around him. "From now on, let me be in charge of the games. You suck at spelling."

His laughter rumbles through his chest. "You got it."

Theo and I are finally admitted into Stella's room, and we sit on her bed, obsessing over her. Her face isn't sweaty, and her cheeks aren't blazing hot anymore. And that damn tube is gone from her mouth. Theo cannot wipe the proud-papa grin off his face. He holds my hand and Stella's and prays over us. He blesses our little family and thanks God for everything.

Dr. Michaels comes into the room. He's beaming also. He has become so attached to Stella that he feels like one of the family now. "She came through the operation splendidly. We closed up her incisions. Her cultures are all negative. I think she's turned a corner."

He looks at Stella. "How do you feel?"

"My throat hurts," she says hoarsely.

"Yes, that mean old tube scratched your throat. Ice chips will help. And soon, you can have ice cream."

He focuses his attention on us. "I want to keep her a few more days, but I think she's ready to taper off the steroids and start on oral antibiotics. As long as her leg appears free of infection and she doesn't spike a fever, she may get to go to a regular room for a couple of days then go home."

I grin at Stella. "Did you hear that? You might get to go home soon."

Stella smiles sleepily.

I stand and hug Theo. He kisses me sweetly on the lips. Stella giggles.

I hug the doctor. "Thank you so much."

"I'm only doing my job. I love it when it works out well." His eyes brim with tears when he pats Theo on the shoulder. "You two seem like a couple now."

Theo shrugs and pulls up the sweatshirt he's wearing. He glances down at his waist then gets an *oh shit* expression on his face. "I, uh... I guess I lost my big-girl panties."

I cover my face. My ears are flaming as I remember the yelp he let out when he zipped up his jeans without first putting his underwear back on. I cannot believe he said that in front of Dr. Michaels *and* Stella.

"Mommy, do his panties have Sleeping Beauty on them?"

"No! I mean, I don't know. I, er, probably not."

Dr. Michaels chuckles. "Ah, big-girl panties, huh?"

Theo giggles like a little girl. "Took me long enough, but I finally put them on."

Dr. Michaels leans in to Theo. "My wife makes me wear mine every day." He fist-bumps Theo and hugs me. "I'll give you some time with Stella, but not long because she needs to rest."

After he leaves, Theo and I are all over her again, showering her with lots of hugs and kisses. Her giggles are music to my ears.

"I'm so glad you're feeling better. I've missed you so much."

"I missed you too, Mommy."

She touches Theo's face. "I got a dimple just like you."

He beams with pride.

"Can you roll your tongue?" she asks him.

He rolls his tongue.

She giggles. "Mommy can't do that." Her poor voice is almost completely gone.

Theo holds her face in his hands. "Did you know that my mommy's name is Stella too?"

"Really?" Her eyes are so heavy that she can hardly keep them open.

"Yep. That's your grandmother."

That woke her up. Her eyes grow big, and she fist-bumps him. "Yes!"

I tickle her. "You're a mess."

"Daddy, can I ask you for something?" Her voice is so raspy, I can hardly make out her words.

I think Theo is a big puddle on the floor. He heard his daughter call him "daddy" for the first time. His face glows, and his eyes well up with tears. He wears a perma-smile. "You can have anything you want, Stella Bella."

She motions for him to come closer. He leans down, and she cups her little hands around his ear to whisper to him. Clearly, this is a conversation not meant for me.

He gets an "oh my God" face. "Really?"

She nods ferociously.

A pink blush creeps over his face, and he giggles like a ten-year-old girl. "Okay, if you're sure. I'll see what I can do."

Oh dear, no telling what she wants. After all she's been through, I might have to find room in my budget to get her a pony.

He smiles at me. "She wants a sister."

In every game, there are winners and losers. But love is more than a game, and if played right, everyone wins. I know the three of us did.

Acknowledgments

Thanks to Kristen House (A Novel Idea) for being beside me from the beginning of this project. I'll never be able to thank you enough.

To Jymie, my favorite writer buddy. You are awesome.

To Kelly Ann Hopkins for your help with back cover content.

To the #ameditingcrew – hugs.

To David Buynitzky for your unique vocabulary.

To Keith Franklin a/k/a Isaac

To the entire Red Adept family, in particular:

Lynne McNamee – thanks for believing in this story and in me.

Erica Lucke Dean – you are the best mentor ever.

Alyssa Hall & Neila Forssburg – my awesome editors. I learned so much from you, and I hope I taught you a few southern phrases along the journey.

Jessica Anderegg & Streetlight Graphics – you nailed the cover design.

To Daisy Mae – the best canine writing partner ever.

To Mark and Maddie – thanks for putting up with me. You might finally get a home-cooked meal. (Don't count on it). I love you.

About the Author

After several decades of writing medical research documents, Cindy Dorminy decided to switch gears and become an author. She wanted to write stories where the chances of happy endings are 100% and the side effects include satisfied sighs, permanent smiles, and a chuckle or two.

Cindy was born in Texas and raised in Georgia. She enjoys gardening, reading, and bodybuilding. She can often be overheard quoting lines from her favorite movies. But her favorite pastime is spending time with Mark, her bass-playing husband, and Maddie Rose, the coolest girl on the planet. She also loves her fur child, Daisy Mae. She currently resides in Nashville, TN, where live music can be heard everywhere, even at the grocery store.